HIDEOUS PROGENY

MARY SHELLEY AND HER MONSTER

VAUGHN ENTWISTLE

MASQUE PUBLISHING

Hideous Progeny: Mary Shelley and Her Monster

Print edition: ISBN 978-0-9828830-9-9

E-book edition: ISBN 978-09828830-2-0

Published by Masque Publishing LLC

First Edition: August, 2020

This is a work of fiction. Names, characters, places and incidents are a product of the author's imagination, or are used fictitiously, and any resemblance to actual persons, living or dead, business establishments, events or locales are entirely coincidental.

❀ Created with Vellum

Note: This book uses British English spellings and grammar throughout.

(As did Mary Shelley).

CONTENTS

GET A FREE SHORT EBOOK!

Get a free copy of my short ebook, *The Necropolis Railway*, by signing up for my occasional newsletter at my author website: www.vaughnentwistle.com

PREFACE

This novel opens with a deeply tragic quote from Mary Shelley herself:

And now, once again, I bid my hideous progeny go forth and prosper. I have an affection for it, for it was the offspring of happy days, when death and grief were but words, which found no true echo in my heart . . . Mary Shelley

This is not the voice of the 18 year old Mary Shelley who conceived the world-changing novel, *Frankenstein*. Rather, these are the words of the mature woman Mary Shelley would become in later life. Sadly, Mary Shelley's story is a bitter dish seasoned with loss and sorrow.

Mary Shelley's legacy.

As the famous story goes, Mary Shelley conceived the idea of her nameless monster during a night of apocalyptic thunderstorms at the Villa Diodati near Lake Geneva in Switzerland. Mary, her husband Percy Bysshe Shelley and Mary's half-sister Claire Clairmont, were the guests of the infamous Lord Byron and his personal physician, John Polidori. This was in 1816, the so-called "year without a summer" caused by a volcanic eruption half a world away. That summer was marked by weeks of rain and violent thunderstorms.

Confined inside, the coterie whiled away the long evenings drinking wine laced with laudanum, holding seances, and reading ghost stories.

Famously, one night Lord Byron laid down a challenge whereby each member of the group would write an original ghost story. Percy Shelley soon declared he had not talent for writing prose and gave up. Lord Byron also penned a few pages before abandong the effort. Dr. Polidori wrote a tale about a woman who peeked in on something forbidden and had her head turned into a skull (which, ironically, struck his audience as humorous rather than frightening. But a few days later, during a night of apocalyptic thunder storms, the idea for Frankenstein sprang fully-formed into Mary's mind.

Astonishingly, Mary Shelley was only 18 at the time, but this young woman's first attempt at a full length work of fiction spawned an entirely new and original tope part horror/part science fiction. Since that day, the name *Frankenstein* has burned itself into the collective consciousness, and has guided the footsteps of many writers who have followed after (including myself), and is a dread name that echoes through the generations.

Mary's legacy of loss

The novel *Frankenstein* explores many themes, including unnatural birth, transgressions against the almighty, abandonment, and retribution. Studying Mary's tragic life, it soon becomes obvious where she drew these themes from.

For Mary the abandonment happened just as she entered the world. Her mother, the famous writer, intellectual and proto-feminist Mary Wolstonecraft, struck with puerpal fever after giving birth to her daughter, suffered in agony for nearly a month before finally succumbing to septicaemia.

Tragedy followed Mary throughout her life. Percy Shelley's abandoned wife, Harriet, filled her pockets with stones and walked into the Serpentine. Mary's half-sister, Fanny, ran away from home and took a room in a tavern where she swallowed a fatal dose of laudanum.

Of Mary's four children, one was born prematurely and died as a babe after only eleven days. Two more children died from malaria and dysentery, and then she miscarried during her fifth pregnancy and nearly haemorrhaged to death. Only one child survived to adulthood, her son Percy Florence Shelley.

As Mary relates in the novel, of the original coterie who had been there that famous night at the Villa Diodati when she wrote her first rough draft of *Frankenstein*, Lord Byron died of fever while fighting with the Greeks against the Turks. Doctor Polidori, Byron's personal physician, lost at the casino and then retired to his rooms and took a fatal dose of Prussic acid. And Mary's famous husband, the romantic poet, Percy Bysshe Shelley, recklessly took his sailboat out during a storm, fell overboard, and drowned. He was 29.

The twin narratives

To save you confusion, let me explain that there are two inter-woven narratives in this book.

Narrative 1 is written in the third person, past tense, and follows Mary on her visit to the home of Andrew Crosse, the gentleman scientist and electrical experimenter who many believe was the proto-type for her character, Doctor Frankenstein. This narrative begins at the book's opening and follows a continuous time line until the end of the book. Mary is 44 years old in this part of the book and is already suffering from the headaches and episodes of paralysis caused by the brain tumour that will take her life at age 53.

Narrative 2 shifts to a first person POV and is written in the present tense. All of these chapters have Star in the title: **Strange Star Ascendant**, etc. In this part of the narrative Mary is 53 years old and her brain tumour is far advanced. In this part of the narrative she passes in and out of a coma, sometimes for months on end.

At the climax of the novel, the two narratives collide and intersect as they do in the mind of Mary Shelley.

Real life characters

Percy Bysshe Shelley is considered one of the major English Romantic Poets. `shelley is best known for classic poems such as "Ozymandius", "Ode to the West Wind", "To a Skylark", "Music",

"When Soft Voices Die", and The Mask of Anarchy. He was also a radical thinker on politics, philosophy and religion.

Andrew Crosse and his young wife Cornelia were both real people. Crosse's electrical experiments terrified the locals who called him the "thunder and lightning man." When an account of Crosse's experiment where he claimed to have spontaneously generated life through electricity, caused and international outrage and Crosse was vilified in the press and attacked and shunned by the local villagers. It is fairly well established that Percy Bysshe Shelley and Mary attended a lecture by Crosse during the time they lived in London, and many credit Crosse as the inspiration for Doctor Frankenstein.

The Reverend Philip Smith was a hellfire and brimstone preacher who regularly preached against Crosse's unnatural electrical experiments and fomented trouble against Crosse, including performing the rite of exorcism outside his Fyne Court home.

Augusta Ada King, Countess of Lovelace was an English mathematician and writer, chiefly known for her work on Charles Babbage's proposed mechanical computer, the Analytical Engine. Countess Ada was in fact a frequent visitor to Fyne court. She suffered from a number of digestive ailments and regularly sought out the aid of Andrew Crosse who provided the electrical therapy that alleviated many of her symptoms.

Now that you have some idea of the real-life background to the novel, I hope you enjoy the book.

Vaughn Entwistle, Cheltenham, England, 2020

THE JOURNEY TO SOMERSETSHIRE

> *And now, once again, I bid my hideous progeny go forth and prosper. I have an affection for it, for it was the offspring of happy days, when death and grief were but words, which found no true echo in my heart . . . Mary Shelley*

T he carriage Mary rode in had been forced to stop several times during the journey from Taunton: the first time to yield to an old shepherd and his dog chivvying a baaing flock of sheep between fields; the second to dodge a dangerously over-laden haywain shedding windblown straws as it swayed past.

The third time, the carriage stopped for death.

At first, Mary did not bother to look up and continued to scribble in her journal:

Due to a surfeit of travellers, I was forced to share a stagecoach from Bath to Taunton with a po-faced magistrate and a quarrelsome couple with their two ill-behaved children and a howling babe. I recuperated overnight in one of Taunton's largest coaching houses, the White Hart Inn, where my enflamed nerves took several drops of laudanum to soothe. But this morning, my prospective host sent his carriage to collect me, and this part of the journey has been much enjoyed as we are now travelling through the lovely Quantock hills made famous by the poets Mister Coleridge and Mister Wordsworth. Surely this region offers the most advantageous of British landscapes, being neither as vast and elemental as the Lake District, nor possessing the dread majesty of the Scottish highlands. Instead the Quantocks offer a pastoral idyll of rolling downs, bosky hollows, and bucolic hamlets of charming thatched cottages. Still, I am ever mindful of the reason for my travels, for even now I feel a presence following—the maleficent shadow that has dogged my steps from the moment of its unnatural conception, and which now precedes me as I trudge the darkening road toward death. When shall I be free of the demon childe I birthed into the world?

She lifted her pen from the page and mopped the nib with an ink-stained handkerchief before it could drip and blot the journal. Over years of travel Mary had learned to write with a steady hand inside jostling carriages and in the queasy cabins of rolling ships. Most of her journeys had been a flight from something dire: poverty, debt, scandal, a jilted wife, a blackmailer, a drowned husband, a dead child. The chapters of the book of Mary's life read like a tedious narrative of misfortune foreshadowed and after-shadowed by a night of apocalyptic storms at the Villa Diodati and the dark nativity of the nameless creature that would make her name famous. All this began half a lifetime ago, back when Lord Byron, Dr. Polidori, and her beloved Percy Bysshe still breathed and walked the earth. Now Mary was the last survivor of that singular coterie and she wandered the world alone, a solitary woman companioned by their ghosts.

The stationary carriage creaked and swayed as the driver clambered down from his seat. He appeared at the window and she leaned out to discover the cause of the stoppage. The driver, who had introduced himself as simply *Tom*, touched the brim of his black coachman's hat in salute and stood on the dirt lane looking up at her.

"Dunno what's happenin', Ma'am. Something bad by the look of things. Best to stay in the carriage. I'll go see what's amiss."

A knot of roughly-dressed men crowded the narrow lane ahead, blocking the way—farmers and labourers given their rustic smocks and straw hats. The carriage driver wandered up to them and spoke to the nearest farmer, which caused the man to turn and point at something in the field at which all were staring at with rapt attention. Although the field gate was swung wide, Mary's view was blocked by the tall hedgerow; however, she could see and smell sinuous tendrils of wood smoke rising from behind. Since childhood, Mary Shelley had been inordinately curious, a trait discouraged in those of the female persuasion, but one she found irresistible. After a moment's consideration, she flung open the door and dropped down from the carriage unassisted. Lifting her skirts and stepping carefully to avoid the mounds of wet dung saucing the lane, she stole up silently behind the group of farm men. But when she peered over the shoulder of the nearest to see what held their attention, Mary instantly regretted her curiosity, as she would later write:

I looked upon a scene of carnage: two dead cows slumped close by; a third cow lay farther away. The nearest had clearly suffered an act of extreme violence. Two carcasses lay close to the blasted trunk of a mighty tree. From the blackened trunk and toppled limbs, the tree had clearly been struck by lightning. Shockingly, a huge rift in the tree trunk showed that the lightning-immolated tree still burned from within, seething red with glowing coals and crackling with flame so that the viewer perceived the scene through shimmering heat waves. Under the tremendous flux of the lightning bolt, the trunk had exploded, hurling jagged splinters hither and yon. Meanwhile, the galvanic current had surged through the ground into the livestock sheltering beneath. The dead cattle were crispened to black and exuded a sulphurous reek of burning hair; one carcass had burst open releasing coils of slippery red entrails at which a murder of crows now pecked, gobbling up choice morsels.

Horrified, Mary looked away, and her eye fell upon the broad back of a man standing out in the field, gazing upon the scene of destruction. He was a giant of a fellow, and the too-tight trousers strained to confine his muscular thighs and buttocks, while the broad, v-shaped back threatened to split the shirt stretched over his thick shoulders. From behind, he had the body of a Greek hero; but then, as if sensing her gaze upon him, the figure turned to look behind . . .

. . . and showed the face of an idiot—the mouth hung slack and the protruding tongue drooled. The eyes were unfocused and each pointed in a different direction. Most disturbing was the head, massively dented in at both temples and then ballooning up hydrocephalically. Mary flinched as a hand touched her arm. It was Tom, the driver: "Pardon, Ma'am, but this ain't no sight for a gennulwoman . . ."

Suddenly a farmer-type in rustic attire ran up, red-faced and breathless, and began to shout aloud, "It's 'im again, ain't it? Mark me, this is the deviltry of the thunder and lightnin' man. He's conjured this. This is what comes of a man dressin' hisself in the robes of the almighty!"

One of the other farmers, Elijah Custard, tried to calm the man, "Now Martin, don't take on so. Ain't no proof of what yer claimin', so don't you be makin' mischief."

But the owner of the cows, Martin Compton, would not be pacified. He lunged forward and snatched an axe from the hands of a farm labourer. The others dodged back as he waved it threateningly. "It's that blasted wire what's pulling lightnin' down from the sky. I'm cuttin' the cursed thing down!"

The other men cried aloud, *No!* and fought to wrestle the axe from his hands.

"Martin, just you calm yourself," Tom the carriage driver spoke in a deep, resonant voice and for the first time the agitated farmer seemed to pay attention.

"I ain't afraid of yer wizard," the farmer scowled back, "or his devilish wire."

"Martin Compton," the carriage driver spoke in a voice edged with threat. "I'll not tell thee again. Put down that axe. You're a tenant of my master, same as the rest. That wire cost more than all your farms fetch in one year. Tear it down and you'll be thrown off your land, family and all. And then what'll you do? Starve, that's what."

For a dreadful moment the farmer's face blackened with rage and he seemed to ready to swing the axe at his tormentor, but then the fight fizzled out in his eyes, his shoulders slumped, and the axe sagged in his arms. "I want comp-say-shun, fer my loss," he sobbed the words more than spoke them. "I'm owed comp-say-shun."

It was only then that Mary noticed the coppery glint of wire, hanging suspended several feet above the highest remaining limb of the blasted tree. Her eye followed the wire as it stretched across the open field to a slender wooden pole, and then leapt to another pole, and from there the wire soared upward into the tops of a dense stand of tall trees and vanished.

Mary, quite forgotten for the moment, took a step back from the fracas and collided with something hard. When she turned to look, the idiot towered over her. Up close she could see that, despite his immense bulk and size, he was not much more than a boy. The idiot boy smiled droolingly down at her and giggled inanely. She took a stumbling step backward as he lurched closer and groped her breast with a huge hand. Thankfully, the carriage driver appeared to rescue her. "Stop that, now Adam," he warned and put a hand to the boy's massive chest, trying to push him back. But it was like trying to push away a fully-grown bull. "Back up, Adam," he repeated, voice hardening, "you're frightnin' the lady." He pushed again, putting all his weight into it, but the massive figure proved immovable. So instead the driver fumbled in a pocket, snatched out a coin and held it beneath the giant's nose. "Here's a shiny penny for you, Adam. Now be a good lad and step away."

The giant moaned excitedly, snatched the coin, and played with it in his huge hands, grinning and gurgling with laughter. Then the massive form stomped backward a step, allowing them to pass.

"Sorry about that, Ma'am," Tom apologised as he escorted Mary to the waiting carriage. "Adam's simple in the head." He tapped two fingers against his temple. "Normally, he's docile as a cow, but like a cow he gets stroppy sometimes and takes a bit of persuading."

Eyes smarting from the acrid smoke, Mary said nothing, her mouth cottony and her heart softly pounding as the driver lowered the step and helped her climb back into the carriage.

"We're almost home," Tom reassured as he closed the carriage door behind her. "It's just up the lane aways." He clambered back up to his seat, gathered up the reigns and cracked the whip over the horses' ears and the carriage rumbled off.

The episode had left Mary in a flux of emotion. She drew off her travelling bonnet and used it to fan her face. She resolved not to look upon the ghastly scene as they drew even with the knot of men who crowded into the hedgerow to allow them to pass. But after the carriage had rattled on another thirty feet she could not help herself and leaned out the window to look behind. Adam, the idiot boy, stood in the middle of the lane, watching them go. For a moment the slack face stretched into a distraught grimace, the broken-hearted face of a child being left behind by its mother. But with distance the features hardened, and the dull eyes lit with animal intelligence and she seemed to hear a voice calling out to her, as if from across the years and many miles travelled: *Creator . . . why do you flee from me? Am I not also your child . . . ?* The colossus reached out a grasping claw toward Mary, as if trying to seize her by a the heart . . . and tear it from her chest.

~

FYNE COURT

I had a dream, which was not all a dream. The bright sun was extinguish'd, and the stars did wander darkling in the eternal space, rayless and pathless, and the icy earth swung blind and blackening in the moonless air. . . Lord Byron

In the time it had been stationary, the air inside the carriage had bittered with the noisome reek of wood smoke. Mary drew a silk fan from the travelling bag on the seat beside her, snapped it open with a flick of the wrist and fluttered it in an attempt to fan the smoke out the open carriage window. It was only then that she noticed a male figure sprawled in the seat opposite who was apparently the true source of the smoke. The man puffed at a long-stemmed clay pipe, his face obscured by a caul of silvery smoke swirling about his head and shoulders. But as the carriage gained speed, the smoke was drawn out the nearest window and she briefly perceived the man's eyes and the smile curled about his pipe stem. It struck Mary with shock that she recognised those eyes, that heart-squeezing smile and realised who the figure was: her husband, Percy Bysshe Shelley, dead now some twenty years. But then the figure blurred, became vague, and dissolved into smoke, which swirled away out the open window, leaving her blinking.

A trick of the mind. Just another of her hallucinations. A wraith conjured from wood smoke and her ever-over-active imagination.

As a mostly solitary child, Mary had been banished from home by her hateful stepmother and packed off to live with relatives in Scotland. With no childhood companions or playmates, invisible friends and imaginary beings provided Mary with solace. But these days, she knew that these tricks of the mind presaged something dire, the way a rumble of distant thunder on a sunny day foretells the violence of the thunderstorm yet to come. She shook her head, as if to shake the lingering after-image free of her mind. But such visitations were worryingly frequent these days. And, inevitably, one of her blinding headaches usually followed on.

Although her hands still trembled, Mary took up her journal and pen and began to scribble an account of the horrifying scene she had just witnessed. But her pen had barely touched paper when she cried out as a red hot needle thrust through the back of her left eye. The pain snatched her breath away, doubling her over, and she whimpered from its extremity. Thankfully, after a few moments of excruciating agony, the pain eased, leaving behind the dull throb of an incipient headache. She would need to take some of her laudanum and soon, before the headache blossomed in full force. Mary lay back on the seat, eyes squinched shut, and willed the carriage to arrive at their destination.

After another ten minutes, the farm fields fell behind, and the enormous trees of an ancient forest rose on either side of the lane. Once again Mary smelled smoke: only this time she recognised the smoke from coal fires. By now her headache had abated to a skipping throb and she peered out the window of the moving carriage, eyes scanning for a nearby residence.

Just then she noticed a figure clad in black tramping the road ahead. The figure walked with his back to her, and did not look behind, but moved to the side of the road—apparently upon hearing the approaching carriage. As the coach drew close, Mary saw that the tall figure was a young man dressed in a prelate's black clothing. He wore a capella saturno, or soup plate hat—a hat with a wide circular brim and a rounded crown of the type typically worn by Roman Catholic clergymen. Mary had seen such hats regularly during her travels in Italy, but they were an uncommon site in England. Still the hat identified the young man as some kind of clergyman. As the carriage passed, the young man turned to fling a look her way and his gaze momentarily locked with Mary's. It was a fleeting glimpse and then the young man whisked by, but his eyes, dark as coffin soil, had seemed to bore deep into Mary's soul and an involuntary shudder shook her frame, as if someone had just stepped over her grave.

And then they were past, and although the sight had been fleeting, for some miles onward the vision of the young's man long and sallow face, with his lank black hair spilling down like black water from beneath the soup bowl hat, and his uncanny eyes left an indelible stain upon Mary's mind.

Just then, the carriage wheel struck a large rock, which was flung up and caromed off the side of the carriage with a *whack!* Mary leaned out the window and peered ahead. Still, the stony lane ahead offered no clue as to the whereabouts of a fine house, and likewise the tall trees screened the view, affording no glimpses of smoking chimneystacks, or high gables. But then the carriage slowed as it reached a set of stone gateposts and turned sharp left into a long driveway hacked through the dense press of trees. The driver slowed the horses to a plod, but it was clear the creatures could smell their stables, for they whinnied and snorted, anxious to be back in their stalls with a feedbag over their noses. The carriage jounced along the gloomy drive, swung sharp right, and burst back into sunlight as they rolled into a wide courtyard with a handsome mansion of two stories on the right, and a carriage house and stables on the left. This was Fyne Court, the country estate of her host. At sight of the carriage, a barefoot stable boy jumped up from the overturned bucket he'd been sitting upon and ran inside the open front doors of the big house. A moment later, the household servants spilled out and assembled into a receiving line.

The carriage clattered to standstill and the driver leapt down to lower the step. As Mary descended, a finely dressed gentleman and a fine lady (no doubt the owners of the great house) came forward to greet her, both smiling broadly. Although she had only seen the man once before, and that had been thirty years ago, she instantly recognised the open face and handsome features. And though the shoulders had acquired a stoop, the gent still enjoyed a full head of hair, although the carefully combed and quaffed waves now shone glossy silver. The young woman who hung close to his shoulder was a ravishing beauty barely out of her teen years, with long chestnut curls spilling about her shoulders.

"Mrs Shelley," the silver-haired man said in greeting, "I am Andrew Crosse and you are right welcome to Fyne Court." Crosse bowed like a diplomat and, taking Mary's hand, kissed it. "I have been an admirer of your writings these many years, and now at last we meet."

Mary smiled and curtsied in reply. "I have the advantage of you, Mister Crosse, in having met you before."

Puzzlement swept the man's face and then he remembered, "Ah, yes, your letter mentioned that you and your late husband attended one of my lectures in London." He shook his head and smiled wonderingly. "All so many, many years ago now."

Mary returned his smile and said, "Nevertheless, the impression you made upon us both was profound and proved an inspiration for my novel."

It was clear Andrew Crosse was a man used to smiling for one rarely left his face, but he looked especially pleased at the revelation. "It is kind of you to say so, but I am sure the imagination of Mary Shelley requires no assistance from anyone."

Mary shifted her attention to Crosse's lovely companion, who had been hanging back. "Ah, but this must be your beautiful daughter . . ." she paused, awaiting a name.

Crosse dropped his eyes with obvious embarrassment and

confided, "I blush to correct you, Mrs Shelley. This is not my beautiful daughter, but my beautiful wife, Cornelia."

Mary's mouth opened slightly and she coloured, aghast at her faux pas. But the age difference was extreme.

Crosse noticed her embarrassment and quickly interjected, "A common mistake, I assure you, Mrs Shelley." He chuckled. "Believe me when I say that I am quite the scandal in these parts."

Mary beamed a conspiratorial smile and said, "I am quite used to scandal, Mister Crosse. I have been the centre of one for most of my life."

All three laughed. "Then we shall all be scandalous together," Cornelia Crosse said and rushing forward embraced Mary with exuberance, kissing her upon both cheeks in the continental style and saying breathlessly, "My dearest, Mrs Shelley, I cannot tell you how thrilled I am to meet such an accomplished woman. You and your mother are paragons and the model for all womanhood."

"Dear me!" Mary exclaimed breathlessly, embarrassed and taken aback by Cornelia's unrestrained show of enthusiasm. "I have barely arrived and already I am a paragon. I tremble at such expectations."

Crosse laughed good-naturedly and taking Cornelia's hand in both of his, kissed it affectionately. His adoration for his young wife was evident. "Although my darling Cornelia be but twenty and five, she has the wit, intelligence and wisdom of a woman twice her age. She has a keen and enquiring mind and acts as secretary and assistant in my experiments. So even though I am the local scandal, it is a price I am happy to pay." They all laughed again and then Crosse seemed to remember his duties as host. "Over the years, Fyne Court has received a number of distinguished guests: the poet Robert Southey, and Mister Wordsworth and Mister Coleridge were frequent visitors when they both took cottages in Nether Stowey. And now we are thrilled to receive the wife of Percy Bysshe Shelley—"

"Not just the wife of a famous poet, dear husband," Cornelia interrupted, her tone, gently scolding, "but the authoress of *Frankenstein*, the most thrilling novel of our time." She leaned close to Mary and whispered, "I have read it three times, but each time I was so afrightened I had to sleep with the bedside candles burning all night."

They all laughed and then Crosse said, "But we must tour you about the house and grounds, Mrs Shelley, and then Cornelia will show you to the room we have prepared—"

"And then we have a special surprise," Cornelia interrupted. "Another house guest who is most anxious to meet you."

"But first shall we will take tea in our flower garden. And then—"

"Mister Crosse," Mary interrupted, "I must crave your indulgence. I have been travelling by coach from London for three days and the journey has taken its toll. I am having one of my headaches. I wonder if I might lie down for a while . . . before the tour."

Crosse's face creased with concern. "Oh, you are unwell? I am sorry to hear it. And here I've been blathering on like a fool. You must forgive my simple country manners, Mrs Shelley, we at Fyne Court are quite out of practice when it comes to entertaining." He turned to his wife. "Cornelia, my darling, would you show our guest to the room we have prepared?"

Mary allowed Cornelia to link her by the arm as they strolled to the handsome front entrance of the grand house, and the receiving line of servants bowed and curtsied as they approached.

Cornelia was as effervescent as glass of freshly poured champagne. She spoke so rapidly her words ran into one another. "Dear Mrs Shelly. I am sorry. So sorry your travels have proved wearisome. We— I mean Mister Crosse and I—receive so few visitors here in the country. And men. Mostly. Our visitors. Mostly men, I am sad to say. Well, I do not mean I am sad . . . Oh, but I am bursting, simply bursting to speak with another woman, and especially one so wise and accomplished."

As they stepped across the threshold, Mary cast a glance behind her. Tom, the carriage driver, stood conversing with his master. Both men huddled close, heads bowed, speaking in a low mutter. Something the carriage driver said chased the smile from Crosse's face and replaced it with a look of concern. Mary guessed he had been told the news of the lightning strike and the death of his tenant's cows.

But then Cornelia drew Mary through the open doorway and into a handsome entrance hall hung with large family portraits. The portraits looked familiar, more by the style of the artist than by their content, but looking up into the light daggered Mary's brain, so she kept her gaze low. The hall smelled of French polish and the fresh bouquets of flowers that bedecked every table and wall sconce. They ascended a handsome staircase of burled and polished cherry, and then Cornelia guided her along a hallway, past a desiccated ficus thrusting up from a large, oriental vase, and in through a open door where she found herself in a large and brightly lit bedroom.

"I do hope you will find this room comfortable."

"Oh, but the room looks lovely," Mary said. "Most commodious," but by now she had to shade her eyes from the light.

"Is there anything I might fetch you?" Cornelia asked.

Mary was mortified to be waited on by the mistress of the house, rather than a servant, but it was clear that Cornelia found her an object of fascination and was loathe to leave her side. "A drink of water, if you please, so I might take my medicine."

The young woman smiled eagerly and bounced out of the room, leaving the door ajar. Tom, the carriage driver, clomped in a moment later, arms laden with Mary's baggage. Following at his heels was the barefoot stable boy, who proudly carried Mary's canvas travel bag in both small arms. Tom set the two large bags upon the floor and gestured for the stable boy to lay the travel bag on the foot of the bed.

"This here's Titch," Tom said, introducing the boy. "He's my help in the stables. We calls him Titch on account of he's so small. Say hello to the fine lady, Titch."

At Tom's bidding, Titch snatched off his cap, said a cheerful "Hallo, ma'm!" and bowed from the waist like a courtier.

Mary smiled at the precious little child. He was about the age that her Willmouse would have been if . . . if only . . .

Tom touched the brim of his hat and shooed the boy out of the room, closing the door behind him.

Mary opened the small travelling bag and began to unload the contents, arranging them on the nearby dressing table. She took out a number of hair combs and brushes, and then began to unpack her personal totems: items she carried with her on all her journeys, and had done since Mary and Percy Bysshe Shelley's first headlong flight to the Continent. First came her green leather journal with its cracked and concertinaed spine. And then a small box with a mother of pearl inlay that contained hand-drawn miniatures: of her second daughter, Clara, of her son, William, and one of her late husband, Percy Bysshe Shelley. The final portrait she set out was of her son, Percy Florence Shelley, drawn when he was a schoolboy of eight years, now a Cambridge scholar at 23. Each portrait contained scissored locks of fine baby hair; the portrait of her late husband contained a single auburn curl shot through with grey strands, which had been snipped after death. She arranged the miniatures on the dresser top in a kind of morbid chronology, from the first dead child to the sole living son. Digging deeper in her bag, she took out a slender smoke-blue bottle whose gummed label identified it is as *Laudanum*. She set the bottle down on the dresser and returned to unpacking. Next, she removed a small wooden box fashioned of ivory-coloured sandalwood and paused to examine it. Carved upon the lid was a butterfly, symbol of the immortal soul. The box was exquisitely made and its cunning carpentry concealed the secret of how it could be opened. Mary's fingers pressed down upon the butterfly and slid the lid to one side to reveal a silk drawstring bag wrapped by a crumpled sheet of vellum covered in straight lines of handwriting. This was the poem *Adonais*, written in Percy Shelley's own precise hand. She set the poem aside and untied the drawstring bag. The object she drew out resembled a fist-sized, shrivelled date. It was the heart of Percy Bysshe Shelley. Calcified from a bout of tuberculosis early in the poet's life, it had failed to burn as the rest of his body rendered to ash upon his funeral pyre. She sat holding the shrivelled heart for a moment, examining it, and then drew it to her lips and tenderly kissed the ossified organ. That ritual performed, she returned the heart to its silken bag, wrapped the crumpled poem about it and settled everything back into the sandalwood box. She rummaged a final time in the travelling bag and brought out a corked and paper wrapped glass bottle. Though the label was torn and faded, the words *Prussic Acid* were just legible. She had purchased the chemical from a Swiss apothecary many years ago, during the darkest and most turbulent time in the marriage with her poet husband, and for reasons she could not admit to, had carried it with her ever since.

A knock came at the door. Mary hurriedly returned the glass bottle to her bag and was just standing up when the bedroom door flung open and Cornelia rushed in. She was carrying a stone jug and a drinking glass and smiled at Mary as he she crossed the room and set both down upon the dresser top. "I had the kitchen maid draw the water fresh for you," she said, slightly out of breath. "It is so much cooler straight from the well."

"Thank you," Mary said. "Most kind." Cornelia's eye drifted from the water jug to the objects arrayed on the dresser top. "Oh, but how sweet. You have set out your trinkets to make the room yours."

Mary grieved from a sense of invasion as Cornelia's eyes roved greedily over her personal shrine. The younger woman's gaze rummaged among the objects and soon settled upon the sandalwood box. With rising concern, Mary guessed what was about the happen but Cornelia was too quick and snatched the box from the dresser top.

"What a pretty box," she said brightly, stroking the wood with her slender fingers, "A box with no obvious catch to open it." She looked coyly at Mary, "But what secret does it contain?"

Mary struggled to restrain herself from the urge to lunge forward and snatch the box back. Instead, she bit her lip and tried to appear unconcerned. "It is a keepsake," Mary quickly said. "A *personal* keepsake. From my late husband." She had made the comment to stop Cornelia's further prying, but instead the younger woman lifted the box to her ear and shook it. The heart inside softly thumped against the sides of the box.

"Could the box contain a stack of perfumed billet-doux tied with a red ribbon?" Cornelia teased. Mary winced as Cornelia's slender fingers pried and twisted at the box, trying to open it. "I do hope it's something wicked."

Mary opened her mouth and strained to say something, but no words came out. Thankfully, Cornelia's gaze next fell upon the smoke-blue bottle, and like a child distracted by a new toy, she set aside the box and snatched the bottle up. "Laudanum!" she said breathlessly.

"Yes," Mary said, struggling to keep the impatience from her voice. "It is medicine . . . for my headaches. The reason I asked for the water." A current of irritation surged through Mary. Cornelia was like a badly behaved child: impolite, impulsive, grabbing things, trespassing upon the privacy of others.

Cornelia gasped dramatically, "I have always *so* wanted to try laudanum." She clutched the bottle to her chest with both hands and spun about the room. "Andrew is very strict on such matters and forbids me. He says drinking laudanum leads to wickedness and licentious behaviour." Cornelia lavished Mary with an arch look. "I have heard stories that much laudanum was taken at the Villa Diodati." She giggled naughtily and added, "And opium smoked? Don't tell me now, but you must confide in me later. You might think I am but a simple country wight, but I grew up in London and I am very hard to shock. And I won't tittle-tattle your secrets. I promise, I will be as silent as the grave."

Mary smiled placidly as if she were indulging a child, which wasn't far from the truth. Cornelia Crosse may indeed have had a keen and probing mind, but it was also an immature and naïve mind that craved to be indulged.

And was I any different at that age? Mary reproached herself. *I was barely seventeen when I eloped with another woman's husband.* She wrenched her mind away before her thoughts could stray farther in that direction.

"Laudanum has its uses," Mary said, "but they are best kept to medicinal ones, such as for my headaches. You are right, though, there was much taking of laudanum at the Villa Diodati. We were young and reckless and delighted in outraging public morals and mocking society and its conventions." When she began her speech Mary had intended it to be a lesson, a warning to the younger woman; but just speaking of those days released a warm burst of nostalgia beneath her breastbone. She ached with a palpable craving for the giddy sense of freedom of that time in her life. Yes, they had been wicked. All of them. Even her. But she had never again felt as free and alive. It was a time when life was an adventure still to be lived. Years before care and worry, loss and grief, and pillowcases stained with tears. Now, at the halfway point of her life, she spent her days looking backward rather than forward.

"But we were made to pay for our excesses," she admitted sadly. "There is always a price to pay, in one fashion or another. There were four of us that summer at the Villa Diodati: Lord Byron, his personal doctor, John Polidori, my half-sister Claire and my beloved Percy. And now . . . " she sighed and continued, " . . I am the only one." She neglected to point out that her half-sister was still very much alive, but estranged from her with a bitterness and vitriol such that she was effectively as dead to Mary as the rest.

Once again, a hot needle thrust again through Mary's left eye, causing her to cry out. She dropped her head and covered her face with a trembling hand.

Cornelia's face grew white. She rushed forward and pressed the bottle in Mary's hands. "Please, forgive me. I am a silly prattling goose while you are suffering. I pray you take your medicine and I shall leave you in peace." She turned and moved to the door, but remembered something and turned back at the threshold. "When shall I awaken you?"

Mary shook her head and forced a smile. Her headache was rapidly worsening, a brutal pressure that threatened to split wide the sutures of her skull. "I doubt I shall actually sleep. I just wish to close my eyes and lie down a while."

"Ah, very well." Cornelia flashed a weak smile, then finally left the room and pulled the door shut behind her. Mary exhaled a long sigh of relief. She moved to the window and looked out for a moment, shielding her eyes against the brightness of the day. Her room boasted an idyllic view over the courtyard stables. From this side of the house it was but a few strides past the stables to a closed gate which invited a walker to step through and wander into the sylvan landscape beyond where the land dropped away into a natural green bowl dotted with the cotton wool shapes of sheep grazing under blue skies strewn with fluffy white clouds. The scene was lovely, but the sunlight was jarring and so Mary dragged the heavy curtains closed. She returned to the dresser and poured water from the stone jug into the cut-crystal glass. Cornelia had been thoughtful: the water was cool and chilled the glass. Mary grasped the slender blue bottle of laudanum. She bit into the resistant cork and twisted and it popped free with a squeak. She splashed three large dashes into the water, paused, and then added a fourth. She swirled the mixture in the glass and then raised it to her lips and gulped it down, eager to ease her throbbing head. Then she recorked the bottle and set it down upon the dresser. Remembering the bottle of Prussic Acid, she placed it in the lowest dresser drawer and piled clothes atop it, to better conceal it from Cornelia's prying hands. Her unpacking finished, Mary lay down on the bed fully dressed, and closed her eyes. After a moment, she noticed something beneath her feet. A spare blanket had been laid on the foot of the bed. She snatched it up and drew it over herself, closed her eyes, and let out a weary sigh. But then a moment later, disturbed by a sudden thought, she opened them again. She rolled from the bed, and groped the dresser top until her fingers closed upon the sandalwood box. Clutching it, she returned to the bed and lay down, her head sinking deep into the goose down pillows, the box clutched in both hands, which she now tucked beneath the pillowcase. Even after all these many years, the contents of the box still exuded the smell of wood smoke. Mary breathed it in, comforted by the aroma. Soon, the laudanum began to take effect. She felt her limbs turn leaden as her body melted into undulating waves of relaxation pulling her down into sleep. From somewhere, far away, she heard a distant noise—a clunk. Her groggy brain grappled with it and finally interpreted the sound as a door opening. With a great effort, she cracked her eyes slightly. With the curtains drawn tight, the room was suffused in gloom, but now a shadowy figure hovered at the open door, one hand on the doorknob.

Cornelia? Watching her?

Should I sit up? Mary pondered. *Let her know I am not asleep?*

Mary felt uneasy to be observed in such a vulnerable state. She feared that Cornelia's curiosity would spur her, that she would tiptoe to the bed and her young and nimble fingers would ease the box from Mary's relaxed grip. The figure took several steps farther into the room. When it reached the foot of the bed, Mary, squinted through her eyelashes as she counterfeited sleep. Even so, she could tell that the woman was not Cornelia. The woman was blonde, much taller, and older. Probably in her thirties. The stranger clutched a armful of bedclothes as she glared down, and Mary could tell from her posture that she was stiff with rage and hatred. Her voice, when she spoke, came out in a whisper as sharp as broken glass.

"Why are you not dead yet?" the woman hissed. "You are nothing but a burden to me *and* to your son."

The words were spoken with unbridled hatred and venom and deeply alarmed Mary so that her heart jolted within her chest. She wanted to fling aside the blanket and sit up. She was quite sure she had never met the woman who was speaking to her so rancorously. Mary wanted to call out, to shout for Cornelia, but she was a swimmer caught in an irresistible undertow and as her eyes drifted shut, her muscles slackened and her mind surrendered, submerging beneath the laudanum waves.

A DISTURBING DREAM

Dreamt that my little baby came to life again; that it had only been cold, and that we rubbed it before the fire, and it lived. Awake and find no baby. I think about the little thing all day. Not in good spirits . . . Mary Shelley

She was walking on a beach. A beach she had never seen before but somehow knew. To her right a great body of water sparkled beneath a Mediterranean sun; gentle waves swelled and swooned onto the sandy shore. The wind carried to her the acrid tang of burning driftwood, and there ahead she saw a large bonfire burning. Drawing closer, she recognised a sombre group of mourners posed before a driftwood pyre, faces she knew: Edward Trelawney, Leigh Hunt, and of course, Lord Byron, proud and aloof as ever. He had just emerged from the water after a swim, his muscular body naked save for a pair of cotton drawers the water had rendered translucent so that she could plainly see his powerful buttocks and slack penis. Then her eyes dropped lower, down to the malformed foot. Byron, noticing the direction of her gaze, lashed her with a contemptuous snarl, and limped away.

The body on the pyre was her beloved Percy. After the sailboat capsized his body had drifted in the water for ten days before it washed ashore. They refused to let her view the corpse and informed her that the face and hands were gone—flayed to the bone by nibbling fish, and so she averted her eyes, looking only at the slender torso she had often embraced, the graceful arms that had once held her.

By now the body was fully immolated. The melting skin of the chest shrank and peeled away and the ribcage surged up from its prison of flesh. Fat crackled and spat as organs burned. And though the flames licked about the heart it remained unconsumed. At that moment, Edward Trelawney rushed forward, one hand thrown up to shield his face from the heat, plunged a hand into the flames, and snatched loose the heart. He dropped it on the sand, where it sat smoking like a stony meteor fallen from the heavens. Trelawney drew out a handkerchief and dropped to one knee. He wrapped the smouldering organ in the hand-kerchief and then offered it up to Leigh Hunt, Percy's friend. Hunt held out both hands and accepted the prize with a solemn bow of his head.

Mary rushed up and accosted him. "Might not I have the heart? He was my love. My husband."

Hunt regarded Mary with a puzzled expression and then silently turned away as if he had not heard her speak. Trelawney and the other members of the funeral party looked upon her with similar indifference. Hunt turned his back and trudged away to the waiting carriage.

"Wait," she called to him. "The heart is mine. You must give it to me."

"Mary!"

She spun at a familiar voice. It was Percy's voice. Something drew her closer to the pyre, and still closer until the heat seared her cheeks and dried her eyes. At that moment, the burning driftwood settled with a roar, ejecting hot sparks that swirled in a crackling vortex about her. The collapsing pyre gave the burning corpse the illusion of animation as it sat up in the flames. But then the skull slowly lifted and gouts of flame flared from the empty eye sockets. "Mary," the corpse spoke.

Transfixed with terror, Mary could neither move nor speak.

"My beloved," the corpse said and clumsily shambled erect, shedding burning timbers.

Mary's throat clenched so she was unable to unleash the scream coiled in her lungs. She swivelled her eyes to seek help from Lord Byron or Trelawney, but the carriage and the other mourners had vanished.

She was alone on the beach.

The corpse, trailing smoke from its charred flesh, stepped from the pyre and tottered toward her. The voice with no tongue to articulate words slurred, "Maaaairrreeeeeee."

As the corpse loomed over her, she was paralysed and unable to move. It placed its skeletal hands upon her shoulders and she felt her skin burn and blister beneath its touch.

"Mary," it hissed. "Embrace meeeeeeeeeeeeee."

DEAD CHILDREN AND A MOTHER'S TEARS

> Thus strangely are our souls constructed, and by slight ligaments are we bound to prosperity and ruin. *Mary Shelley*

S he awakened as a sleeper does when jolted awake by a sudden summer storm: not having heard the thunder while asleep, but with the rumble still echoing in her ears once conscious.

Mary Shelley opened her eyes to find a face hovering over her. Although her body was still a vassal of sleep, her mind was fully aware. She knew she had just torn free of a nightmare, but the dream still gripped her in its thrall, reluctant to let go.

"Mary?" the face hovering over her was a younger woman's face, not a monster's. "Mary, are you awake?"

Long seconds passed as slowly, gradually, Mary repossessed her body, piece by piece, until at last she was able to find her lips, her tongue, and eventually her voice. "Dream," she gasped. "Horrid dream." Her body returned in a rush so that at last she sat up creakily in the bed, the last images of the beach, the pyre, the monstrous face lapsing from her memory like a dissipating fog. It took a moment to recall who she was. Where she was. And then it all returned in a rush: the coach from Bath, the carriage ride to Fyne Court, and the young woman who now wrung her hands, bit her lip and looked down upon her with helpless solicitude. The author of *Frankenstein* wiped crusts of sleep from the corners of her eyes. "I am sorry to frighten you. I did not think I would slumber."

"You have slept for four hours," Cornelia said. "That is why I came to awaken you. Whatever were you dreaming? You were trying to cry out in your sleep and your face was a mask of terror. What dread nightmare troubled your slumber?"

Mary swung around on the bed and set her feet on the floor, then stripped off the blanket she had wrapped herself in and tossed it on the bedside chair. "The nightmare?" she let out an ironic laugh. "All my life has been a tragic and portentous dream that keeps coming true."

"My dear, Mary," Cornelia fretted, "do not speak so. I know you lost your husband, but you have your children."

Mary looked up at her wearily. "My first child came two months early and lived but a few weeks."

Cornelia's eyes left Mary's face and drifted to the portraits set out upon the dresser. Mary guessed which miniature she was looking at.

"That was my second child, William," she continued, her voice taut. "Willmouse, I used to call him. He died of malaria when he was three. My second daughter Clara died of dysentery. She was but two years old. And then there are the losses I have no keepsakes to remind me of, save the tattered rag of my soul: my mother who died three weeks after giving birth to me; my husband's first wife who took her own life after he eloped with me; my half-sister Fanny, who fled our family to a rustic inn where she drank a fatal dose of laudanum; Lord Byron who died of fever while fighting the Turks, poor Doctor Polidori, who lost a card game at the casino, retired to his rooms, and swallowed Prussic Acid. All who have ever been close to me have died. Died young. Died tragically." Mary's still-handsome face distorted with anger and woe as she cast a pitiful look at the younger woman and asked, "Am I not cursed? For grief walks forever at my side, holding my hand."

"Oh, my dearest, Mrs Shelley," the younger woman said. "I feel your loneliness. It crushes my heart with the weight of gravestone. Have you no one left?"

Mary smiled sadly, feeling tears spring in her own eyes. "I have my son, Percy Florence." She picked up the miniature from the dresser top and handed it to Cornelia. "It was painted when he was a boy," she explained. "Now he is a young man at Cambridge."

"A *handsome* young man," Cornelia said, admiring the picture. "Is he very like his father?"

A normal mother would have said yes. A normal mother would have painted a flattering portrait. A normal mother would have gushed and cooed. But Mary Shelley was the daughter of Mary Wollstonecraft, and though by a cruel dagger thrust of fate the two had never met, Mary had grown from girl to a woman reading her mother's books and letters and private journals so that her mother's voice was a ghost that haunted her from within; thus schooled, she had learned to prize honesty above sentimentality.

"Percy Florence is a wonderful young man, and as he is my child I love and treasure him. Indeed, I have sacrificed everything for him." Mary's head tremored slightly. "But he is not like his father." Her eyes dewed and her voice softened as she looked back through the long tunnel of years. "For Percy Bysshe Shelley was like a star fallen from the heavens. But the earth is no place for a star . . ." She smiled bitterly, and added in a broken voice, " . . . and shooting stars burn brief but bright and shed their transient glory."

But even as she spoke Mary wondered *Why am I baring my soul to this stranger? To this flibbertigibbet of a girl I have just met?*

But then her mind echoed the answer:

Because no one else has ever wanted to listen.

Cornelia's eyes suddenly filled with hot tears as her face collapsed. She covered her mouth with a hand but a huge sob burst out that wracked her whole body. And then a second sob followed close on, so violent it threatened to break her in two.

Mary, looking deep into Cornelia's troubled eyes, immediately guessed the truth. "You, too, have lost a child?" she asked softly.

Cornelia had both hands clamped tight over her mouth and could only nod frantically.

"Oh, my poor lamb," Mary said.

Cornelia flew into Mary's arms and hugged her desperately, the way a heartbroken child hugs her mother, seeking consolation. When the sobs that wracked her thin frame finally subsided, she spoke in a choked voice. "My babe also came too early. Fu-fu-five months. A gu-gu-girl." Her voice cracked and failed. "I would have named her Emily." She covered her face with her hands and squeezed out a keening sound.

Mary slipped her arm around Cornelia's slender shoulders and hugged her. "But you are young," she consoled. "And strong. You will have others."

Cornelia broke from Mary's embrace and shook her head. She looked up at Mary, her eyes bright with tears, her lower lip aquiver. "But don't you see? My situation is extreme. I am but 25 and Andrew is 70. I had hoped to be a good wife and present him with a child." And then she added in a tragic voice, "even though he will not live to see that child grow up."

"But you will be a mother, Cornelia. You are in your prime childrearing years. Many women lose their first as I did. Do not despair yet."

Both froze at a voice calling from the other side of the bedroom door. "Cornelia?" It was Andrew Crosse. "Cornelia, is our guest awake yet?"

Cornelia threw a questioning look at Mary who answered the question with a quick nod. "Yes," Cornelia called back. "We will join you shortly, husband."

"Very good then, I shall await you in the parlour," Andrew Crosse replied and the floor creaked as he moved away.

"Oh, look at us," Mary said, affecting a carefree air she did not feel. "We are being maudlin and sentimental when we have just met and become firm friends." She smiled and said, "Although we women are strong, men flatter themselves that we are weak. We must not give them any reason to question our womanly strength," And with that Mary picked up the water jug and poured a short glass of water and then removed the laudanum bottle from its drawer, uncorked it and splashed two large drops to the water. "Here," she said, offering the glass to Cornelia."

Cornelia eyed the glass longingly, but hesitated. "Oh, I must not. It is for your headaches."

"Take it," Mary insisted. "A small dose. It will lift your spirits as it lifts mine."

Cornelia received the glass eagerly, touched the rim to her full lips, and took an experimental sip.

"Ugh!" she said, as her face spasmed with disgust. "It is bitter as poison."

"Do not sip it. Drink it down all at once."

Cornelia lifted the glass to her lips again and this time gulped it in three long swallows. She dabbed her wet lips on the back of her hand and shot Mary a quizzical look. "But I feel no different."

"It takes time. But you'll see. Soon your worries will be lifted. But you are sworn to secrecy. You must not tell your husband. It will be our secret . . . as we are new friends."

The younger woman smiled with mischievous delight. "Yes, I love secrets. It will be our secret." She seemed to become aware of the time. "Oh, but Andrew is waiting for us." She appraised Mary's dress a moment and asked, "Have you a wrap? Evening draws apace, and the country air cools noticeably with the dusk."

Mary took a wrap out of her bag, threw it about her shoulders and held out her arm to once again link arms with her host. As they stepped through the door, Mary paused and cast one last glance at the sketches of her husband and children, living and dead. For a moment she questioned if she had really loved any of them. Was her life real, or just a narrative she was composing, arranging characters and action for the best dramatic effect? Before the door swung fully shut, the shaft of light spilling into the room illumined the blanket she had carelessly tossed aside, and for a moment the rumples and folds were transmogrified by light and shadow so that the blanket formed a hideous face with a jutting forehead, a prognathic jaw and a cavernous black eye socket where a spark of light betrayed the presence of a lurking eye. It was a face she knew only too well—the face of the thing that had dragged its rude form in a slow and tedious pursuit across the decades and followed her to this place . . .

. . . where, hopefully, she could at last lay the ghost to rest by the same *dread engine* that raised it.

STRANGE STAR ASCENDANT

> *Between two worlds life hovers like a star, twixt night and moon, upon the horizon's verge . . . Lord Byron*

I awaken, although whether from sleep into into wakefulness, or from wakefulness into sleep, I cannot tell.

Am I dead? Is this the Afterlife? Am I in the Bardo?

My mind stretches out, straining to find my extremities, like a hand stretching to fill the fingers of a glove, but finding nothing.

I am bodiless. Inchoate. A spark of awareness floating in a dark void.

My eyes—if indeed I possess eyes—seem to be open, although the only way I can tell is by the solitary star that burns a hole in the fabric of night, so bright it throws all other stars into eclipse. My vision remains fixed upon that solitary point of light, so intense, so dazzlingly brilliant.

I seem to be floating in a flat calm sea. I want to turn my gaze, to look away for one instant, but I am filled with dread to do so—as if I and the strange star rely upon one another for continuance. As if I looked away for one moment the star would burn to ash, its light extinguish, and I would drown in my solitary darkness. But now, as I watch, the star coruscates, its light dimming almost to darkness as it threatens to fizzle and die; but then it flares bright, and then brighter still. And so with each passing moment the light shifts, dims and flares, flares and dims, ever changing. I cling on, sensing somehow that, as long as my starry companion burns, I will endure.

THE WIZARD OF BROOMFIELD

I am fearless, and therefore powerful . . . Mary Shelley

When Cornelia conducted Mary into the parlour, Andrew Crosse was waiting but distracted. They found him stooped over, his rapt attention fixed upon a large barometer hanging on the wall beside the chimney breast. He was tapping on the barometer glass with a fingernail.

"There is my husband," Cornelia muttered to Mary, "ever the scientist, toying with one of his instruments."

Startled, Crosse looked up, his expression of frowning attention brightening to a delighted smile.

"Andrew, dearest," Cornelia said, presenting Mary as if she were a prize won at the local fair, "our guest is awakened."

Crosse swept back the tails of his coat and bowed. "Mrs Shelley. I do hope you are feeling rejuvenated."

"Yes, thank you," Mary agreed, smiling back. "After my nap I am myself again."

There was an embarrassed pause as no one could think of what to say next, and then Cornelia plunged in: "What does your barometer tell you, dear husband?"

"What? Ah, yes. The barometer is falling rapidly."

"Then we should hasten to catch it," Mary said, a quip which caught husband and wife off guard and made them chuckle.

"See," Cornelia said, "Mary is learned in both letters and in natural wit." She cast a quick glance out the nearest window. Outside, the day was blue skied and bright. "Perhaps we should quit the house and begin our tour of the grounds while we still have the light?"

After Cornelia collected her wrap, the three left by the front entrance hall. The day was balmy, and the autumn air carried the sweet scent of ripening apples from the cider press in the stable. The stable doors were swung wide and swallows flitted in and out, and now Tom stepped from its shadows. He had stripped off his shirt in the heat and carried a brown leather horse collar slung over either muscular shoulder. Like any good servant he stopped and froze upon seeing his lord and lady and deferentially dropped his head. At the sight of a naked male torso, Mary also dropped her gaze, but a moment later she could not resist a quick peek. But when she looked up, her eyes locked with Tom's, which caused both parties to hurriedly look away.

The party of three crossed a courtyard swarmed by a living carpet of the most colourful cocks and chickens Mary had ever seen, their fabulous feathers ranging from black and white to rich russety reds and golds. As they waded through the clucking mass, the two women giggled with scarcely suppressed hysteria as the chickens pecked at their fingers and plucked at the trailing hems of their skirts.

Suddenly Mary sensed she was being watched and threw a glance over her shoulder. She was quick enough to catch movement in one of the second storey windows. A slender hand had parted one of the curtains and someone was peeking out. Evidently, the observer knew he or she had been caught spying and Mary saw the hand hurriedly snatch away and the curtain fall closed.

Mary speculated that this might be the mysterious house guest

Cornelia had hinted at upon her arrival, but before Mary could ponder further, Andrew Crosse led them through an arched brick portal at the side of the stables. They now trod a loamy footpath that gradually ascended into the arboreal gloom of the ancient woodland surrounding Fyne Court.

"But what does it mean," Mary asked Crosse as they trudged up the steepening trail, "if the barometer is falling? Is that a good thing?"

The amateur scientist's face lit up a the opportunity to wax eloquent upon matters scientific. "A barometer measures the pressure of the vast ocean of air pressing down upon the earth. When the pressure rises, it means that fair weather is headed our way. And when the pressure falls—"

"Storms ahead?" Mary asked.

Crosse tilted his head to show the ambiguity such a reading might produce.

"Possibly. It generally means we are headed into a spell of changeable weather. However when the pressure falls very rapidly, as it is now, the chance of storms is highly likely."

"With lightning?" Mary asked.

Crosse's smile betrayed his excitement. "Very possibly thunderstorms. It is unseasonably hot for the end of summer and the past two weeks have been dry. Now the winds have shifted from the East as a sea breeze blows onshore. When the cool sea winds are forced to rise over the Quantocks and the airy mass of cold sea air collides with the hot stagnant land air, it might bring thunderstorms, potentially violent ones. As it did last night with so-called, dry lightning, with no rain."

"When might that happen?" Mary asked.

Crosse shook his head. "That is something the barometer cannot foresee. It could be tomorrow. It could be this eve." He smiled forlornly. "And it might not happen at all. Winds are capricious and often shift. The storm may never happen."

Cornelia laughed. "So there you have a scientist's best prediction: something might happen now, something might happen later, or nothing at all may happen."

The three of them shared a laugh as they strolled the path into a walled garden and Mary let out a gasp, "Oh, but this is enchanting!"

The garden was large and laid out in a series of stepped terraces each terrace burgeoning with huge rose bushes, rhododendrons, and every form of English flower. A folly in the Arcadian style had been built at the highest point in the garden. Its dark alcoves were supported by Greek columns providing an ideal spot to rest and survey the gardens protected by an overhanging roof to shield viewers in times of inclement weather.

"Surely you have recreated Kublai Khan's pleasure dome," Mary said.

"On a very modest scale," Crosse conceded. "But speaking of Kublai Khan, you might be interested to know that Mister Coleridge and Mister Wordsworth were regular visitors to Fyne Court when they took cottages in Nether Stowey. It is a very pleasant walk from here."

Cornelia butted in before Crosse could continue, "I think you have told Mrs Shelley that story already."

Crosse looked chagrined, "Oh, I have?"

"Yes, husband. But come," Cornelia urged, "We have much more to show you and then on the morrow you might linger where you like."

They left the walled gardens and proceeded on a path that climbed deep into the dense forest. Here and there Mary glimpsed a slanting ray of light streaking through the tree tops and finally realised what it was: the same shiny copper wire she had seen that morning suspended above the lightning-blasted tree. And now that she had been made aware, when her eyes searched the treetops she noticed the coppery flash of wire stitching paths here and there through the forest canopy.

"I see you have noticed my wires," Crosse said. "I call them my 'explorers.'"

"Yes," Mary agreed. "I saw one of your wires this morning, some distance from here, suspended on poles as it ran across a farmer's field."

Crosse stopped walking and the two women also halted as he

explained. "Yes, I have added wires over the years and now the system spans more than a mile and a half. They are part of my experiments in electricity. The wires gather the great flux of positive and negative charges churning in the atmosphere." He pointed back to the house. "If you look, you can see a number of wires that converge at a single pole. From there they are run into my laboratory." He smiled whimsically. "It used to be the music room, but now it makes music of a rather discordant fashion, which I hope to demonstrate to you tonight."

At the mention of electricity, excitement surged through Mary's veins. This was the reason she had sought out Andrew Crosse and made the long journey from London to Fyne Court. She was grateful that Crosse had brought up the subject without necessitating her to do so.

The party set off again and soon a large pond hove into view. The pond was coloured a vivid emerald green from a skimming of weed and scum floating atop its surface. From the elation of a moment ago, Mary's spirits sank at the sight.

"This is our dragonfly pond," Cornelia said, and scurried toward it. When Cornelia noticed that she and her husband had left Mary behind, she threw a puzzled look behind. "Mary dearest, come closer. You must see the pond. It is alive with dragonflies. But fear not, for they shall not bite you."

Mary answered coyly, "Thank you, but I can see well enough from here."

Mary's eyes were riveted to the green-scummed surface, which even now stirred from an object—a large object—moving beneath. And then something slowly surfaced: the crown of a human head, covered in weed and slime, soon the face emerged, a woman's face, ghastly green and rotten, the eyes glittering within the bruise-black eye sockets. The shoulders next appeared as the woman walked straight toward Mary. The others seemed not to notice. As the figure waded ashore it raised an arm and pointed an accusatory finger at Mary who suddenly realised who the figure was: Harietta Westbrook, the wife Percy Bysshe had callously deserted to elope with Mary.

Later, abandoned by her husband and pregnant by another man, Harietta had filled her pockets with stones and walked into the Serpentine. Hers was the first death in a list of many that festered like wounds in Mary's soul.

"Mary?" Cornelia's call broke the spell. Mary looked to her host who had been standing at the pond's edge, but who now hurried back to join her. With her face a mask of concern, Cornelia snatched up Mary's hands and pressed them between her own. "But are feeling quite well? You suddenly seem distracted?"

Mary risked a nervous glance at the pond. The horrible figure of Harriet Westbrook had vanished.

Another hallucination.

She hesitated a moment and then stuttered, "I, I . . . have a dislike of water."

Cornelia laughed gaily at the comment. "But, whatever for? It is merely a small pond—" She caught herself before she could go any farther. "Oh, oh yes. How thoughtless of me . . . I . . . am so dreadfully sorry . . ."

Mary realised that Cornelia had incorrectly assumed that Mary's loathing of water had been caused by the manner of her husband's death. It was not the case, but she did nothing to dissuade the notion.

"Come along ladies," Crosse urged. He stood waiting at the edge of the pond.

"Mary is fatigued, husband," Cornelia called back. "And suppertime is drawing near. We should not tarry."

Crosse looked baffled, but strolled back to join them. "Shall we return to the house?"

"No, no," Mary said. "I pray that we continue. I am most delighted at what you have shown me and anxious to see more."

And so they continued on the footpath, which rewarded them with delightful woodland vistas at each turn. With his longer stride, Crosse soon left the women far behind as they chatted together and sauntered. When Cornelia looked up and noticed her husband was out of sight around a bend, she threw her arms about Mary and kissed her full on the lips. It was more than a friendly buss, but a deep and lingering kiss, and when they finally broke apart, Mary found her hand resting upon Cornelia's firm and girlish hip. Cornelia whispered, "I feel utterly sublime," and then broke free and skipped away up the path, giggling like a schoolgirl. Mary was shocked and taken aback, and quickly decided she would not share her laudanum so freely again; but as she followed after her hosts, she could still feel the pressure of Cornelia's soft lips upon hers.

The two women finally caught up with Crosse as they summited the top of the woodland loop. Crosse left the path and led the way through a slot cut through the trees. Beyond the tree line, a dry stone wall marked the end of the woods and the beginning of grassy farm fields.

"Look there," Crosse said, pointing to the undulating humps of the Quantock hills in the far distance, "storm clouds over Wales, and moving this way by the look of it."

Sailing across the far horizon was a fleet of dreadnought thunderclouds capped by cauliflower shaped crowns boiling high into the sky. The cloud bottoms were the colour of lead, and were lit here and there by jagged flashes of lightning. "And there we have our approaching storm," Crosse announced, his voice taut with excitement.

It soon became apparent just how far away the storm clouds were. After a prolonged delay of many minutes, the ground gently shook with the low, slow rumble of thunder, muffled by the miles. Moments later, they were hit by a ferocious gust of wind that lashed the treetops and stung their eyes with grit and dust. Both ladies shrieked as the wind lifted their skirts and mussed their carefully quaffed hair.

"Did you feel that?" Crosse asked unnecessarily. "Gusts of wind such as that often presage the coming of a storm." He smiled with manic intensity. "With any luck, we shall have our lightning, and before midnight if my guess be true."

Although the storm was far from imminent, they returned to the woodland path and set off down the sloping trail that led back to Fyne Court. After five minutes, the stony wall of a ruin hove into view. The roofless shell had arched openings at either end, through which a tiny beck ran.

"Oh, but what is this?" Mary asked, "An antique ruin?"

"It is a folly," Crosse explained. "We call it the boat house, although, I assure you, there is no boat inside."

"No," Cornelia said. "Nor could any boat sail upon such trickle of water, save for a paper boat."

Mary winced at Cornelia's mention of "paper boat." Since he was a child, her late husband, Percy Bysshe Shelley, had indulged a mania for paper boats and had even had the crazy idea of distributing his political pamphlets by folding them into paper boats and setting them afloat upon the sea.

The party of three lingered a moment at the boathouse, but the folly was merely a hollow shell that served as a focal point for the eye and held little of interest. Cornelia linked Mary's arm and they set off again. The path descended toward the house, but then turned sharp left through a deliberate gap in the screen of trees. As they stepped through it, Mary gasped at the sight of a squat stone structure. "A castle!" she cried with genuine delight. "A tiny castle!" She shot a look first at Crosse and then Cornelia. "Pray, is it real?"

"It is another folly, I am sad to say," Andrew Crosse confessed "I had it constructed as a playhouse for my children when they were young."

Cornelia quickly countered, "Ah, but it is *my* playhouse now. Andrew keeps a telescope in the right-hand turret for his astronomical observations, but the left-hand turret is my refuge. I read in there and do needlepoint . . ." She laughed gaily, ". . . queen of my own domain."

"How delightful!" Mary said.

Cornelia leaned close and whispered in Mary's ear, "You and I will sneak out later and I shall show you."

They left the castle and strolled to the long driveway where they lingered a moment. Crosse pointed to the rising ground at the rear of the house. "There, Mrs Shelley, if you care to note the tall pole."

She looked and finally spotted what he was pointing at. "Yes, I see that a large number of your wires converge upon it."

"Precisely," Crosse said. "From the pole a thick bundle of wires passes through a high window in the old music room and down to an apparatus where the collected electrical charge is stored. Are you familiar with Leyden jars and galvanic cells?"

Mary nodded. "Somewhat. My late husband was a great enthusiast for scientific discoveries. In his rooms at Oxford he had a solar microscope and various electrical apparatus. And then during our travels we both attended lectures by scientists such as yourself and Galvani and—OW!" Mary cried out at what felt like a sharp sting to her shoulder. A moment later, both Cornelia and Crosse cried out in a like fashion. It took a moment of confused wonder before it became clear that the three of them were under attack, as small stones rained down upon them.

When Mary looked, she saw three shabbily dressed men standing farther up the driveway where they were scooping up stones and flinging them.

"You there!" Crosse shouted to the men. "You're trespassing upon my land. Begone with you!"

But the men ignored Crosse's threat and hastened to snatch up more stones, which they continued to hurl at Mary and the Crosses, stony missiles whizzing through the air about their heads, sharp and deadly, but luckily missing all three. At that moment an angry shout came from behind, and Tom came running along the pathway toward them. He had hold of the leads of two large grey lurchers, which were barking ferociously and dragging him along with such force as if to tear his arms from their sockets. When he reached Crosse, the driver struggled to wrestle the dogs to a standstill.

"It's them troublemakers again, Mister Crosse," Tom said breathlessly. "I seen them gathering at the end of the drive so I fetched the dogs. A few are local villains I recognise, but the rest are lame and broken down labourers, no doubt poured full of strong ale and cider at the *Three Tuns* in Bridgwater. I didn't reckon they'd be cheeky enough to come down the drive. Shall I let Zeus and Thor have a taste of them?"

But there was no need, for at first sight of the dogs the three men dropped their handfuls of stones and took to their heels, running pell-mell back up the drive.

Crosse shook his head. "No. Hold the dogs. As I am a Christian I must first try to reason with these men, fools or no."

And so with Tom and the dogs leading, Crosse and the two women trudged up the drive toward the lane where they found a huddle of seven or eight men loitering. Standing in the midst of them, and obviously their leader, was a tall, thin figure dressed in a clergyman's black weeds. Mary recognised him as the same young man in the cappella saturno hat she had seen from the carriage.

The dogs surged at sight of the men, barking furiously, and Tom strained to hold them back. "There's that damned black crow Smith," Tom spat. "I'd like to have known he's behind this!"

"Crosse shared an angry look with the women. "The tall, thin fellow is the Reverend Philip Smith. He is the instigator, come here to stir things up." He looked to his driver. "Come, Tom, let's you and I see off the scoundrels."

"Oh, no!" Cornelia said, throwing her arms about Crosse and trying to restrain him. "Please, husband, do not risk your safety. Those men look like ruffians!"

"Aye, sir. "Tom agreed. "Ye best stay behind. I'll let the dogs give 'em a good sniff. That'll put the wind up 'em!"

"*I* shall go speak to them," Mary announced.

All looked at Mary with amazement. Crosse shook his head and said, 'I would not be a man worthy of the name if I allowed a guest, and a fine lady at that, to fight my battles for me."

"Listen," Mary said, laying a comforting hand on Crosse's arm, "men respond to other men with violence. But I doubt they would be brazen enough to attack an unarmed woman. They would be transported for it and I believe they know it."

"No! Mary!" Cornelia cried out, reaching for Mary's hand, but it was too late, as the author set off at a fast walk toward the waiting mob. A few more stones whizzed past her head, but the clergymen must have said something, because the fusillade suddenly ended. As she reached the roadway, the cleric raised the Bible toward Mary and began to read aloud the rite of exorcism:

"Most glorious Prince of the Heavenly Armies, Saint Michael the Archangel, defend us in our battle against the principalities and powers, against the rulers of this world of darkness . . ."

Mary ignored him and fixed her attention on the rough posse. From a distance they had appeared threatening, but up close she saw that the Reverend's cohort were less than formidable. The youngest was Rory, a shoeless street urchin of maybe six or seven, while the rest were old and stooped duffers: shabbily dressed men who looked ill or on the point of starvation. "You men," she snapped, "put down those stones at once. Tom knows all your names and we have written them down for the local magistrate."

It was a lie, but Mary gambled that such a pronouncement would strike fear into a mob of uneducated tavern idlers and it worked. The men hastily emptied their hands of the stones they had picked up and many dropped their heads and stared at their feet, anxious to avoid being recognised.

Mary now turned her appraising gaze upon the Reverend Philip Smith. He was a young man, probably straight out of seminary school and, by his pious pout, brimming with self-righteousness and religious zealotry.

"What are you doing here?" she directed her question at the clergyman, "a man of the cloth who should be saving souls, not causing dissent and strife? What gives you the right to molest Mister Crosse and his wife?"

"Smith paused in reciting the rite of exorcism to snarl, "I am here to exorcise the house and woods of the devils that Crosse and his unholy works have summoned from hell."

"The reverend's right," said Walter Furse, a stumpy man with wiry white whiskers. "I done seen the devils dancing on the wires: Cob, Mob, and Chittabob."

And then a local farm labourer, Eli Custard chimed in, "None dare pass the house after dark for his deviltry."

And now all the men wanted a say:

"Aye, and such deaf-making bangs and booms that fright the cattle and cause the ewes to drop their lambs early."

"The Wizard Crosse conjures storms that spoil our corn and barley."

A stout, bald man stepped forward and shook an angry fist. Mary recognised him as Martin Compton, the farmer she had seen just that morning. A fat blue vein throbbed at his temple and his angry words strained through a snarl of crooked teeth, "Crosse's devilish wire summoned the lightning that killed three of my cows just this last night."

Reverend Smith flourished the Bible high. "Andrew Crosse is an atheist who freely boasts he has supplanted the Creator. Such acts of blasphemy shall damn him for eternity."

"Mister Crosse is *not* an atheist . . ." Mary interrupted, and lavished the clergyman with her most beatific smile, ". . . but *I* am."

The young clergyman hissed with shock and spat, "Jezebel!"

Mary shook her head softly. "My name is not Jezebel. It is Mary. Mary Shelley. I am the creator of *Frankenstein*. Does that dread name echo with you?"

Although all the farm labourers were illiterate, over the years the fame of Mary's monster had spread far and wide, and garbled versions of the story—whispered in front parlours and church pews, in ale houses and shearing sheds—were familiar even to those who had never cracked the spine of a book, and who could not as much as scrawl their own name.

The Reverend clearly recognised the name *Frankenstein* and now he raised his Bible and orated as if from the pulpit: "I prophesy that this house of wickedness will die in flames and damnation—"

"Here is a prophesy for *you*," Mary interrupted. "My creature will walk the earth tonight. Here, at Fyne Court. So go home. Bolt your doors. Bar your windows. But it will not stop a monster sewn together from pieces of dead men stolen from a charnel house, and brought to life by a lightning bolt. Sleep if you can. But likely you will awaken with a monster's hand gripping your throat, squeezing the final breath from you."

At her threat all the men shrank back. Rory, the young urchin boy whimpered and plastered his hands over his ears so as not to hear the scorching words Mary uttered.

The vicar held the Bible up to Mary's face like a shield, his hand trembling as he proclaimed, "Hussy, you are damned before the Lord!"

"Yes," Mary agreed mildly, "I am damned." She pushed the holy book aside and leaned into his face. "And I am already burning!"

The men released a collective gasp at a finely dressed gentle-woman boldly blaspheming; their mouths dropped open as she continued, "I am damned as is my undead creature, who will wander the earth until the last man draws breath. When my monster comes tonight, shall I whisper your names to him?"

She looked around at the huddle of men who recoiled and trembled at her gaze. Then she singled out the clergyman. "What say you, Reverend? Shall I whisper your name to the monster? You, Philip Smith of Bridgwater?"

The young Reverend's eyes widened, his nostrils flared with fear and the Bible in his hands lowered in a series of jerks. The gang that had been full of beer and bravado moments ago was suddenly full of nothing but terror. Several men loitering at the back quietly melted away. And then others, noting that their comrades had deserted them, skulked after. Suddenly only four remained. And then three. And then two. Finally, the reverend's sole remaining companion was Martin Compton, the farmer who had lost his cattle and who no doubt helped raise the shambolic posse. His amazed face showed that he recognised Mary from the events of the morning. Even though she said nothing to him, her piercing look was sufficient to drive him stumbling backward and then, with a torn cry, he ran away. The Reverend shrank back from Mary, and looking about, suddenly found himself a priest without a flock.

Smith raised the carved wooden cross that hung around his neck by a stout cord and chanted, "The Lord is my shepherd, I shall not fear—"

At that moment, thunder rumbled in a deep and resonant groan that seemed to percolate up from the bowels of the earth. Moments later, a tremendous gust of wind lashed the treetops with a great cracking and snapping of limbs. It sucked up a yellow vortex of fallen leaves, which swirled about them like a corn devil. Smith's voice shrivelled in his throat and his eyes darted wildly about. It looked and sounded as if something enormous blundered toward them through the forest, smashing trees as it came.

"My monster is early," Mary said, her dark hair blowing wildly about her face. "Reverend Smith, you shall be the first to meet him."

The True Believer now truly believed that a monster was coming for him. The young clergyman let out a piercing shriek and turned to run away down the lane, his black vestments flapping wildly.

Mary suddenly found herself alone. After a lifetime of scorn, calumny, and public opprobrium she had finally struck back, and now she trembled with exultation. She turned and walked back to the others, floating along the drive like a woman in a dream, all the while repeating to herself a line she had penned many years ago:

"I am fearless . . . and therefore powerful."

"What happened?" An astonished Crosse demanded when Mary rejoined the group. "We saw the rascals run away as if pursued by all the devils in hell."

"Yes, tell us, dearest Mary," Cornelia pleaded. "What did you say to them?"

Mary pondered a moment, a strange and mysterious smile upon her lips, and then calmly replied, "I merely told them a story."

A DRAWING ROOM CONFESSIONAL

> My dearest Mary, wherefore hast thou gone, thy form is here indeed—a lovely one— But thou art fled, gone down a dreary road that leads to Sorrow's most obscure abode. For thine own sake I cannot follow thee. Do thou return for mine . . . Percy Bysshe Shelley

And so the party of three returned to Fyne Court in good spirits, with all marvelling and loudly praising Mary's temerity in facing down the Reverend Philip Smith and his lackeys.

Once inside the house they dispersed to change for dinner. Mary practically skipped up the stairs, her slight headache forgotten as pride and exultation flowed through her body.

As she ascended the top of the stairs, Mary encountered one of the servants who was carrying a basket of clean linen. As decorum dictated, the servant froze on the spot and dropped her gaze to the floor. Mary smiled at her as she wafted past, still filled with *bon homie* and daring from her recent victory.

All the doors along the corridor looked identical and for a moment Mary feared she would have difficulty locating the room she had been given. But then she spotted the large oriental urn that held a stand of desiccated grasses. She remembered passing the urn as she was first shown to her room . . . or did she pass the urn as she left her room? It was impossible to be certain, as Cornelia's constant chatter had been a distraction.

She reached the door immediately adjacent to the urn and rapped timidly with her knuckles. When no one replied, she twisted the knob which turned easily. The door opened and she slipped inside. To her surprise she found the room in darkness. Had she left the curtains pulled after her nap? She could not recall. However the room felt overheated and close. Plus the space held the queasy aroma of a sick chamber where an invalid has been confined for some time. Her nostrils flared as she scented an overflowing chamber pot and the funk of an unwashed body. But overarching all was an acrid tang of burning and when Mary looked at the fireplace she noticed the feeble remnants of a fire guttering in the grate. Why on earth would someone light a fire on such a warm summer day? And then, upon stepping closer she saw that the fireplace held not a bed of cherry coals ebbing out of life, but a poorly burning object of some kind that someone had flung upon the fire grate and which lay half-consumed and still smouldering. By the charred leather cover it looked like a journal. And then, heart-stoppingly, Mary noticed its remarkable resemblance to her own green leather journal! But before she could look closer, she heard a moan from the bed behind her and spun around. To her mortification she found that the room was occupied. In the smoky gloom she could make out few details, but as her eyes adjusted she saw the wasted form of an older woman huddled beneath the bedclothes. Her long grey hair was fully unpinned and fanned out about the pillow in an unkempt sprawl.

Mary felt a jolt of panic. In her haste she had chosen the wrong room and bumbled in upon a sick relative of the Crosse's. At that moment, the woman's eyes flickered open and fixed Mary's face with a frightened and astonished gaze.

"Oh, excuse me. I am so terribly sorry," Mary blurted. "Wrong room."

"So, step-daughter, are you so impatient?' the older woman hissed thinly. "Have you come to watch me die?"

The woman suddenly lunged forward, as if to grab Mary's arm, who flinched back and then fled from the room.

As she hurriedly pulled the door shut behind her, a familiar voice said, "Ah, there you are, Mary." It was Cornelia, who now fixed Mary with a puzzled look and asked, "But are you not dressing for dinner?"

"Ah, yes," Mary said, blushing. "I appear to be lost. I am sorry but I mistakenly entered the wrong room and blundered in upon someone who I imagine must be a relative of yours."

Frown lines of puzzlement spoiled Cornelia's pretty features. "Relative? Whatever do you mean?"

"An elderly lady. Lying in her bed."

Cornelia looked at the door with a stunned expression. "But this is *your* room." To prove it, Cornelia snatched the doorknob and flung the door wide. To Mary's amazement, the room was well lit with sunlight. She looked inside and saw the bed and the dresser that held her arrangement of mementos. No invalid woman lay in the bed, which was neatly made. No charred journal smouldered in the grate.

Dull terror wrapped about its clumsy hands about Mary's throat and squeezed, so that for several moments she could summon no words.

"I, I am sorry," she finally stammered. "It must be my headache coming back, Forgive me. I am so scattered these days."

As Cornelia fixed her with a look of concern, Mary laughed off the event and hastily slipped into the room. Her hallucinations were becoming more frequent and she fought down a surge of dread. The doctor had warned her that this might be the case, and if so, it marked a worsening of her ailment. What if she were losing her mind? She decided that that line of thought was too dreadful to pursue and busied herself changing clothes.

Although the room was not overlooked, Mary felt exposed and so she lit the two candles on the dresser and drew the curtains closed.

But as she pulled on her finest party gown, Mary could not shake the image of the invalid woman. The room had been dark, the light so dim she could barely make out the female face. And yet it had felt strangely . . . familiar.

She startled at a knock at the door. Cornelia called out from the hallway, "Might I help?"

"Yes, please," Mary assented. The younger women slipped into the room and began to help lace the back of Mary's gown, oohing and ahing at its prettiness. Mary had fetched one of her finest gowns— perhaps a little too ostentatious for a simple country house and its denizens—with a low neckline that showed off her graceful white shoulders, one of her best features. And then she took out her prettiest floral scarf and draped it across her shoulders, the better to effect the grand reveal at a key moment.

"You look lovely," Cornelia said, without a trace of ironic jealousy.

"Thank you," Mary replied. "But you have youth and beauty, which no fashion can upstage."

Cornelia offered her arm. "Shall we go torture our male guests? There is one, in particular, whom I suspect will be most taken with you. As they both made to leave the room, Cornelia paused to blow out the candles, carefully cupping a hand behind the flame as she blew each tapir out. "Andrew insists that we are mindful with the candles," she explained to Mary's unspoken question. "He says the old house would burn like a straw bale if fire ever broke out."

When the two women floated into the parlour on a rustle of silk, they quoshed the voices of two men lounging on a horsehide sofa, deeply engaged in conversation. Upon sight of the ladies, both men sprang to their feet and hastily adjusted their dress, pulling up trousers, shooting cuffs, and tugging down waistcoats.

"This is Josiah Phipps, our much-beloved local vicar, " Cornelia said, introducing a short, middle-aged man with a bald head who was dressed in a churchman's black vestments. In contrast to the tall, black-clad scarecrow Reverend Philip Smith, this ambassador of The Almighty seemed cheerful and cherubic, the ruddy-cheeked model of what a jovial village holy man should be.

"A pleasure to meet, you, Mrs Shelley." The reverend said, ducking a bow. "As I was just explaining to the doctor here, I am looking forward to some frank and stimulating discussion with the daughter of Robert Godwin and Mary Wollstonecraft."

The cleric had begun his introduction by invoking both of Mary's parents, infamous as they were for their outspoken views on politics, religion and the role of women. She did not know quite how to take his comment. It seemed likely that the cleric's first words were a warning shot fired across her bows, and Mary suspected she would be defending herself very soon.

Mary smiled sweetly and offered her hand, which the prelate held with the delicacy of a china teacup, before surrendering it.

Cornelia gestured to the man at his side. "And this is our local physician, Dr. Richard Freestone."

While awaiting his own introduction, the doctor had struck what Mary considered a carefully rehearsed pose, one hand gripping the lapel of his own jacket in a martial fashion, the other resting nonchalantly upon his hip. He was younger than Mary by fifteen or more years; he possessed a handsome, almost Byronic head of auburn curls, and was clean-shaven apart from a pair of geometrically precise side-whiskers. In his tight-fitted jacket and drop-front trousers, he cut a dashing figure, and his brown eyes held a sparkle of deviltry about them. Mary had little doubt that the ministrations of Doctor Freestone were much sought after by the local ladies of the parish.

"Charmed to meet you doctor—"

"Richard!" he interrupted. He swept back the tails of his frock coat and proffered her a courtier's deep bow. "Please call me, Richard. I am not wearing my doctor's hat tonight." He made a gesture to the black leather medical bag at his feet. "Although I never go anywhere without my little bag of wonders."

"Then we must hope that you shall not called upon to use it." Mary quickly put in, which brought a polite chuckle from all.

She offered her hand and the doctor swept it up in his and kissed it, softly pressing his lips to the space between her knuckles. It was a deeply sensual kiss, and Mary felt her cheeks flush and her heart flutter.

The ladies delicately settled into their seats and the men dropped back onto the horsehide couch. All waited politely as Andrew Crosse drew up a chair next to his wife and settled himself into it. When she judged the moment ripe, Mary casually loosed her hold on the scarf allowing it to droop and reveal the alabaster whiteness of her shoulders. It had the intended effect, and without looking, she felt the young doctor's appraising gaze.

When everyone was settled, Andrew Cross nodded to the pimply-faced young butler to step forward and begin serving sherry from the silver salver he was holding. When all had their glasses charged, Andrew Crosse rose to his feet and raised his own glass, "I offer a toast to our good friends and neighbours the Reverend Phipps and Doctor Freestone, and to our most illustrious guest, Mary Shelley, the famed authoress."

Everyone chimed in, "here, here," and sipped their sherries. The warmth of the liquor rushed down Mary's parched throat and a blush rose into her cheeks.

The doctor leaned forward and addressed Mary in his rich baritone, "Perhaps you can assuage my curiosity, Mrs Shelley." How is it that a lady as lovely and refined as you came to write such a grim tale as your *Frankenstein?*"

"You have read it?" Mary asked, unable to conceal her skepticism.

The doctor nodded his handsome head in reply. "Indeed, I have my own copy."

"You mean *my* copy, Richard," the clergyman corrected. "He borrowed it from me some time ago . . . " and then he added in a good-natured jibe, " . . . and has *yet* to return it."

"I also have my own copy," Cornelia added in an excited voice, "I bought it on our last trip to London, and I have read it three times, although it gives me horrid dreams each time." She sighed loudly, reached out and put her hand atop Mary's. "What an imagination. However do you think of such things?"

The clergyman's smile dripped with scarcely restrained skepticism, "Of course, I am sure the lady's husband, the great poet Shelley, had a great hand in the writing . . . especially with the more, ahem, gruesome passages. I very much doubt a gentle woman's upbringing and natural female squeamishness on such matters would allow her—"

Reverend Phipps' patronising tone caused Mary's back muscles to tighten. "Squeamish?" she challenged. "Precisely what matters do you refer to?" Mary had not meant her voice to sound so harsh, but the words burst out from her.

The violence of Mary's response knocked the clergyman onto his back foot. "I, er, I merely refer to those descriptions of death and mortality, which I am sure no gentle lady such as yourself could have any experience of—"

Mary's jaw clenched as she fought to imprison her tongue and bite back the rage she felt curdling in her brain. The others all noticed her rising dudgeon and shot anxious glances back and forth, but the clergyman alone seemed oblivious. Soon her temper was an iron bear trap, the wicked jaws spread wide and straining to snap shut. Mary might still have managed to restrain herself, but then the clergyman insisted on planting a foot firmly inside the trap.

"I have read both the poetry and the philosophical writings of your late husband, Mrs Shelley. Tell, me, are you an atheist as well?"

Mary had guessed the question was coming, and so was not surprised. She made a show of calmly sipping her sherry as she corralled her anger and composed herself, and then dabbed her lips with a napkin and squarely met the Reverend's gaze. "At this point in my life I confess I am not sure if I believe in the Almighty. However, after all my travails one thing seems clear: if God exists, then he hates me."

It was a shocking pronouncement, and in the silence that followed, the ticking of the clock in the corner obtruded into the room. The Reverend's eyes opened wide with shock at her pronouncement, while the Doctor had difficulty concealing an amused grin.

"Why do you say that, my child?" Reverend Phipps leaned forward in his seat and reached out a comforting hand toward Mary, but his grasp fell short and he withdrew his hand awkwardly. "Why do you feel as through God has turned away from you?"

Mary then recited her long litany of loss and grief. "You speak of female squeamishness at death and mortality, Reverend Phipps? Well, let me see." She paused a moment as she wrestled her voice an octave lower, softening the consonants. "My mother, Mary Wollstonecraft, died three weeks after giving birth to me, so I have never known maternal love and cosseting. Then your gentle God chose to take three of my four children from me. One a mere babe of a day; the other two as children by dysentery and the sweating sickness. I lost my fourth child by miscarriage. I haemorrhaged and would have bled to death but my husband Percy made me sit in a bath filled with ice water. I shivered through the long night in agony, praying only for the release of death."

A look of profound discomfort flashed across the faces of her audience, but Mary cold not hold back the torrent of words fountaining up from her soul. "My husband was twenty-nine when his sailboat capsized and he drowned. My half-sister Fanny, ignored, unloved and unwanted by my family . . ." Mary's voice cracked and dried, and her lips quivered a moment before she regained the power of speech, and when she finally spoke her voice creaked out as a hoarse whisper. "And for that I acknowledge my portion of the blame . . ." She paused to snatch a sip of sherry and began again, "Fanny ran away to Wales, took a cheap room in a tavern and wrote a farewell letter before she swallowed a fatal dose of laudanum."

Mary's torrent of revelations drove an audible gasp of shock from the assembled group. Cornelia dropped her head and stared at her lap, her eyes sparkling with tears.

"But that is not all. My husband's first wife, Harriet, after being betrayed and abandoned by Percy . . ." She trailed off and attempted a smile, which showed more as a grimace. ". . . because of me," she corrected. "Harriet filled her pockets with stones and walked into the Serpentine. There were five of us in Geneva the summer I fastened upon the idea of my creature: my husband, Percy, my half-sister Claire, Lord Byron and his personal physician, John Polidori. Of those five, only my sister and myself still draw breath, although by poisonous estrangement we are as good as dead to one another. Lord Byron died of fever while fighting for the Greeks and Dr. Polidori . . ." her lips twisted in a wounded smile and she continued in a hoarse voice. "Poor, poor Polly . . . Much to my shame for we all took pleasure in ridiculing this bright young man. After losing at cards, John Polidori retired to his rooms and swallowed a fatal dose of Prussic Acid." For a moment Mary's thoughts soared up through the ceiling to her room and the dresser drawer that held her own bottle of Prussic Acid, the label tattered and worn with the miles travelled and the years passed since she purchased it; and she wondered if she would have the courage to follow Polly's example—should her trip to Fyne Court fail to answer her prayers.

When her minor tirade had finished, Mary seemed to collapse into herself, and suddenly seemed a very slight figure. She dropped her gaze to the rug, blinking back tears. No one spoke for several long moments, although the silence begged for a voice to fill it. Mary realised what she had just unburdened upon the room, and searched her scattered mind for something to lighten the mood, to walk back what she had just unleashed.

Just then someone coughed and Mary looked up. The sound seemed to come from the direction of the entrance hall, but the corridor leading toward it was pitch dark The young butler was moving about the house, lighting candles and lanterns, but had yet to light the candles in the entrance hall, and so from where Mary sat it appeared as a gloomy cavern drowning in shadow. It seemed that someone was lurking there in the darkness, listening in on their conversation. But it was likely just a curious servant eavesdropping, and so Mary tried to ignore it, although it made her ill at ease.

After her confession the conversation lagged. And as she had caused it, Mary was anxious to speak again, but just then, something set the teacups and the best china to jinkling in its hutch. Then the floor beneath their feet squirmed as the room began to quiver. The shiny brass weights in the Grandfather clock began to sway and clonk against the insides of their wooden cabinet and finally came a long, low resonating drum roll of thunder that poured into the silence like a thick syrup and grew progressively louder until it set the window glass rattling in its casements. At that very moment the light from the windows faded and the room darkened ominously as the shadows surged from their hiding places and sponged up the light.

Mary smiled sheepishly and quipped, "Apparently Reverend, your side has chosen to have the final word."

Her joke broke the tension, and everyone laughed.

"It seems the storm we witnessed earlier is nearly upon us," Andrew Crosse noted. "Apparently my barometer faithfully foretold the future this time." The butler appeared and Crosse beckoned him closer, "Jasper, we are drowning in darkness. Light more candles . . . and have more candles brought to the dining room . . . and then go about the house and make sure all the windows are shut fast—there is a storm approaching."

The young butler dithered a moment, but then dipped a bow and vanished on his errand.

The physician spoke up, "I must say, Mrs Shelley, that as a doctor, I was most struck by your description of Victor Frankenstein reanimating your corpse. From what did you take your inspiration for that dreadful image?"

Mary turned her head and fixed Andrew Crosse with a smile. "Why Mister Crosse here deserves that accolade."

The revelation evoked cries of surprise from the guests and Mary quickly explained: "Many years ago my husband Percy and I lived in London. While there we often attended the talks given at Garnerin's London Lecture rooms. I remember clearly one particular lecture. The first part of the evening featured a display of phantasmagoria—coloured lanterns projecting fantastic images upon a screen. But then we witnessed Mister Crosse discourse upon his experiments with electricity. My husband had long been a keen follower of advances in science and we were both thrilled and amazed by Mister Crosse's lecture."

"See, my darling husband," Cornelia Cross burst out, clapping her hands together, "your work has inspired great literature!"

Andrew Crosse was clearly a humble man and embarrassed by such a pronouncement, he dropped his head bashfully and said, "No doubt a great exaggeration."

"Oh, but you must not be so modest," Mary countered. "For your experiments fired my imagination and I never forgot them. So it came to fruition on one night in 1812. You might remember that dreary summer, plagued by storms and incessant rain?"

"The so-called 'Year without a Summer?'" the doctor offered. He smiled ruefully. "Yes, I was a young boy travelling through Europe. I fully remember the dreadful weather." He flashed his winning smile at the group and added, "I was camping in the Black Forest. We very nearly drowned."

Mary nodded. "Percy and I were in the Swiss Alps. The days tended to be gloomy and wet, with the weather gradually deteriorating as evening crept on. Most nights were lit up vividly by the most tremendous thunderstorms. Often we would draw up our chairs near a window to watch the ferocious forks of lightning lashing the sky and the sizzle of reflections on the lake below. It was . . ." she paused and searched for the right words. ". . . elemental . . . terrifying . . ."

"Like Creation?" Reverend Phipps offered.

Mary's expression turned inward, as she looked back across the years and watched the fiery skies. "More like the Apocalypse. We could have been witnessing the old world dying or a new world being born in violence and fire."

"And the lightning inspired you?" the question was asked by Andrew Crosse in a voice taut with suspense.

Just then a coal in the fireplace cracked and popped, spitting a red-hot ember into the room. It landed on the hearthrug and Crosse jumped up from his chair and stamped upon it to smother it.

The vile stink of burning wool swirled in the air. Mary sensed her audience was rapt, hanging upon her every syllable. Now was the time to reveal her secret and the true reason she had come to see Andrew Crosse.

"With the days rain-soaked and dreary, we took to staying up late at night, where we would discuss all manner of forbidden things in philosophy and politics." She paused and fixed the Reverend with an arch smile. "We were young and had the young's conviction of our own genius." She looked back at the rest. "On many dreary evenings Lord Byron and my Percy wrestled in profound discussions of the meaning of life and what gave things conscious animation—wild notions that galvanism could somehow reanimate dead flesh. Back then I was a young woman of 18, shy and less outspoken. So I listened in silence. But I took in every word and my mind seethed with fantastic thoughts and wild imaginings. When one topic had been thrashed to exhaustion, they latched upon another. And on one such stormy evening, Lord Byron produced a book of German ghost stories translated into French. It seemed a deliciously daring entertainment and so we took turns reading the stories aloud by candlelight. The allure of all things macabre and eldritch thrilled our senses. Sometimes we held séances, and seated about a round table we would hold hands and try to summon spirits of the dead."

The Reverend cleared his throat with obvious disapproval, his expression grave and vexed.

Mary met his gaze and asked, "You disapprove, Reverend?"

The reverend's face turned grave. "Ghosts and discorporate entities, such things are not to be trifled with," he said in a scolding voice. "I have had personal experience of the dangers—"

"Dangers?" Mary interrupted. Although she was nearly as much an atheist as her husband, her experiences with the uncanny had left the door to her mind firmly ajar. "Please, Reverend Phipps, do explain."

The reverend's expression spoke eloquently of his immediate regret at having broached the subject. "I merely mean to say that awakening certain entities poses a very real danger." The next words he uttered in a brittle whisper, "Demonic possession. Attracting the attention of unclean spirits." He flashed an undertaker's smile. "I think you know what I speak of."

But Mary would not let the reverend off so easily. "But you spoke of *personal* experiences?"

Now all faces turned toward the reverend so that he was

compelled to continue. "I have, on rare occasions, been called upon to perform certain rites . . ." he trailed off.

"You speak of the rite of exorcism?" Mary asked.

The reverend rolled the sherry glass in his hand, evidently finding something fascinating in its umbrous depths.

"There is a story that lingers hereabout of a place a mile or so hence called Ruborough. The story has it that, many years ago, a certain Doctor Farrer . . ." the reverend's glance momentarily alighted upon Doctor Freestone, but then he went on, "I should first describe the local legend about a lost fortune. Ruborough has many large stones—the remains of a camp of the ancient Romans. But more intriguing is a story of a great treasure reputed to be buried there. One night Dr. Farrer searched for the treasure using a hazel stick as a divining wand. He soon discovered a void in the earth. When the divining wand jerked, the doctor believed he had discovered the hiding spot of the gold. He marked the place and determined to return the next day with his servant. When the moon was full, he and his servant returned to the spot and began to dig. The earth suddenly gave way beneath the servant's pick revealing a hole descending into the depths. Suddenly there was a great roar and a chorus of hideous groans as if from all the devils in hell. Then something reached up and grabbed the servant's ankle and began to drag him beneath the earth. Fortunately the Doctor had brought his Bible and held it aloft, praying to God as he struggled to pull his servant free. When, at last, the servant kicked loose, the two men ran away as fast as they could back to Broomfield."

A silence followed the reverend's telling of the story. Having narrated his cautionary tale, the Reverend pursed his lips and sat back, content to let his warning sink in. But then the Doctor said, with clear amusement in his voice, "'Tis a pity the unfortunate Doctor Farrer chose the night-time to dig in. Perhaps he would have had better luck had he attempted the dig during the day."

Now that the doctor had raised an obvious flaw in the tall tale, the others could not help but poke more holes in the story.

"I am surprised he could hold the Bible aloft while reaching down to pull his servant free," Crosse added, before drowning a sardonic smile in his sherry glass.

Now Mary could not resist and put in, "And also fortunate he had chosen to bring along his Bible, as one is want to do on a treasure hunt."

At her remark, Doctor Freestone slapped his knee and laughed uproariously, which triggered an outburst from the Reverend.

"Only a fool laughs at such danger!" the Reverend had leapt up from the sofa and his face purpled with passion. "Dowsing, card reading, prophesy—all are proscribed by the church. Only the foolish risk their immortal souls toying with elemental forces they are ignorant of."

The Reverend's tone made it obvious that Crosse and his guests had overstepped the bounds of common courtesy and all quickly muttered shame-faced apologies.

"No, no, it is I who should apologise," the Reverend said, calming himself. "Yes, the story might just be a foolish folk tale told in taverns by uneducated labourers and simple farm folk. But I must add a postscript. As a young man, just after being ordained, I determined to visit the place myself. As the story goes, there is indeed a jagged void that leads into the earth. As soon as I approached, I felt a great malevolence radiating from the place. So I took out my Bible and began to read aloud from the scriptures. Soon, I found myself growing short of breath and seemed to feel a pair of hands clasped about my throat, squeezing until I could not breathe. My vision darkened and I began to feel faint. By God's grace I barely staggered away from there. I later returned with some local farmers and we bricked up the hole in the ground, so that none may accidentally stray there."

For a moment no one said anything, and then Mary cleared her throat and spoke up. "I too have some experience with the uncanny," she paused and put a hand to her bosom. "I must tell you the full story of how the idea for my novel about Doctor Frankenstein and his monstrous creature came about."

Cornelia sat up in her chair and blurted, "I have read in the preface to your book of the competition that Lord Byron set—a challenge to write a ghost story."

Mary nodded. "That is how it began. But you cannot know the full particulars, as I chose never to disclose them. Nor has any living soul heretofore heard the full accounting. But I will tell it plainly now, for it touches upon the reason for my trip to Fyne Court." She fixed Andrew Crosse with a piercing look, "And why I have come to seek the aid of Mister Crosse, who is intimately connected to the story in a way he could not conceive of."

Andrew Crosse was just putting the sherry glass to his lips, but now he drew it away and threw an astonished look first at Mary, and then at his wife, Cornelia.

Mary began, "You know the beginnings of the story. In the long nights at the Villa Diodati we were ravaged by such tempestuous storms whose thunderous roaring shook the house, rattled the windows in their casements, and rendered sleep impossible. And so we whiled away such nights taking turns reading ghost stories aloud. When we had exhausted the collection, Lord Byron threw down his challenge: we should each undertake to write a ghost story and then he would judge which was the best. My husband Percy attempted a few pages, but soon tore them up in a fit of pique and proclaimed that he was a poet and had no skill at prose. The same was true of Lord Byron, who penned some lines but quickly became bored. Dr. Polidori wrote a tale about a woman who peeked in on something forbidden and was punished by having her head turned into a skull. It was meant to horrify but to poor Polly's chagrin the tale struck us as comical and drew gales of laughter from us. I, too, cudgelled my brain for inspiration but none came. But then, several days later, during another storm-wracked night, I lay upon my pillow in that state of half-waking, half-sleep where eldritch images loom up in the mind. My imagination, unbidden, possessed and guided me, fitting the successive images that arose in my mind with a lurid vividness far beyond the usual bounds of reverie. I saw with eyes shut, but acute mental vision, the pale student of the unhallowed arts kneeling beside the thing he had put together. I saw the hideous phantasm of a man stretched out and then, on the working of some powerful engine, show signs of life and stir with an uneasy, half-vital motion."

Mary paused a moment, gathering herself, which allowed the room to snatch a breath, while the reverend gulped down the last of his sherry and quickly crossed himself.

Mary raised her head again, smiled a mysterious smile, and the candlelight glimmered in her dark eyes as she continued. "The entire story flowed into my mind in a sudden rush. Anxious to write down my half-dream before it evaporated, I threw off the bedclothes and sprang from the bed. My journal lay open upon the writing desk before the window and I hurried toward it. But at that moment came a doom crack of thunder and I beheld a stream of fire reach down like a fiery finger and touch one of the oak trees growing outside the window. In the next instant the French doors burst open as the thunder flash, raw and elemental, rushed into the room. I felt the flux coursing through my body and was flung high into the air. Some time later, I awakened to find myself lying on the floor. Before I could collect my wits the door to the bedroom flew open and my husband and the rest rushed in. They had all heard the tremendous report and witnessed the flash of lightning strike near the house. Outside nothing remained of the oak tree save for a blasted stump, peeled into smouldering ribbons. Doctor Polidori examined me, but apart from a racing heart and a few singes upon my nightgown I seemed unhurt."

A gasp of astonishment burst from Andrew Crosse and all turned to look at him. "Dear lady, it is miraculous that you survived! Such a lightning bolt contains a deadly amount of flux, enough to vaporise a tree. Had you not been knocked off your feet by the electricity, you most certainly would have perished."

Mary nodded in agreement. "Yes, but instead I felt charged with an uncanny energy and commanded the others to leave. With great reluctance, especially from my darling Percy, they quit the room whereupon I seized my pen and fell upon my journal and let the story of Doctor Frankenstein and his reanimated monster pour out of me. I wrote for hours through the night with nary a pause for rest. But it was not as if I wrote the story, but rather as if the story possessed me and used me to write itself."

Mary's mouth had dried up, as had her voice. She took a quick sip of sherry and then drained the glass in one gulp. "But days later, as I read through my scribbled pages, they awakened in me a memory,"

"A memory?" the doctor asked.

Mary nodded, her eyes fixed upon the empty air as she looked back through the dark tunnel of years. "As the lightning bolt hit the tree and transfigured it with fire, I felt something pass through me."

A silence fell into the room with the weight of a dead body slumping to the floor.

"Su-something passed through you?" the reverend's voice was as fragile as spun glass.

Mary struggled to find the right words. "It felt like . . . like giving birth."

The reverend scowled at the pronouncement. "But surely it was just the galvanic force passing through you—"

"Have you ever given birth, Reverend?" Mary asked mildly.

The Reverend shifted in his seat, suddenly uncomfortable. "Wu . . . why . . . uh . . .well . . ." he smiled, flummoxed with embarrassment ". . . obviously, no—"

"I *have* given birth," Mary countered. "Four times. It was the same feeling: one life stepping out from another. And then I saw, in the instant before I was knocked off my feet, the hulking figure of a man standing in the fiery core of the thunderbolt that consumed the tree."

Andrew Crosse moved forward and dropped heavily onto the couch his wife sat upon. "Dear lady, what are you saying?"

"I believe that something came through me that night. Something strange and terrible. A malignancy. My imagination turned it into a creature of fancy—one of my airy nothings. But something has stalked me since that day and brought grief to me and death and misfortune to all those around me. I believe it is a kind of curse."

The room fell into a deep silence as Mary's terrible pronouncement continued to resonate in the minds of her audience like a struck bell.

"Shu-shu-surely not," the doctor finally stammered. "My dear lady, this is all a series of unhappy coincidences."

"It might be . . ." the reverend spoke up, his voice grave and urgent. "But it might *not* be. Sometimes, when we are at our most vulnerable, there are invisible forces lurking all about us that seek to break into the prison of our souls."

"Oh, that's superstitious nonsense, Reverend," the doctor scoffed. "Surely an educated man such as yourself cannot believe that sort of thing."

The Reverend turned earnest. "Richard, I have spent my life believing in the ineffable, for that's what's God's Kingdom is. It lies somewhere beyond the ken of human imagination. In a place we cannot reach on the physical plane. And if the kingdom of God exists, as I believe it does, then the reverse must follow. There are lower intelligences, beings, demons, devils—call them what you will. I felt myself being attacked by one that day at Ruborough."

The doctor laughed, a little too loudly. "Oh come now, surely you don't really believe—"

"I felt it Richard, as strongly as I see you now before me. It was real. Palpable. I felt it latch upon me, and I knew if I surrendered to it I would be lost . . . forever!"

Andrew Crosse jumped up from the sofa, clearly agitated. "But I fail to understand, Mrs Shelley. If it's an exorcist you need, surely it's the Reverend you want. What could I possibly do?"

Mary set her empty glass down on the table next to her, and carefully smoothed the lap of her dress before speaking. "I believe this ghost, demon, entity, monster—whatsoever it may be—was raised by electricity . . . and can only laid by the same dread power."

Andrew Crosse gasped. "But that's impossible. You would be killed! It is a miracle you were not destroyed in the first instance. No. I could not possibly. It would be far too dangerous . . ."

The reverend quickly jumped in. "A ghost must be summoned before it can be laid. And even the most innocent can be possessed. Taken over. Made a puppet. Like water, evil assumes the shape of any vessel it is poured into. You face a greater danger than death,

Mrs Shelley." He paused for effect. "You risk the loss of your eternal soul."

Before the reverend could continue, he was interrupted by a disembodied voice: a woman's voice, young and full of music, which seemed to come from everywhere: "Ghosts? Discorporate entities? Whatever am I interrupting?"

Mary heard soft footsteps approaching and turned to look. The passageway from the entrance hall into the parlour was a gloomy tunnel lit by a single guttering candle, and now a clearly feminine silhouette moved along it toward them. When the figure emerged into the light of the parlour, Mary discovered to her surprise that it was a beautiful young woman.

Apparently, this was the surprise mystery guest.

But in the next few moments, Mary's surprise turned to dread.

The woman, who Mary guessed to be in her late twenties, boasted the most spectacular head of auburn curls that had been carefully primped and curled into giant ringlets that framed her exquisite face.

Crosse jumped up from his seat and moved quickly across the room to greet her.

"My dearest Countess," he effused, bowing from the waist. "You must excuse our country ways. Had I known you were up and about I would have had a servant escort you and introduce you properly, rather than leaving you to grope your way unattended through the darkness."

Crosse looked around at the assembled group shame-faced and confessed, "I am afraid we run a very disorganised household here at Fyne Court." Crosse offered his hand and the lady gripped the very tips of his fingers as he led her forward into the light where she smiled at the assembled party.

"I wish to announce our mysterious house guest. It is my honour to present Augusta Ada King-Noel, Countess of Lovelace."

At his words the woman slipped into the room, as silkily as the fluttering violet dress she was wearing. Mary was conceited about her own curls and her ringlets had set perfectly. But her thinning hair and mousy ringlets paled in comparison with the Countess's thick and shiny coils of auburn hair. But even before her name had been announced, and even though the two had never met (by Mary's careful design) the author of *Frankenstein* guessed who the stunning young woman was and inwardly despaired. She recognised her instantly by the mouth, the nose, and those unforgettable smoky grey eyes as the only legitimate daughter of Lord Byron. She also knew of the woman's growing reputation as a mathematical genius possessed of a formidable intellect. It was precisely these traits that struck fear into Mary, for it was common knowledge that Countess Ada had a fascination for the father she had never met. Now Mary knew that she would soon be interrogated by that fearful intellect, who would wish to pry every nugget of information from Mary she could.

Then Mary remembered the mysterious cough she had heard. She had attributed it to one of the servants, but it seemed likely that it was Ada who had coughed. She had been lurking in the hallway for some time, listening in on the conversation. How long had she lurked there? How much had she heard?

Ada's gaze moved from person to person as she smiled and greeted them in turn. Then the doeish, smokey grey eyes finally settled upon Mary's face and the younger woman's smile betrayed her genuine excitement. "You must forgive me, Mrs Shelley. I suffer from a number of ailments and had taken to my bed for most of the day."

As the Countess approached, Mary rose from the sofa and curt-seyed as the two clasped hands in greeting. "But when I heard of our famous houseguest," Ada added, "I simply had to rouse myself. Oh, but I am beside myself to finally meet the redoubtable Mary Shelley, daughter of such esteemed parents, a mother who is the heroine to all women and who herself is a literary giant . . ." she paused a moment and then added a disarmingly casual insinuation. ". . . and a lady who knew my late father *intimately*."

The young Countess so obviously stressed the last word that Mary could not conceal the look of unease that flashed across her face, but she quickly recomposed herself.

All the men jumped up and offered the Countess their seat, but

Ada chose to sit on the sofa, in the middle, which forced Mary and Cornelia to move over to make space.

"Dearest Ada," the doctor quickly interjected after the Countess had settled herself, "poor Mrs Shelley has just finished unburdening her soul to us. Please do not interrogate her further."

Although he had clearly come to Mary's rescue, the doctor addressed the Countess with a degree of familiarity such that she could not help but feel a twinge of jealousy.

The countess now continued, "I have already heard the tale of your heroism under fire, Mrs Shelley, and was wondering what could invoke such temerity in a member of the tender sex, but then I remembered that you are the daughter of Mary Wollstonecraft. It must have been she who gave you the heart of a lioness?"

Mary hid behind a false smile and said, "If my heart is resilient, it is merely because it has been broken so many times. Now there is enough scar tissue to render it as hard as tortoise shell. There have been many things that have broken my heart. But I confess that most of them were men."

Countess Ada laughed delightedly at the comment. "Bravo, Mary, spoken like the true daughter of Mary Wolstonecroft."

Mary swallowed and smiled, grateful for the respite the doctor's question had afforded her.

"Everything that came to me from my mother came second-hand," Mary explained to Ada, and then to answer her puzzled looks, she continued, "for I never knew my mother, except through the voice I heard from her books, the tone of voice I read in her letters, from the locks of her hair and the too few remembrances of her I pried from my father. My mother died three weeks after I was born. So you see, it was I that killed her."

At her comment, the doctor quickly leapt in. "My dear lady, you have earned no blame in that tragic occurrence, nor can you lay claim to any. I have found that Nature can be cruel and kind in equal measures and with equal equanimity. I have attended to many such lyings in where, despite the best attentions of doctors and mid-wives and the prayers and solicitations of our wisest holy men, and despite the best wishes of friends and loved ones, tragedy outraces us all. Thus, too, has been my own wretched experience—"

At that moment, Reverend Phipps interrupted him by quickly leaning forward and placing a hand on the doctor's shoulder.

"Richard," he implored in a comforting tone, "do not probe the old wound. It benefits no one."

Just then Jasper, the young butler, strode into the room bearing a fully-lit candelabra in either hand.

"Behold," Andrew Crosse said dramatically. "Here comes our Prometheus bearing illumination."

"More like our Lucifer," Richard Freestone jibed.

The young servant bowed his head and announced. "Ladies . . . gentlemen. Dinner is served. If you would follow me I shall lead you to the dining room."

STRANGE COMPANION

Yes, love indeed is a light from heaven. A spark of that immortal fire with angels shared, by Allah given to lift from earth our low desire . . . Lord Byron

Slowly . . . gradually . . . I became aware. My mind had wandered somewhere else, but now it had returned and I existed in the moment. When I looked, the star was still there, burning brightly—my constant companion. Had I slept? It felt like sleep, for this now felt like a familiar awakening. And then I thought I heard something. A noise. No, a human voice, distant and indistinct. I listened for long seconds, but no sounds recurred. But then I felt a movement, a drift, an ineluctable undertow that seized hold of me and drew me with gravitational force, like a tide, like the pull of the oceans upon the seas. And now I recognised it: sleep. It was calling to me, lulling me with its caresses. I looked for my companion star. Ever faithful, it burned in the darkness, although now and then it twinkled and faltered. I resisted the tidal pull a moment longer. I wanted to remain with my star, to be comforted by its presence, but exhaustion swept over me and I finally relaxed and surrendered myself, once more, into the arms of morpheus.

THE WAGES OF SIN

Those who will not reason are bigots, those who cannot, are fools, and those who dare not, are slaves . . . Lord Byron

The Reverend Philip Smith had run a long way down the lane with the sun descending at his back, so that he trampled the feet of his own lengthening shadow. As he reached the high street of the village of Broomfield, his wobbly legs buckled and he sprawled full length on the dusty lane. Here he lay, face down, chest heaving as he fought to catch his breath. Finally, when his ragged breathing slowed, he dragged himself to his knees and began smiting his own chest with his fists. Flinging his gaze up at the darkening skies, he cried aloud, "I have failed you my Lord!"

Hot tears left trails down his dusty cheeks as he wailed with anguish. He had set out that day as a crusader for righteousness, but on his first confrontation with the devil's dam, his nerve had failed and he had run away like a faithless coward.

"I am an unworthy to carry this cross!" he shouted aloud and seizing the crucifix that hung about his neck, tried to snatch it off. But the cord was too stout to break and he nearly succeeded in guillo-tining himself. After the third unsuccessful attempt, he let go of the cross and clasped his hands in prayer.

"Help me, Lord," he blubbered, snot dripping from his nose. "I am unworthy to serve you. Give me strength that I might vanquish evil. Show me the way, Lord. Show me!"

He sank back on his haunches and drooped his head. It was no good. He had failed, and was no better than the tavern-idling sinners he had inveigled to join his cause. But then he noticed a figure hobbling along the road ahead. It was a figure he recognised by the man's bald head and shambling gait: Martin Compton.

"Judas in the flesh!" Smith spat, for Compton had been the last to desert him.

He watched as the stoop-shouldered farmer limped up to a cottage, opened the front door, and went inside without knocking. Strangely a lit lantern hung above the door, even though it was hours before dark. It took the Reverend Smith a moment, but then he realised what the abode was: Meg Pollard's Parlour. Broomfield was more of a hamlet than a village proper—too small to support a tavern. But Meg Pollard's Parlour was the next best thing: a drinking house that freely sold ale without a license. Moreover, it was a house of infamy, known for selling strong ale and liquor, dicing and gaming, cock fighting, and all activities both unsavoury and unchristian. Although Smith had never personally visited the notorious den, he had preached against it from the pulpit of his church in Bridgwater.

"Sinners!" Smith spat. "Sinners seeking to sin." And then Smith realised the truth: God had heard his prayer and had given him an answer.

He staggered to his feet, knocked the road dust from his knees and marched toward the farmhouse stiff-backed, his religious ardour rising up within. The devil had won the first battle, but the war of righteousness had just begun.

The rough iron latch lifted beneath Smith's thumb and an over-powering reek of alcohol crashed into his face as he stepped across the threshold into the dimly lit room.

The space was narrow and low with forehead-bruising beams that required all but the shortest man to duck beneath. The room's few windows had been bricked up to prevent the prying gaze of customs men. A giddy, quavering light came from a number of smoky tallow candles so that the unhealthy air stank of wax, pipe smoke, unwashed bodies, and spilled dregs of beer and cider. When the Reverend Smith stepped farther into the room, he found Martin Compton already ensconced at a lopsided table, his still-trembling hand just raising a mug of scrumpy to his lips. And when the clergyman looked around, he saw the rest of his faint-hearted posse, likewise drowning their grizzled faces in a mug of ale.

"Oh, yea of little faith!" The Reverend proclaimed, silencing the morose chatter and turning all heads in his direction. The clergyman took a step farther into the room. "Here I find you, supping up the courage you lack in the face of the Lord's enemies. When your day comes and you stand before God to be judged, you will not be able to hide in the bottom of an ale jug."

The Reverend Smith swept the room with his soul-scorching gaze and most of the men dropped their heads in shame.

A large, slatternly woman in a stained apron who had almost as many hairs sprouting from her chin as the men, stamped her foot on the flagstones and snarled, "What right have ye fer to come here molesting my customers, Reverend? I don't come to your Church on a Sunday selling my ale."

Smith glared at the woman and sneered, "Silence, woman, I am here on a mission from the Lord." He glared around the room with such virulent intensity that the men shrank into themselves. "Listen to me. You men will be my army and together we will return to the Godless Crosse house and shrive the devil in his den."

But in response the men just shook their heads and groaned dismally.

"Best leave it, Reverend," Martin Compton said. "Most men in these parts are afeared to walk past the Wizard's house in daylight. None but a loon would dare venture there after dark."

"Not with devils dancing on the wires," Walter Furse said. Years of hard work in the fields had worn him to a thin frazzle of meat and bone with a scabrous, sun-peeling bald head. "I seen 'em many a night: Cob, Dom, and Chittibob."

Another member of the lapsed posse: Philip Yardle, a mousy-looking man who twitched now and then from a touch of St. Vitus' said, "I ain't never going back there—not with a witch what can summon monsters." The man had been taciturn before and barely uttered a word, but his slurred speech suggested that several pints of ale had lubricated his jaws.

This gave Philip Smith an inspiration. He cast his flinty gaze upon the slovenly taverner, a straggle-haired, lumpen crone in a filthy apron.

"You . . . woman."

"Me name's Meg."

"God knows your name even if I don't. Answer me. Have you anything stronger than ale or cider?"

"Mebbe," Meg squawked, wrinkling her prunish mouth. She scratched the tuft of white hairs sprouting on her chin for a moment, as if thinking, and finally said, "Rum. But it'll cost ye. And I'll want the coin up front."

The Reverend Philip Smith did not hesitate but reached into his vestments and drew out a drawstring purse, which he banged down on the nearest table. The audible chink of coins threw the room into silence.

"For rum I'll join your crusade," said a man who had been sitting in the shadows of the chimney breast.

"Aye, me too," his companion said.

Smith eyed the pair. These two were strangers. Farm labourers most like. They were younger men, fit and strong looking, although both sported noses that had been broken and ears pounded to cauliflower shapes. No doubt the men were the lowest sort of tavern brawlers. But as such they would be valuable allies and less likely to run away than the ancient duffers he had recruited.

"Are you righteous men?" Smith challenged, fully doubting they were.

The two men struggled to hold back the oily smiles that floated to their lips.

"Friends of righteousness," the taller ginger man answered in a strong Cornish accent. His companion was an Irishman who agreed, "Arr, to be sure I am a God-fearin' man meself."

In truth the pair were anything but righteous. They were transients: part-time labourers and full-time-ne'er-do-wells who were currently working at the farm that neighboured Fyne Court. In fact, they had both signed on with the farm using false names. Ryd Thorne and Nessan O'Rourke were former soldiers who had deserted the English army after repeated floggings and imprisonments due to their drinking, whoring, thievery, and endless insubordination. Since then the pair drifted from place to place and county to county, only staying in one locale long enough to wear out their welcome before committing another outrage and then fleeing in the night with the local hue and cry hot on their heels.

"I have no love of Crosse and his blasted conjuring," said O'Rourke in a guttural Irish accent as thick as treacle.

His companion flashed a gap-toothed grin. "Rum now and rum after and we're your men." His Cornish accent was accented by a lisp from his missing front teeth. Thorne's clothes were as filthy and tattered as his friend's, but strangely he wore a fancy silk scarf knotted around his grubby neck.

The Reverend Smith regarded them with a baleful stare, his sallow cheeks sucked in. He fully suspected that the pair were anything but honest men. The Irishman's crooked nose clearly had been twisted one way and then another by a fist or two. The Cornishman, although tall and broad-shouldered, was missing both front teeth, likely to the toe of someone's boot.

But after a moment's consideration, the young clergyman nodded his agreement and then addressed the proprietress. "Rum for any man who will join my holy crusade."

A roar of approval went up from the men and Meg breathily waddled to a large barrel at the back of room, tipped up the lid and scooped the first dipperful of liquor and ladled it into a short metal cup. She began to pass around tots of rum, which the men greedily snatched up and tossed down their gullets, then thrust out their grog glasses for a refill.

"We will need lanterns," Smith said. "Axes to break down fences, and pitch and tinder to kindle fires."

"Fire?" Martin Compton replied, looking alarmed. "I want no part of burning. We'll be gaoled or transported."

"Be not faint-hearted," Smith replied. "We are doing God's work." He raised the Bible before him, "And the Lord will be our shield."

THE WAR ACROSS THE DINING
TABLE

A king is always a king — and a woman is always a woman, his authority and her sex ever stand between them and rational converse . . ." Mary Shelley

⤳

The young butler led the procession into a large dining room where the table was set with places for six. The long table already had two candelabra burning, and when the butler set down the two additional candelabras, the room glowed with light and seemed to expand in size.

In recognition of her title, the Countess was seated first at the foot of the table, opposite Andrew Crosse who as host, was seated at the head. Cornelia was seated at her husband's right hand. As Mary waited for the butler to pull out her chair, she turned to glance out the window. She was curious to see how far off the storm clouds were. To the west, a great wall of black cloud advanced, a leviathan that threatened to crush all beneath it. The clouds screened the setting sun and tinged the world with a sickly purple twilight, so that here and there the brightest stars prematurely blazed in the sky. As the light outside was failing and the dining room was so brightly lit, she found herself looking through her own reflection. But as she looked another face seemed to swim up from beneath hers: a hideous face, male and monstrous. The effect was startling and Mary cried out and stepped quickly back, covering her mouth with a hand. The others looked at her in alarm.

"Dearest Mary!" Cornelia said. "Whatever's wrong? You look as if you've seen a ghost?"

"A hideous face!" she cried, "outside the window, looking in at me."

The doctor quickly stepped forward and looked out the window to see what she was seeing. "Ah!" the doctor said. "I am sorry you are startled, but be not afeared. That is Adam. He lives with a family in the village and I have his keeping for Adam is my . . . responsibility. I brought him with me and told him to wait in the stable, but he has clearly become curious." The doctor threw a look of contrition at the others. "Please forgive me, I shall attend to this and shan't be a moment. Do carry on without me." And with that, the doctor rushed from the room. Mary continued gazing out the window and watched as the doctor rushed up to the hulking figure that towered over him. Then he took Adam by the hand and began to lead him away, back toward the stables. As the giant meekly followed, the huge head slowly swivelled on the thick neck, and Adam's disturbing gaze seemed to be staring straight into Mary's soul. And then Mary remembered where she had seen him before: he was the monstrous child she had met just that morning, when he had groped her breast on the lane.

Mary looked at the others with puzzlement. "I do not understand. What has the doctor to do with that boy . . . Adam?"

The others avoided each other's eyes, and looked about the room with obvious unease. Crosse finally stuttered. "The uh . . . the boy . . . Adam . . . his mother had been a patient of the doctor's—"

"The poor soul died in childbirth," the vicar interrupted. "Complications. It was . . . all quite . . . tragic . . ."

"Oh, but there was nothing the doctor could do." Crosse jumped in, finishing the thought. Mary might have questioned why the doctor's acquaintances were so rushed to explain the circumstances behind Adam, but at mention of the mother dying in childbirth, she was for a moment cast back to the tragic circumstances of her own nativity.

"At any rate," Reverend Phipps interrupted, "it is hardly a cheerful topic of conversation for the dinner table."

However, Mary's curiosity had been piqued and she sensed that there was much more to the story, but her curiosity would have to wait as the butler drew out a chair for her, unnecessarily dusting it with the flick of a cloth, before saying, "If ma'am would care to sit."

Mary took her seat and the butler draped a napkin across her lap and then eased her chair in. A few moments later, the doctor re-entered the room, slightly out of breath.

"Terribly sorry about that," the doctor apologised. "Again, do forgive me. I have returned Adam to the stable and instructed Tom to keep better watch over him. I have promised Adam a plate of shepherd's pie from the kitchen so we should not be interrupted again."

"I saw Adam this morning . . . " Mary blurted out before she had time to think better of continuing the conversation, ". . . in the field where several cows had been struck by lightning. He . . ." she thought of the giant boy's hand groping her breast, but could not bring herself to say that. "He . . . affrighted me . . ."

The doctor looked at Mary with concern. "Dear lady, I am right sorry to hear it. Adam may seem monstrous because of his size and appearance. He is simple of mind, but in truth he is a gentle soul and would not harm a bedbug. Even though his entry into the world was not gentle . . ."

"How so?" Mary asked. She was still curious about what the doctor had been about to say in the parlour before Reverend Phipps had shushed him.

The doctor's mouth opened, and he seemed ready to continue his explanation. His eyes flickered to look at the clergyman, who shook his head to say *no*. Freestone then bowed his head and said, "Well, that's a discussion for another time—"

Dinner commenced, although conversation was at first stilted as the party sat silent while the butler, maids, and kitchen staff carried in salvers bearing their first course. After the Reverend said Grace, the clatter of silverware and forks scraping china took the place of conversation as at the party ate.

All through the early courses, and quite despite herself, Mary found her gaze lingering upon the Doctor's face. Richard Freestone was a handsome man and, despite the normally sober calling of his expression, he was quite the dandy. His clothes were far too fashionable for a simple country doctor. And his dark brown hair shone lustrous in the candle light with all its waves and curls. (Mary had no doubt that he employed curling papers and pomades to produce such a spectacular mane.) The cut of his breeches was suggestively tight and the silken white cravat looped about his throat tied with enough precise care so as to appear careless. Although he spoke modestly and seemed humble, there was an excess of dash about him, a little too much devilishness for a doctor. He was handsome and clearly knew he was handsome, and his facial expressions seemed rehearsed and carefully controlled, such that Mary quickly decided that he could not be entirely trusted. Men already had so many advantages over women in power and money and social ranking such that masculine beauty struck her as a vulgar excess. In marriages a male partner more attractive than his mate almost inevitable led to wanderings and affairs, whereas a fat and ugly man would be steadfast and faithful. Her own experience had shown it to be true, and Mary shuddered to recall the many times she had been inveigled by the allure of a handsome male face, only to be jilted, betrayed, and even blackmailed over love letters she had written in earnest.

Cornelia had been watching Mary during the meal and noticed the constant glances she threw the doctor's way and while the butler and kitchen maid were clearing away the dinner plates she spoke, "Oh, but I think you have made Mary curious, Richard, with your mysterious hints."

But before the doctor could answer for himself, Reverend Phipps weighed in. "My dear child, such a tale is hardly likely to aid the digestion of our wonderful meal. Do you not think?"

Cornelia clearly did not like being referred to as "a child" and there was a barb in her voice when she replied. "But we have with us Mary Shelley, one of the greatest story tellers in the world. Having tantalised her, it would be impolite if Richard did not assuage her curiosity by telling his own story."

A moue of disapproval rippled across the clergyman's features. He was clearly put out, but he was forced to swallow his disapproving scowl along with a mouthful of claret.

Dr Freestone smiled ruefully and then began. "Well, mine is a sorry tale, but now I must tell it." He took a quick swallow of his wine and began. "When I first became a doctor, I returned home to see my family who hail from this Bourne. I was soon approached with news of a woman in the village who was large with child and the baby so overgrown that all feared she would perish. Of course, I attended upon the woman and examined her. The gossip was true: her pregnancy was enormous, frighteningly so, and after listening at her belly, I thought I detected . . . no, I *did* hear twin heartbeats. And so I deduced that she was carrying twins. But then, as her labour continued into the next month, I again examined her but this time heard only a single heart beat. By now her labour was a month early and the woman had already begun to bleed. I feared that the one babe must have died and that the labour must be immediately delivered before the dead child poisoned the womb. The poor woman's laying in lasted three tortuous days of agony. But when I attempted the delivery, I found only one monstrous child so huge it could not be drawn from the birth canal. In retrospect, I should have used my scalpel. But I was young and arrogant and thought I could do better. I tried by every means I had been taught to extract the baby, but after hours of fruitless manipulations and much suffering by the mother, I failed time and again. At last, desperate to end the woman's ordeal, I sent to a nearby farm for a set of forceps of the type used to deliver calves." The doctor's voice suddenly failed and he fell silent. His brown eyes gleamed. A muscle twitched in his jaw. It was clearly a painful memory for him, but he eventually resumed. "The result was that the mother died and the child was made into an idiot by an excess of pressure on the skull. And so I, the young and gifted doctor, killed a mother and made a simpleton of the babe. To this day, I have never seen so much blood at a birth. And I will never wash my hands clean of it. The child was Adam, who I made my ward. And so I determined to remain here, in Broomfield, and do my doctoring here, as penance for my youthful arrogance." He smiled weakly at Mary. "So you see, tragedy is what we endure in this life, be we high or low born."

The Reverend Phipps shook his head sagely and added, "These are trials sent by the Lord to test our faith."

There followed an awkward silence which betrayed the fact that no one else in the room agreed with the vicar's platitude.

The silence was broken when the domestic staff appeared, carrying trays of all manner of decadent pastries and cakes. But Mary's mouth was filmed with a bitterness she doubted that confectionaries could sweeten.

BEATIFUL MEN

I do not wish women have power over men; but over themselves . . . Mary Shelley

Mary remembered the first time she clapped eyes upon Percy Bysshe Shelley.

As the maid opened the front door to his knock, the young man had stepped inside, ducked a quick bow, and asked to see Mister Godwin. He was carrying a bundle of books bound up in brown paper tied with twine, and now he tucked them beneath one arm as he presented his calling card to the maid and announced himself as Percy Bysshe Shelley.

Percy Bysshe Shelley.
Percy Bysshe Shelley.
Percy Bysshe Shelley.

Mary had rolled the name around her tongue like a kiss of sticky-sweet honey.

Even his name was beautiful.

Back then, she had been a pigtailed girl of 14, gawking at the handsome boy through the bannister railings. He had caught her spying and grinned and wiggled his fingers at her teasingly, as a brother does to a younger sister.

The maid curtsied to the new visitor and then led him along the hallway toward the study where Mary's father worked every day at his writing table. As they passed the stairs, Mary saw the young stranger's face up close, and was instantly smitten.

William Godwin was a famous journalist and philosopher who received many visitors, but these were normally fusty old men with grey whiskers and bald heads. By comparison, this young man seemed like a vision. In the old church of St. Pancras, where Mary's mother was buried, and where Mary's father took her to service every Sunday, there were stained glass windows that glowed with images of androgynous angels crowned with golden halos. For Mary, Percy Shelley seemed like an angel who had shed his halo, stepped down from his window, and pulled on a rake's clothes to walk the earth. Shelley had a poet's luxurious, wavy hair, finely arched eyebrows, high cheekbones and an ethereal voice to match—surely a stained glass window somewhere was missing its angel. In his handsome, cinch-waisted jackets, drop-front trousers, white cravat and lace-cuffed shirts, he captured the attention of all women as he entered a room. Small wonder that he was already married with a child. (Did she know that back then?) For two years, he had been a not-infrequent visitor to the Godwin home, encouraged by her penurious father, who saw in the future baronet and heir to £6,000 a year, a source of revenue.

But then he came to call one sultry summer's day when Mary was 16 years old, a girl ripening into a young woman. In careful anticipation, Mary had dressed in her finest dress, coiffed her hair, pinched colour into her cheeks and arranged to be leaning against the hallway bannister in a posture of careless lassitude when the maid announced the arrival of "young mister Shelley." He had entered smiling, handed his hat to the maid, and looked about him. His eye had been drawn to Mary, and for the first time Percy Bysshe Shelley actually *saw* Mary Wollstonecraft Godwin.

By now the young aristocrat was firmly insinuated into the Godwin household, and so it did not seem indecorous when Shelley began to escort Mary on long walks to Old St. Pancras church, where Mary would leave a small bouquet of posies on her mother's tomb. During their strolls, the young man spilled out his thoughts on life and death and art and poetry with such breathless passion that it left Mary dizzied for days. As their walks became more frequent, it soon became apparent that Percy Bysshe Shelley harboured feelings toward her. He would take her arm as they crossed uneven ground, and their hips frequently jostled one another in their perambulations around the churchyard. And then a day came when Percy took Mary by both hands, stared deep into her eyes, and professing his love for her, kissed her full upon the lips.

In the weeks that followed, Percy became an ever more frequent visitor to the house, although by now it was clear that he was coming to visit her, not her father. And so, after a desultory visit paying respects to Godwin (to share Percy's latest pamphlet or poem) he and Mary would walk out together.

As they strolled the St. Pancras churchyard, nodding to the other mourners, in the odd moments when they were alone, the two would steal sly, furtive kisses. Most of what Mary knew about love and romance had come second-hand from her half-sister Claire, or through a few scandalous French novels she had read late at night when the rest of the house was asleep. And so she knew a little about men and their passions. With each visit Percy's kisses grew deeper and hungrier, and she responded with wanton abandon, her heart fluttering like a bird in its cage. Although a young girl with a young girls's naïeveté, she was besotted with her handsome beau, and knew what this dance would lead up to. And so one day she found herself with her buttocks pressed up against her mother's headstone while Percy slipped his tongue into her mouth and she sucked upon it thrillingly. She could feel his arousal pressing hard into her belly and in the next instant felt a hand lifting her skirts and fumbling in her petticoats. Mary took his hand and guided it to the spot, releasing a dreamy sigh as he found the special place. Moments later he entered her. As it was her first time, there was pain, but it was over quickly as Percy soon groaned and spent himself. As he withdrew, their commingled essences—semen and blood—dripped out and ran down the rough granite face of her mother's gravestone.

As they left the churchyard, arm in arm, Mary floated as if in a dream. She was sixteen years old and now she was a woman and felt for the first time the gathering power of her own feminine mystery. In that moment, Mary sensed that she had won. That Percy Bysshe Shelley would now be forever hers.

And the loss of that belief would be the first of many disappointments.

A DESSERT OF ASHES

> *Women are systematically degraded by receiving those trivial attentions which men think it manly to pay to the sex, when in fact, men are insultingly supporting their own superiority . . . Mary Wollstonecraft*

To Mary's surprise, Countess Ada managed to restrain herself from pestering Mary about her famous father, but as the dessert was being served, the young woman leaned over, put her hand atop Mary's and spoke in a low whisper, "You knew my father first-hand," was her first breathy question in what Mary guessed would be a prolonged interrogation, "was as he as great as they all say?"

Mary wanted to say that Ada's father played angel or devil as his quixotic mood took him, but mostly he was of the demonic persuasion. He loved to shock people and openly boasted of his sexual conquests, including his scandalous relationship with his half-sister. In fact, Lord Byron revelled in his infamy and openly encouraged the public's bad opinion of him. As a man, he could be cruel one moment and kind the next, praise and mock in one sentence. When Percy and Mary Shelley first became part of the Villa Diodati quorum (Mary's half-sister Claire played no role apart from concubine and lapdog to Byron, curled at his feet, forever fawning for scraps of attention), for the most part, Mary had kept silent and was ignored. But that soon changed after Byron read Mary's first rough pages of *Frankenstein*. From then on, Byron finally looked—truly looked—at Mary in the same way he looked at Percy Bysshe—as something close to an equal. It was a gaze that recognised her genius—and not at all grudgingly. Byron even said so, loudly, and in the hearing of others, much to the dismay of Percy and Claire, and especially poor Polidori. Mary's story of a man who usurped the almighty by creating life, had elevated her in Byron's eyes to the lofty stratosphere that hitherto had only been shared by Byron himself, Percy Bysshe, and poor dead consumptive John Keats who was present in spirit only.

And so Mary had no respite from the importuning voice which ceaselessly bombarded her with questions through the dessert course (dulling Mary's already modest appetite). Of course, every question from Byron's only legitimate daughter concerned her infamous father. And much as any child who has never once been in the same country as her parent, let alone the same room, Ada's curiosity was unassuageable.

Dessert was a selection of jellies and blancmanges. Ada deferred as she said sweets did not facilitate her digestion as did Mary whose headache, a constant pulsing in the right hemisphere of her head, was threatening to return in force. After the rest of the party had indulged, Crosse called for the servants to clear the table.

"And now I think the gentlemen will join me in post-prandial brandy and a pipe or two," Crosse announced brightly. And then he turned to Ada Lovelace, "And, of course, as a lady of high rank, the Countess must also join us."

All the women exchanged looks of deep disappointment. Ada's cheerless frown suggested she did enjoy politely sitting and looking on as the men sipped brandy and puffed at pipes; likewise, Mary felt aggrieved that she and Cornelia were being dismissed as *mere women*, and wanted to remain with the others for conversation. For his part, Doctor Freestone seemed to read her mind because he also objected, "Oh, surely, Andrew, we must not stand upon that old convention? Not when we are graced with the presence of women with such outstanding minds—"

"Do not discomfort yourself," Crosse interrupted, raising a placating hand and smiling cheerfully. "We will imbibe but one brandy and then you and the Reverend will accompany me to the music room where I must prepare my apparatus for the evening's demonstration." He flashed a paternal smile. "Countess Lovelace may then rejoin the ladies so they might converse on *feminine* topics at their leisure.

It was obvious from the expressions around the table that no one save the Vicar seemed happy with this arrangement, but as Crosse was the host, it was not seemly to argue the point farther, although Mary shared a look of umbrage with poor Cornelia, who dropped her gaze and picked morosely at her napkin.

STRANGE STAR ECLIPSED

> *Oh! What a miserable night I passed! The cold stars shone in mockery, and the bare trees waved their branches above me; now and then the sweet voice of a bird burst forth amidst the universal stillness. All, save I, were at rest or in enjoyment; I, like the arch-fiend bore a hell within me, and finding myself unsympathised with, wished to tear up the trees, spread havoc and destruction around me, and then to have sat down and enjoyed the ruin . . . Mary Shelley*

I awaken abruptly, dizzy and disoriented, the way a sleeper awakens from a sleep that has been too long, too deep.

I stare once again at at my star, taking comfort in its companionship. It seems the only thing constant and familiar in my darkness. But then, as I watch, the star falters, flickers, and begins to fade. My terror vaults as it dims to the point of extinguishment and a noise accompanies it: a human wail of grief. Suddenly I realise that I am the source of that wail. *I have a voice!* I think. *I can see and I have a voice!*

As if sensing my discovery, the star burns brighter momentarily, but then dims worse than before, flickers . . . and goes out.

No! I think. *Without my star I cannot endure.*

I reach out with my mind to where the star once hung, only to touch the scratchy fabric of night. And then I realise that I am reaching out with a hand, and that my fingertips have touched something real and tangible. At my touch the star illuminates and jiggles about in a dizzy dance. My fingertips encircle the star and I try to draw it back to me . . . and at that moment a corner of the night sky peels loose and lets in a dazzling shaft of light. I moan and squint at the painful brightness. But a moment later I realise that the light is streaming in through window glass, and that the fabric of night I had grasped is just a heavy curtain. As my befuddled senses reel, I finally see that my lone companion, my strange star, is nothing more than a moth hole eaten in the curtain.

With a trembling hand, I push the curtain aside and gaze through the window. I am amazed at what I see beyond the glass and for a moment my mind tumbles in distraction. The bright world beyond the window glass seems familiar, but my clumsy tongue cannot find words to describe it.

And then, in a flash, my name rushes from the depths of me and trembles upon my tongue, crying to be spoken. And finally, after long months of quiescence, I remember who I am and where I lie.

DARK FORCES ASSEMBLE

*If I am a fool, it is, at least, a doubting one; and I envy no one
the certainty of his self-approved wisdom . . . Lord Byron*

To avoid detection, the Reverend Phillip Smith and his
shambolic posse had trooped the long away around through
the farm fields, which necessitated clambering over
numerous stiles, and sometimes tramping along dusty farm tracks to
make any forward progress. The way was slow and laborious, but they
had no choice—they were on an errand of mischief, and stealth was
essential. The sallow-cheeked Smith led the procession. He had found
a shepherd's crook left lying against a hedgerow by its forgetful owner
and snatched it up, deeming it a sign of God's approval. Thrown over
one shoulder was a rough hessian sack which sagged with the weight
of clinking and clanking bottles—more rum to buoy the courage of his
disciples when the fateful struggle against evil seemed imminent. His
motley crew of miscreants weaved and shambled behind, depending
upon their level of infirmity and how much they had already drunk.

The two rough fellows dogged Smith's heels, exchanging furtive glances and snaggle-toothed smirks. Finally Smith's Christian soldiers reached the field where the slot in the trees had been cut which led to the woodland path that Mary, Andrew Crosse and Cornelia had perambulated earlier. They had reached the highest point in the landscape and the rabble of men stood looking down upon the dense woodland cover.This was the only vantage point that allowed even a partial view of the house at Fyne Court, its lit windows, and the copper tracery of wires that converged at the music room like the nexus of a spider's web.

As the Reverend Smith surveyed the lay of the land, the two army deserters stood apart from the rest, their heads close together as they conversed in guttural whispers. "What say ye now?" asked the Cornishman.

"You stay close by the good Reverend," the Irishman replied. "The fool has a purse of money that will soon be ours. At first chance, I shall slip away, toward the house, scouting."

"A-scoutin' fer what may be thieved?"

The Irishman answered with a wicked smile, "The King's army taught me well. We will need money to flee this Bourne. That fine house must've plenty things worth thieving.'"

"Aye, nay doubt. But what about the gamekeeper and his dogs?"

O'Rourke turned and spat. "I been stealing from the English all my life, dogs or no."

In response, the Cornishman slipped something out of a pocket and held it close to his body so that only the Irishman could see: a six-inch bladed knife with a wicked sharp blade. "The gamekeeper and his dogs'll get my knife if they get a sniff o' me."

"Come brothers," the clergyman called to his followers, and began to lead his posse into Crosse's field. As they clambered over the stile, the Cornishman turned to say something to his crony, but Nessan O'Rourke, like any good thief worth the name, had noiselessly vanished.

"Like a ghost, that lad is," Ryd Thorne smirked, knowing it was likely that there would be many throats offered up to the cutting edge of his blade before the night was done.

A DEATH IN THE MANGER

> *Here I swear, and as I break my oath may ... eternity blast me, here I swear that never will I forgive Christianity! It is the only point on which I allow myself to encourage revenge... Oh, how I wish I were the Antichrist, that it were mine to crush the Demon; to hurl him to his native Hell never to rise again - I expect to gratify some of this insatiable feeling in Poetry . . . Percy Bysshe Shelley*

A dam was sitting on a hay bale, eating from a stoneware plate when Tom entered the stable carrying a huge metal tankard of ale. The giant, half-wit boy noisily slavered down the last of the shepherd's pie and began licking the gravy from the plate and moaning with pleasure. Tom walked up to him and tugged the plate from his huge hands. "Lemme take that, Adam," he said, "Afore ye lick the pattern off." Adam started to blubber like a child deprived of his toy, so Tom quickly pressed the ale tankard in his huge hands. "Here's some ale for thee," he said. In truth the ale was very weak and Adam would have needed to drink a gallon to feel its alcoholic effects. Still, the giant man-child set to noisily guzzling the drink. He drained the tankard in four huge gulps and belched loudly, and then shook the empty tankard at Tom and moaned, wanting more.

"You stay here and be a good lad until the doctor comes to get ye, and I'll give you some more," Tom said.

Adam whined like a scolded puppy, but Tom was unbending. He snatched the empty tankard from Adam's grip and wagged a finger at him. "Like I just said, you sit there like a good lad and you can have some more. Right?"

Adam chundered and grumbled, but folded his huge arms into his lap and became docile. Tom gave him a final admonishing look before he walked out of the stable, bound to check the kennels where the dogs had begun barking again. He was certain the hounds had sniffed out poachers lurking in the woods.

The barefoot stable boy, Titch, had been standing in a corner, silently watching, and now he crept forward from the shadows. Titch was only five and small for his age. Even sitting down, Adam towered over him like a giant stone idol.

"Adam," Titch said. "Let's play the game."

Adam, upon seeing a familiar friend, grinned and gurgled with laughter.

"The game," Titch repeated. "Come on, let's play the game."

Again, Adam chuckled, but remained sitting.

"Come on, Adam. It's fun. Let's play the game!" The little boy grabbed the giant by one hand and tugged, but Adam's bulk was immovable.

The stable boy paused a moment and then said. "You like ale? I can get you ale." He mimed drinking from a cup. "Ale, Adam? You want ale?"

Adam groaned and nodded excitedly.

"Play the game and I'll get you beer."

This time, when Titch tugged at Adam's huge hand, the giant rose and allowed himself to be meekly led to a spot in the middle of the stable. Titch looked up. He stood directly beneath one of the main roof joists.

"Now," Titch commanded. "Throw me, Adam, until I fly high enough to touch the joist."

And so, gurgling with laughter, the giant reached down and encircled the little boy's waist with his massive hands. They had played this game before, but only when Tom wasn't around. The Gamekeeper had caught them playing the game a time or two before and had been harsh in forbidding them from playing it. But Titch was canny enough to know that what Tom didn't know wouldn't kill him.

"Throw me, Adam," Titch urged. "Toss me high."

The giant effortlessly lifted the boy and then heaved. The boy sailed several feet into the air, blond hair lifting and small legs kicking as he fell, and then the giant gently caught him.

"Again!" Titch cried.

The giant tossed him a second time, higher. Titch squealed with delight as he fell back and was caught.

"Higher, Adam, higher," he demanded. "Throw me until I can touch the roof beam."

Adam threw him a third time, so that he flew even higher. Titch reached to touch the beam but his fingers swished through thin air an inch short. In the shadowy gloom of the stable ceiling, the stable boy could not see the rusty eye hook that protruded a good six inches from the bottom beam. The hook was used to haul things up into the rafters. A rope would be passed through the eye hook so that heavy horse collars could be hung from it.

"Higher! Higher! The boy shouted between squeals of laughter.

This time Adam released a grunt as he flung the boy skyward with all his might. Titch sailed much higher than before, legs kicking. And this time his head slammed into the bottom of the roof truss, punching the rusty eye hook through his skull and into his brain. As Titch fell back into Adam's arms, his body flopped limply. But Adam didn't notice and threw him again. The boy soared up high and then fell in a loose sprawl of limbs. When the giant caught Titch, he saw the red blood runneling down his face. Adam paused and gaped at the boy's face in puzzlement. He knew this wasn't right although he had no idea what had happened. He grunted and shook the boy, whose bloody head tossed back and forth.

A wail of alarm tore from the giant's throat. He shook Titch harder, so that the small head flailed back and forth, spraying blood. Titch remained flaccid and silent. Adam now saw the blood gushing from the open wound and running down the boy's face. With a moan of fear, Adam realised he had broken the boy, the same way he broke the kittens and puppies and chickens he petted too hard. Adam let out a keening cry. He had been bad again and knew that everyone would be angry with him and shout at him and beat him with a switch for breaking the little boy. He looked about the stable, howling with fright, uncertain of what to do. He had only a vague sense of what he had done wrong, but knew he must hide the stable boy where no one would find him.

STRANGE STAR OCCULTED

> *Why I came here, I know not; where I shall go it is useless to inquire — in the midst of myriads of the living and the dead worlds, stars, systems, infinity, why should I be anxious about an atom? . . . Lord Byron*

I lie still for an age, waiting for the world to piece itself together again. For my memory to return. Somehow I sense I have slept for hours.

No . . . days.

No . . . . . . weeks.

A single thought bursts to the surface of my awareness.

What is my name?

I sense that the answer is there, lurking just beyond my reach. A shy ghost that flits away each time I draw near. Finally, a name shuffles forward from the darkness, like a geriatric servant hobbling from the dusty corridors of a grand house in answer to the bell pull.

Cornelia?

I tumble the name over in my mind for several moments, but then cast it away. It has the ring of familiarity, but it is not the missing puzzle piece that, when slotted in place, completes the picture.

But then a stray recollection floats to my consciousness like an air bubble rising from deep in the ocean and suddenly bursting to the surface.

Mary. For some reason I feel sure that *Mary* is my mother's name. I try to conjure her face but, strangely, I cannot. How can I know my mother's name and yet not recall her face? I repeat the name over and over: *Mary, Mary, Mary* and it seems to fit. But then it strikes me, *I am also named Mary.*

At last, I have my name. Surely I must now reclaim my past.

The bedside lamp has burned out, and the room hangs in oppressive gloom. I will my right arm to move toward the curtains. To draw them back and let the light spill in. But the bedclothes has been tightened with such ferocity I can barely move and after several seconds of straining I abandon the effort, breathing hard and sweating.

Exhausted.

Suddenly I hear a voice calling the darkness.

Distant.

Muffled.

At first it is an unintelligible jumble of words, but then the voice approaches and grows louder.

"I am just about to check on mother." It is a woman's voice. A familiar voice. Although I cannot name its owner, the sound of her voice makes my stomach clench with anxiety.

A door knob rattles in the darkness. A crack of light flares and dilates as the owner of the voice pushes the door wide and enters the bedroom. Acting on some instinct, I say nothing and lie still, my eyes mostly shut so that I dimly perceive shapes filtered through my eyelashes.

Floorboards creak as a shadowy silhouette floats into the room and hovers at my bedside. Although my eyes are barely cracked, I can just make out a human shape peering down at me.

"Are you awake, mother?" the woman asks.

I feel a hand touching my throat, slender fingers moving up my neck. Probing. Exploring. The fingers slide further . . . searching.

Checking for a pulse, I think. *She's hoping I'm dead.*

After several moments of breath-held silence the woman unleashes a disappointed sigh. And then her voice mutters close to my ear. "Why are you not dead, old woman? You are nothing but a burden to me *and* to your son."

The words are uttered in an-under the breath curse. Upon hearing that jumble of syllables, spat at me like a mouthful of poison, I suddenly remember who owns the voice: Jane, my son's wife. I always felt deep unease when Jane insisted upon addressing me as "mother," expressing a filiality that failed to mask her seething resentment. Now, thinking that I was still unconscious, Jane had been unable to cage the hatred and contempt roiling inside of her.

The probing fingers find the artery on my throat and measure its thin, erratic pulse. Then Jane huffs in vexation and the hand removes itself. A few moments later floorboards creak as she retreats and the soft thump of the door bumping shut lets me know that I am alone again.

This time when I open my eyes, the room is warmly lit. Jane has turned up the lantern to examine me and forgotten to turn it down when she she left.

For the first time in weeks I am able to look about my sick room in full light. It's only then that I notice my green leather journal on the bedside table and the pen and bottle of ink. I realise I must finish my story while strength in me remains. It takes an enormous effort to squeeze loose of the bedclothes, which Jane had cinched tight again before leaving. By the time I drag myself upright on the pillows, I am trembling and sweating through my nightgown. With my remaining strength I drag the journal from the bedside table into my lap, and then pull the ink-pot closer, setting it unsteadily upon the bed. Finally, my pen freshly dipped in the inkwell, I open my journal, turn to where I left the story hanging in mid-sentence, then touch the nib of my pen to the paper and begin to write the rest of my tale.

ONWARD CHRISTIAN SOLDIERS

Every day confirms my opinion on the superiority of a vicious life — and if virtue is not its own reward I don't know any other stipend to it . . . Lord Byron

When they reached the stone wall that marked the edge of Crosse's property, the Reverend Smith raised a hand and his ramshackle militia stumbled to a halt.

Martin Compton marched at his shoulder and now he muttered in the prelate's ear, "This be it. Yon field with the sheep be Crosse's and so be the field of corn agin it."

The Irishman slapped the Reverend Smith on the back with excessive force and grinned a slack grin. "Why not mix the two?" he suggested. "That will vex Mister Crosse greatly."

Smith thought on it for a moment, his gaunt cheeks sucked in. And then he called out in a strident voice "Tis a godly thing to do to one so ungodly. Men, take up your axes. Your staffs. Pick up stout field stones and smash the fence. And then we shall rend—" Smith's next words were drowned out by a deep rumble of thunder. All the men stopped and turned to squint at the black storm clouds sweeping toward them from the West, towering, massive, and hideously black, like a premonition of hell. Even though he felt certain of his righteousness, fear prickled beneath the Reverend Smith's breastbone. It was a sight reminiscent of something from the Old Testament: the judgement of God upon Sodom and Gomorra and he gripped the Bible tighter to his chest.

"I dunna much like the looks of that," muttered one of the men and received rumbles of agreement from the other men.

"Be not afeared!" Smith shouted. "It is a sign! A sign of God's wroth. A sign that we do his work."

Muttering morosely, and with clear reluctance, the men set to their mischief, all except for the Cornishman Ryd Thorne, who giggled with wicked glee as he took his axe to the gate, hacking through the leather cords the gate hinged upon, so that it fell flat upon the ground with a heavy thunk. Others smashed fence pales with stones until, with a prolonged cracking sound, the spine of the fence twisted and the entire length toppled to the ground. Then the men chased the sheep about the field, arms spread wide, shouting and whistling as they drove the bleating herd into the ripening corn. At first, the panicked sheep crashed among the stalks, trampling and flattening. But sheep will not intentionally push deep into a cornfield and most refused to move farther and contented themselves to graze upon the fallen corn. When it became clear the sheep would be driven no farther, all looked for guidance to Reverend Smith.

"Now what?" Martin Compton challenged.

Smith's jaw clenched and unclenched several times. And then he looked to the Cornishman who was carrying the lit lantern. "You there, fellow. Kindle fire. Set the crop alight."

Thorne smiled slackly and strode into the corn. Seizing a fistful of dry chaff, he raised the lantern glass and kindled it to life. Then he dropped the burning fistful among the dry stalks. Grey smoke plumed up. The Cornishman moved farther along, kindling fire at multiple points. Soon, several columns of dense grey smoke rose up, and then they all heard a dry crackle and saw tongues of yellow flames licking at the air.

Martin Compton swallowed dryly. Fear danced in his belly. He hated his landlord, but burning a man's crop went against all his instincts. And if his master were ever to find out that he was part of the group that did such wickedness . . .

The wind suddenly gusted and the flames leapt and grew with a *whoof!*, until a wall of corn burned steadily and the heat of the fire pushed the bleating sheep and the watching men into backing away.

The sky darkened miserably as the first black raincloud floated overhead and the freshening wind strengthened to a gale. At first it blew from the East, but then suddenly veered, blowing from the West. There was a soughing exhalation as the winds aloft collided and formed a whirlwind spinning about them, a vortex choked with dead leaves and spiderwebs and burning clumps of straw. Then the black cloud menacing above seemed to inhale, drawing the air vertically skyward, snatching hats from the farm hands' heads and sucking them up into the darkening sky. The Reverend Smith stood at the centre of the whirlwind, watching wild-eyed, his face ecstatic, part from terror, part from trembling anticipation. One hand clamped the black saturno hat to his head, the long strands of black hair whipping about his sallow face. Most of the farm labourers had dropped to their knees and were crossing themselves and praying fervently, or cowering blindly and blubbering with fear. And then a dazzling bolt of lightning sizzled down from the cloud above and touched its crooked finger to the top of a tall larch tree. Thunder boomed as the bolt of lightning pulsed on and off, the vast current boiling the water and sap within the tree to super heated steam. A moment later the trunk of the larch tree exploded with a cacophonous roar. Their ears ringing painfully, it drove the men into a panic and they fled, abandoning Reverend Smith as all ran blindly into the deep woods. Even the army deserter, Thorne, was stricken with terror. As he sprinted past the Reverend, the Cornishman shouted, "You're a dead man if you linger here."

Smith watched them go, terrified to run away, but terrified to stay.

And then the whirlwind descended into the centre of the cornfield where it flattened the crop, forming a perfect circle, while the air above it whirled with broken stalks and burning detritus. Then something seemed to break out of the circle. Something invisible that weaved a zig-zag pathway through the corn. Smith watched, slack-jawed as the thing threshed through the crop toward him. "It's just a whirlwind," he told himself. "Just a corn devil." But the very name *corn devil* unnerved him and even if it was just a whirlwind, the Bible was full of stories of whirlwinds and the voices that spoke from them. It could have been made by a number of unseen sheep stampeding through the stalks; the toppling corn seemed to mark the progress of an invisible presence ploughing through the crop with inhuman speed. Thoughts of the witch's threat about a monster surged to the surface of Smith's mind. Suddenly his nerve buckled and he turned and ran pell-mell after the others into the dark shelter of the forest.

DOPPLEGÄNGER

"I will revenge my injuries; if I cannot inspire love, I will cause fear, and chiefly towards you my arch-enemy, because my creator, do I swear inextinguishable hatred. Have a care; I will work at your destruction, nor finish until I desolate your heart, so that you shall curse the hour of your birth ... Mary Shelley

By now the storm clouds were but a few hours away as evinced by the giant thunderheads boiling high into the sky. The booms of thunder were louder and closer as Mary and Cornelia stepped through the front doors of Fyne Court into the cooling evening. With half the sky hung with a black curtain of clouds, an unnatural twilight reigned, so that when Mary and Cornelia stepped away from the house, they found the sylvan paths leading into the woods dark and gloomy.

As the chill air caressed her bare shoulders, a shiver rippled through Mary's slender frame. "Oh, but I have left my wrap," she said. "Tarry a moment, dearest Cornelia, whilst I run and fetch it." And with that, Mary ducked back indoors, leaving Cornelia waiting alone in the deserted courtyard, for the chickens had all fled back into their roosts.

Mary rushed through the house to the parlour, where she found her wrap crumpled on the sofa. She quickly gathered it up, draped it about her bare shoulders, and was about to leave when she heard voices coming from down the hall. The men: Mister Cross, the reverend and the doctor were holding forth in the dining room and Mary could scent their pipe smoke in the air. But then she heard a female voice: the Countess Ada. The voices were muffled by the dining room door, but she heard Ada say something about how the world was about to change. Mary was intrigued and wanted to listen further, but just then Jasper, the young butler, entered the parlour carrying a silver salver. He moved about the room picking up the discarded sherry glasses and settling them on the tray, but then he noticed Mary silently lingering. He shot her a jaded look and cleared his throat peremptorily, letting her know that her eavesdropping had been noticed. Ashamed to be caught in such a compromising position, Mary quickly uttered, "I left my wrap behind and the dusk brings a chill to the air," and then fled the room.

Cornelia was nowhere to be seen when Mary stepped from the front door. Mary lingered a moment and then, growing impatient, she wandered across the empty courtyard and entered the woodland path where she remembered seeing the castle folly. It was very much darker between the tall trees, and she crept along following her own vague sense of direction. But as she rounded a bend, the gloom deepened. She hurried along the loamy path as quickly as the poor light would allow, hoping to catch up with Cornelia. Eventually she made out a figure in the near distance, strolling the path ahead, walking away from her.

From behind it appeared be the slender figure of a young woman and believing it to be Cornelia, Mary quickened her pace and called out, "Cornelia! Here I am. Do wait up." At her call, the figure stopped and turned to look behind. But as she moved closer, Mary saw that the figure was not Cornelia, but another young woman who was strange to her. Or yet, who wasn't strange. And with a shocked intake of breath, Mary gasped to recognise her own face: or at least, the face that had looked back from the mirror when Mary was a young girl of seventeen. The figure was alarmed to see Mary, and stood mute, regarding her older self with a wide-eyed look of horror.

"Mary?" a woman's voice called from behind. "Oh, there you are." The voice was familiar, and when Mary spun around, she saw Cornelia hurrying along the path toward her, a lit lantern swinging in her hand. Stunned, Mary turned back to her younger double, and only then saw that what she had perceived as a human figure was, in fact, the foreshortened stump of a storm-broken tree. For Mary, it was a moment of infinite terror. Her husband Percy had seen his own doppelgänger on several occasions before he drowned, and Mary knew that such apparitions were regarded as an omen of death.

"Mary," Cornelia gasped, panting from her exertions. "There you are. But—" she looked at Mary with concern. "But what is it, dearest Mary? You look as if you've seen something horrible!"

Mary realised how she must appear to Cornelia: mouth agape and staring wide-eyed like a mad woman and made an effort to brush it off. "Oh no," she said. "I thought I saw something in the woods. But, it was just a strange shadow."

"Oh my," Cornelia said, "Looking about herself with unease. "Do not speak of strange shadows and such things when it is going dark. You will quite unnerve me. Anyway" she added, "I had to return to the house to fetch a lantern and when I stepped outside you had vanished. I thought the woodland goblins had snatched you away."

Mary laughed and smiled, attempting to make light of things. She linked arms with Cornelia and together the women strode off down the darkened path, the lantern swinging in Cornelia's grip peeling loose the shadows and forcing them to slither behind nearby trees and ferns—all except for the shadow of a man lurking behind a tree, a shadow that now dropped to a crouch, ready to spring.

As they silently trod the loamy path, Cornelia finally offered, "I am so very sorry my husband vexed you."

Mary stopped, broke loose of Cornelia's arm, and turned to face her. "Apparently I have neither intellect nor the advantage of a man—even with a man of science. A man of intellect whom I would have believed to be more enlightened."

"Please," Cornelia begged. "Andrew is of another generation. Do not be angry for the fault of his upbringing."

Mary bristled a moment longer, but then relented. She looked at the other woman's face, her eyes bright with tears and was pierced by guilt." Oh, but I am not angry with you, Cornelia, or Mister Crosse. It is the world I am vexed with."

She hugged the younger woman and said brightly. "Please, do not let my ill temper spoil our time together."

Concealed by the wide trunk of the tree, the Irishman slowly rose to his feet. The women were almost within reach. He had but to step out and he could grab them both . . .

Cornelia's face suddenly lit up. "Oh, but now is our opportunity to steal away."

"Steal away? But where?"

"As I said earlier, to my secret place where women may speak freely."

The Irishman's heartbeat thundered in his ears. He had but to take two strides. He would surprise them both. A roundhouse punch would knock the older woman senseless. Then he'd be free to hurl the young one to the ground, lift her skirts and petticoats and tumble her on the spot. When he was done he would cut both their throats to keep them from squawking like chickens and then make for the off. He had done much the same before. It would be the work of a few moments.

As the women passed, the Irishman tensed. He slipped the knife from his right hand to his left and balled his right hand in a fist. He had just started to move when a livid white flash ran jagged across the base of the approaching thunderclouds, lighting him up. He snatched back, flattening himself against the tree trunk. Seconds later the rolling drumbeat of thunder shook the ground. Unaware of the danger they were in, Mary paused a moment, her hand upon Cornelia's arm, arresting her as she stopped to study the heavens. The sky to the east was prematurely dark due to the boiling black mass of approaching thunderclouds. To the west and north, the sky was a hideous colour bleeding from a sickly unnatural green to the deep purple of a bruise.

Cornelia saw the storm approaching and looked at Mary. "We should not tarry. By the time the storm reaches us we must be safely ensconced indoors."

The women hurried on and the Irishman faltered. Startled by the lightning, he had missed his moment when he could have taken them both swiftly, cleanly, and now he watched in impotent rage as the women escaped into the twilight.

ZEUS CATCHES A SCENT

My present situation was one in which all voluntary thought was swallowed up and lost . . . Mary Shelley

Tom strode from the stables to the kennels. The dogs had been barking steadily for the last hour and upon seeing him, they went into a frenzy: leaping about inside their kennels, scratching at the doors and whining to be let free. Tom had a short barrelled shoulder-gun tucked under one arm—a blunderbuss with a flared muzzle—and now he set it down upon the ground as he stooped and talked to the fretful dogs in a calming voice.

"All right you two, hold yer howling." He dug in a pocket, pulled out a chunk of pork fat, tore it in two and tossed a piece to Zeus, the older, larger lurcher. The dog snaffled it down in one bite and then Tom tossed the remains to Thor, the younger dog. Both dogs wagged their tails and barked for more.

"You be patient Thor," Tom gently scolded, "I'm just takin' Zeus with me this time. I can't hold ye both and shoot straight—" He thought about it a moment and then added to himself: "If'n I need to shoot."

Tom unlatched the kennel door and deftly slipped a lead around the larger lurcher's neck.

"Come along, Zeus," he said to the dog, pausing to take up the blunderbuss and sling it over his free shoulder. "I think there's poachers in the woods, so you and me are gonna flush 'em out."

And with that Tom set off with the lurcher. From the way the dog pulled at the lead, Zeus seemed to have picked up a scent. Tom had little doubt there were miscreants roaming his master's woods. The blunderbuss he carried was loaded only with rock salt and some fine gravel. The aim was not to kill but merely to scare poachers off with a scorching backside peppered with rock salt. Often the roar of the blunderbuss' report alone sent poacher's fleeing.

Although Tom was a seasoned outdoors man, the skies overhead were strange and unlike anything he'd seen before. The day turned from gloomy twilight back to brilliant sun and back again as wave after wave of black thunderheads cruised overhead.

The dog pulled all the way along the path running through the flower garden, past the emerald pond, and up the highest point of Crosse's land where the woods fell away and the countryside transitioned to open farm fields. As he climbed to the top of the stile Tom saw immediately the toppled fence, the burned corn, and the scattered sheep, most of which had drifted back into their own field. At the sight of the wilful damage, Tom cursed and spat.

Not poachers, then. This was the not first instance of vandalism that had been visited upon Crosse's land. Tom had no doubt that the Reverend Phillip Smith and his lackeys were behind this. Tom stood at the top of the wall, surveying. It was clear that the vandals had been here recently. As in previous attacks Tom had little doubt that they had done their misdeeds and run away, but he could not be certain that they were not still lurking nearby. He dithered for a moment, torn between searching the woods, but felt it might be wiser to stay closer to the house to protect it.

In the end, the weather made the decision for him. A rolling crack of thunder roared frighteningly close as a black thundercloud tumbled overhead and lightning flashed. With a jolt of fear Tom realised that he and the dog were standing at the highest point in the land and were in danger of being struck at any moment. And so he jumped down from from the stile and clicked his tongue at the dog.

"C'mon boy," he said and set off down the path, heading back toward the house. But they had not gone ten feet when hail began to fall, heavy and stinging. Tom stooped and lowered his head, but both he and the dog were suffering a lashing. They hurried down the paths until they reached the flower garden where Tom led the lurcher into the shelter of the Arcadian Alcoves. Here they were at last free of the stinging hailstones. Wiping the icy water running down his face, Tom watched the ferocious fall of hailstones stripping petals from the rose bushes and piling up in icy drifts a half inch thick in places.

His shirt was soaked and Tom was wracked with shivers. First the vandals and now this. He combed the wet hair from his eyes and peered out, his mood blackening.

CASTLE OTRANTO

> Vivid flashes of lightning dazzled my eyes, illuminating the lake, making it appear like a vast sheet of fire; then for an instant every thing seemed of a pitchy darkness, until the eye recovered itself from the preceding flash . . . Mary Shelley

"Where are we going?" Mary asked, finding it necessary to speak in a whisper, even though she didn't herself know why.

"As I promised, to my secret place." Cornelia replied and tittered. She had both hands cupped over Mary's eyes, blindfolding her. "See," she dropped her hands allowing Mary to see the stout stone structure looming ahead.

"Your castle!" Mary cried.

But although the folly had seemed a charming child's delight in the bright daylight, in the gloom it leered back at them like a giant stone skull, the windows transfigured into dark eye sockets spilling shadow.

The folly was, in fact, a much-attenuated castle. Its centre section was little more than a raised stone porch covered by a lean-to roof where a wooden bench provided a convenient place to sit and rest. On either side, flanking the central porch, was a half-round stone turret with a crenellated top. Four arched windows were set into the curving facade of each turret. A wooden door on either turret provided access and now Cornelia produced a heavy iron key and unlocked the door to the left-hand turret.

"My husband keeps his telescope and stores some of his electrical apparatus in the other turret," Cornelia explained. "But this side is all mine."

The key turned, the lock rasped open, and they stepped inside. The circular space was sparsely decorated: a small writing desk against one wall, a horse hair sofa against the other. A fur rug flayed from some kind of animal (wolf?) thrown upon the floor offered the only creature comfort. The centre of the room was occupied by a round table with four chairs set about it. And, of course, as befits any castle, a full suit of armour menaced from a shadowy alcove. Mary let out a gasp when she saw it, almost expecting it to come of life and take a lumbering step toward them, the shiny metal arms outstretched and grasping.

"Oh," Mary gushed. "You have your own Castle Otranto!"

"What is *Otranto*?" Cornelia asked.

"It is a book. A novel. A wonderful gothic tale filled with ruined castles and dark dungeons and ghosts rattling chains, and all things that thrill and raise gooseflesh."

"Ooooh!" Cornelia said, hugging herself. "Again, Mary, do not speak of ghosts and spectres!"

Both women laughed as Cornelia moved about the room with a tapir kindled from the lantern, lighting the melted stubs of candles of varying lengths and thicknesses and soon the space was illuminated by their warm, pulsing glow. Mary settled into one of the chairs as Cornelia lit more candles about the room and then set her lantern down in the middle of the table beside a crystal decanter that contained some kind of amber liquid. Scotch?

Cornelia perched on the chair opposite Mary's. In the buttery glow of the candlelight, both women's dark eyes and fair-skinned faces took on the glow of Renaissance women painted by Caravaggio. Cornelia reached across the table and took both of Mary's hands in hers, gave them a squeeze, and both women burst into infectious laughter.

"Oh, but I think we are the ones having the adventure," Cornelia said in the voice of a wicked schoolgirl.

"Yes," Mary agreed. "We are the queens of our own castle, while the gentlemen and the Countess are locked in a stuffy drawing room."

"I am so glad I am not with them," Cornelia said. "I have no doubt a lady as clever as you could hold your own in conversation, but I feel so dreadfully dull in the presence of Countess Ada." She paused a moment and then ventured, "Do you not think it unseemly in a lady to be so . . . so . . . ?" She hesitated, struggling to find the word.

"Educated?" Mary interrupted. "No, I do not. Although I know that most men think women inferior and are threatened, not fascinated, when they meet a woman who is their intellectual equal." As she said it, a memory sprang forth into her mind. An image of Lord Byron standing in the parlour of the Villa Diodati in the harsh morning light. For once the curled lip, the narrowed eyes, and all the trademarks of his normal hauteur had been wiped from his face as he handed back the rough scribblings of Mary's first draft of *Frankenstein*. And then, Byron awarded her with a stunning gift: a look of artistic admiration. It was the first time—perhaps the only time—he had looked upon her with the kind of filial admiration his face displayed when he and Percy Shelley talked of poetry, philosophy, and all matters esoteric and sublime. Byron was a rakish cad, and an imperious bully, but he was foremost a poet and like any artist, recognised true talent when he saw it. Although she did not care to admit it, when she received that look from him—from *Lord Byron* no less!—she felt as if she had been catapulted to the Elysian heights where only demigods such as her husband and Byron were allowed to tread. And breathing such thin and rarefied air made her giddy.

Despite the burning candles, the room was still dull, and so

Cornelia adjusted that lantern, giving the wick a quarter turn. It was then that Mary noticed something and released a sharp gasp.

Cornelia looked at her with concern. "What is it, Mary?"

Mary was staring at the far wall, her mouth open, lower lip aquiver. She extended her arm jerkily, and pointed with a trembling finger. "Look!" she breathed in a thin whisper.

Cornelia looked at the direction of her gaze but could make nothing out. "What?" she asked.

"The light," Mary replied. "The light from the lantern. See how it is bent by the crystal, so that the image thrown upon the wall seems to resemble a face."

"What?" Cornelia said. "I don't see a . . . oh . . . wait." She studied the light prismed across the wall. "Oh, yes, I see it now. A kind of face." Cornelia laughed, but as the women continued to look, the abstract image conjured from light refracted through the crystal flask did indeed seem to form a monstrous face, and once seen could not be unseen, unnerving them both. Cornelia jumped up from the table and flew to Mary's side, but as she rose, she bumped the table with her hip. The motion made the face jiggle and shift, the eye seeming to roll in its socket, the slash of the mouth tautening into a snarl.

"Oooh," Cornelia asked breathlessly. "It is just a trick of the light is it not?"

"Yes," Mary agreed. "It's just a trick of the light, refracting through the crystal decanter."

They both laughed nervously.

"Look," Cornelia pointed. "There is an eye, a mouth, a rudimentary nose . . . ." She trailed off as her voice dried up.

"It seems to be looking at us," Mary observed, doubling the tension.

At that moment the light outside dimmed theatrically, and the room shook from a long, rumbling drumroll of thunder that made both women shriek with surprise, but their cries were soon drowned out by something hammering at the windows to get inside.

"Oh look!" Cornelia said, point at the windows where a fusillade of hailstones were striking with such force they threatened to smash through the glass at any moment. The hail storm grew louder and more intense but then trailed off and ended as abruptly as it had begun,

"The hailstorm seems to be ending," Mary observed.

But then both women let out another shriek of surprise at the sound of a fist hammering on the door.

"Who could that be?" Mary asked.

"I cannot image," Cornelia replied, looking at her companion, mouth open, eyes wide. She threw her arms about Mary and buried her head in Mary's shoulder. "Oh, please, let's not answer it, I beg you. But the hammering grew more frantic: *bang bang bang bang bang bang . . .!*

Holding onto each other, the two women crept to the door where the knocking was thunderous.

"Who is it?" Mary shouted through the door.

The knocking abated for a moment and then a muffled voice shouted back.

"It's me! It's me!"

Cornelia was just turning the key in the lock when Mary cried out a warning, "Wait! Stop, Cornelia. We do no know who you are letting inside!"

But the warning came a moment to late as the door flew open and a man barged in, knocking Cornelia aside. Startled by the rush of motion, both women screamed. The dishevelled figure stumbled in, breathing hard, But then they saw who it was: the Doctor.

The normally dapper figure had been lashed by the hailstorm. The shoulders of his jacket were epauletted with melting hailstones and the nest of his curly auburn hair sparkled with fat drops of melt water. As he staggered inside, face flushed red, breathless and battered, a tremor of cold shook his frame. He struggled to barge the door shut against the gusting wind and once it was closed, Cornelia leapt forward to turn the key in the lock, securing them from the storm.

The doctor looked at the women's concerned faces and laughed. "The seasons are topsy-turvy. A December hail storm in August? I quite thought I would be battered to death!" He paused as he used his fingers to rake melting hailstones from his hair.

"Oh you are frozen, poor thing!" Cornelia laughed, "But I have just the thing to warm you."

Moments later the three were seated at the round table. They watched as Cornelia produced glasses from a shelf and poured brandies from the crystal decanter.

"Surely such a storm presages the end of the world!" Dr Freestone said.

"How is it you managed to escape from the drawing room, Richard?" Cornelia smiled as each sipped their brandy.

"Ah yeesssss," the doctor drawled. "I told them I had to check on Adam."

"And how is Adam?" Cornelia asked.

The doctor quaffed his drink and shrugged. "I am quite sure he is fine. He is safely in the stable where Tom is looking after him."

"So you abandoned poor Ada to the company of the reverend and my husband?"

"Actually, *she* was the one holding court when I left," Richard said. "The Countess has some of the most astounding beliefs. Do you know she was actually talking about building herself some kind of flying machine?"

The women shared in a amused gasp of astonishment.

"And do you know," the Doctor continued. "I think she just might very well succeed. At any rate, if anyone could—man or woman—I believe the Countess Ada could."

A knock came at the door. At first so timid, that all three fell silent and sat listening, unsure of whether they had heard it.

"Was that—?" the doctor started to say when the knocking resumed.

This time, the doctor got up to answer the knock at the door, which proved to be none other than the Countess herself. Around her, steam was rising from the ground as the hailstones melted into the warm ground, giving her the illusion of being a goddess newly risen from the earth.

"Ada!" Cornelia exclaimed. "I thought you were busy putting the men to rights."

"I was, but now your husband and the Reverend have adjourned to the music room. The storm is almost upon us and they are readying the apparatus." The Countess favoured the three with a look of penetrating curiosity. "Now what have you have been up to without me?"

Moments later all four were seated about the small round table.

Doctor Freestone had brought his black bag with him and now he reached in and drew out a smoky green bottle. "Absinthe?" he offered.

Ada tut-tutted. "Richard, I do hope you have something more interesting in that black bag of yours."

The doctor smiled sheepishly, replaced the bottle of absinthe, and rummaged deeper in his leather bag. A moment later he brought out a lump of something resinous which he slowly unwrapped from its papers. He looked up at the others, smiled, and said, "And now for the most important part."

He reached into his bag a third time and drew something out wrapped in a cloth. He placed the mystery object in the middle of the table and then dramatically snatched off the cloth, revealing an artefact decidedly Asiatic in appearance. It was made of brass with a bowl at its centre and was attached to a black hose which terminated in a silver mouthpiece. Although it had been many years since that summer of '46 in Switzerland, Mary recognised it instantly.

"A hookah pipe!" she exclaimed.

"Yes," Ada Lovelace agreed. "I understand that my father always travelled with one." Ada fixed Mary with an arch look. "You must have seen him indulge during those long, bleak days at the Villa Diodati?"

Mary dropped her eyes and blushed. Every word that fell from Countess Ada's lips seemed an interrogation.

"I do recall seeing it," she replied meekly and then blushed at her unintended double entendre.

"Bravo!" Richard said, "Then you know only too well its sublime effects."

They watched in silent anticipation as the doctor cut a chunk of the sticky brown resin, packed it into the brass bowl, and then he lit the resin with a splint kindled from the lantern. He placed a pipe between his lips and drew in upon it as the pipe gurgled and the hashish in the bowl crackled and glowed red as it released copious clouds of pungent grey smoke.

Dr. Freestone drew heavily on the brass mouthpiece of his hose, filling his lungs deeply, and then jetted pungent smoke out both nostrils. He smiled and nodded to Ada, who eagerly took up a free pipe, placed it between her lips, and drew in deeply. She held the smoke in her lungs for maybe thirty seconds, and then languorously exhaled a plume of smoke.

Ada caught Mary's expression and giggled. "You look so shocked, dearest Mary. I confess that I also habitually indulge. Sometimes, especially after a long day of mathematics, it is the only way I can salve my overactive mind."

Mary Shelley was indeed shocked, but she resented letting Ada know just how much. Feigning indifference, Mary snatched up a free pipe, put it to her lips, and drew deep. The smoke filled her lungs and then seemed to funnel straight up into her head as though her body were a hollow glass vessel. She was immediately hit by the effects of the drug. She tried to hold the smoke inside her lungs as Ada had, but after a moment she felt a tickle in her lungs that exploded from her in a hacking and spluttering cough.

Cornelia leaned forward anxiously and importuned, "Please, might I try next?"

When Dr Freestone handed her the pipe, she placed it to her lips and drew in mightily. Mary expected her to likewise cough and splutter, but the young girl held the smoke for longer than anyone and then jetted it from her mouth. "Oh, but is sublime," she gushed, and hurriedly drew again upon the pipe.

Mary took a second turn at the pipe. It had years since she had indulged—back in the Villa Diodati days—but the smoke stirred familiar sensations as it diffused through her entire body, relaxing her. All conversation lagged as the party each took turns drawing lazily upon the pipe. Mary took a third draw from the pipe, although she feared she might levitate from her chair and float out the window and into the sky, much like a hot air balloon.

At that point, Ada leaned close to Mary and whispered in her ear. "He had you, didn't he? My father?"

Mary flinched and looked away, trying and failing to keep the apprehension from her face.

Ada touched a hand to Mary's arm. "Do not take on so. I know my father's powers made him irresistible to either sex. I knew it the moment I set eyes upon you. My father left a mark on every woman he encountered."

Mary felt her face colouring. She wanted to deny it. To say it had never happened. But she was deep in thrall to the hashish, her tongue was heavy and languid in her mouth, and she could not summon her voice to speak. Yes, Lord Byron had had her. But it had not been entirely with her consent.

It happened in the context of one of those dissipated evenings at the Villa Diodati. The inclement weather had confined them indoors for a full week. Rain hammering at the windows. Gutters singing. It was an evening when the laudanum was brought out and passed around freely, plus whatever wonders Polidori fished out of his medical bag: sticky lumps of hashish that would be dropped into Byron's elaborate glass hookah and the pipe passed around.

Mary had been reclining slackly upon a sofa, feeling flushed with warmth and drowsied by the laudanum she had drunk, As her mind skimmed in and out of sleep, she listened to Shelley and Byron discussing the notion of Free Love. And annoyingly, Claire's voice wheedling into the pauses in the men's conversation, which often incurred a curt rebuke from Byron for having the audacity to speak, spoken in a tone one uses upon a naughty dog . The next thing she knew there was a body pressing down upon hers—a man's body. Thinking it to be Percy's her mouth opened to the lips pressed to hers and admitted the probing tongue. But the kiss seemed unfamiliar— hard and libidinous—and when her eyes flickered open she found that it was Byron. Had her mind not been slackened with laudanum and hashish, her inhibitions lowered, she would have screamed, spat in his face, pushed him off her—or so she told herself a hundred times since that night. For to Mary there was something simultaneously attractive and repulsive about Byron, like a shiny red apple whose outer beauty concealed the squirming maggots feeding upon the corruption within. But whatsoever the reason she felt she had complied by dint of her passivity. Later, she would have reason to regret this as evinced by the condescending looks Byron had visited upon her each morning as she took her place next to Shelley at the table to break her fast. It was a look of condescension Byron bestowed on all he considered beneath him, a man for whom every conversation was a negotiation that established his superiority in class, rank, poetical genius or intellect. Mary threw a look to her side, seeking Percy Bysshe, only to find him on the floor, atop Claire, her dress pulled up over her bare buttocks, her black stockinged legs wrapped about Shelley's waist, her hips thrusting back against his wantonly. Standing over them, watching the proceedings with abject lust, was Dr. Polidori, who had removed his trousers and was stroking his erect penis, anxious to see if his master would allow him a place at the table in this feast of flesh.

In mid-thrust, Byron turned his head to see what Mary was looking at and cried aloud, "Not you, Polly. Not you! There are no *servants* allowed to partake at an orgy. Be content that I allow you to watch."

A pang of despair jolted through Mary at the memory. It was a recollection that made her flesh crawl.

Mary looked up to see Countess Ada's interrogative gaze fixed upon her, almost as if she was reading the thoughts and memories projected onto the back of Mary's mind.

"Your father . . ." Mary hesitated, trying to choose her words scrupulously, the way a drunk person must focus all attention in order to walk a straight line without weaving. "Your father was a dominant personality, in all ways . . . good and bad."

The latter words sprung an ugly fold to form above the bridge of Ada's nose, spoiling the otherwise pretty face. "Precisely what do you mean . . . bad?"

Mary's mouth opened and she felt herself colour as she struggled for a reply.

"Do not berate Mary, so," Richard spoke up, coming to her rescue. He smiled ironically. "Ada is fixated upon her father. As a doctor I find it most unhealthy."

Mary Shelley had been a young and naive girl back then. But even then she had feared that Percy's and Byron's lofty talk of the bankruptcy of marriage and Free Love was nothing more than a mask for male lust, an excuse to fornicate with any woman they desired. All her life Mary had been savagely disappointed in her romantic aspirations. She merely wanted to be loved.

Desperately.

Totally.

But each love affair had ended badly. She knew that Shelley had been unfaithful. With his first wife, Harriet. With her. With her half-sister Claire. And then, in Italy, with Jane Williams, a member of the English coterie and a companion with whom he became infatuated and wrote poetry for.

Mary knew too well the vagaries of men. But she had been even more disappointed that her own sex could be equally fickle. She herself had become besotted with Jane Williams when the two women returned to England and shared a house in London. They had delighted in setting tongues wagging by attending the Opera together, unescorted by a man. Mary had once entertained notions that, with Jane, she he had at last found someone to share a life with. To share a love as two equals. But then Jane had become pregnant by a military man she was secretly having an affair with and cast Mary aside most cruelly. It was another intimate betrayal, and all the more despicable for it. And so Mary moved through her life with no companion save for her young son, her own broken heart, and, of course . . . her ghosts. It was in this time, the lowest period in a life filled with tragedy, that the headaches ensued and Mary began to see things.

More precisely, her monster.

It would appear in a darkened closet, a rude form sketched by shadows limning the clothes hanging there. The hideous face would surface in the random finger smears on a fogged-over window pane. Coalesce in an oily stain on the cobblestone pavement after rain. She acquired the notion that the creature was following her, for in a crowded street, or in an empty house, she would catch a fleeting glimpse of a hulking form lurking on the periphery of her vision. A fleeting shape that would vanish when she turned her gaze toward it. A hideous face quickly plunged beneath an upturned collar. And she soon realised that the baleful visage staring after her from a crowded railway station or from a stand of trees in Kensington Park, was the face of her nameless creature. It was the monster whose malign presence had dogged her steps through the years, visiting ill-fortune at every turn. As if to remind her: *You have abandoned me, but I will follow in your footsteps and make your life tedious with loss, heartbreak and despair.*

By now the hashish in the hookah's bowl had burned down and the doctor took another wrapped block of the resinous drug from his bag along with his knife and prepared the pipe again. Although Mary had had more than enough, she soon found the hookah pipe being gently pressed between her lips. By now she felt as if she were sitting at the top of a wobbly pole. And as the room revolved around her on a pivot, faces loomed one by one from the smoke: Doctor Freestone, Cornelia, Countess Ada. She suddenly noticed that the others were laughing and playfully caressing one another in a most inappropriate fashion. And then Doctor Freestone turned to Ada sitting at his side and kissed her full on the mouth. She was shocked that the Countess not only did not object, but responded by clutching Richard by the hair at the back of his head and grinding her mouth aggressively against his. Cornelia objected to being left out, and Richard pulled his face away only to have Cornelia take the Countess' place, clamping her mouth greedily upon the doctor's. Mary was shocked but at the same time felt jealous to be left out of the kissing game, but then Richard broke free again and, leaning across the table, pulled Mary close and pressed his lips against hers. Mary closed her eyes and fell deep into the kiss, which faltered and suddenly became the soft pressure of a woman's lips upon her own. She opened her eyes to find a familiar pair of smoke-grey eyes staring into hers and found that it was Countess Ada who was kissing her, and who now pulled away to say in a husky voice, "I must kiss the lips that once kissed my father's lips." Ada resumed and the kiss deepened as the Countess pushed her tongue deep into Mary's mouth, so that their tongues embraced and wrestled. Ada's kiss was the same as her father's, and despite herself, Mary found herself succumbing to the kiss, and pressed her own lips harder against the younger woman's.

Bang . . . bang . . . bang . . . bang . . .

Mary's eyes sprang open at the sound of insistent knocking. The others sat around the table as before, but were laughing and conversing politely—apparently the kissing game had ended as if it had never begun.

Or had it all taken place in Mary's mind?

The turret door swung open and Jasper, the young butler eased his tall form into the room. Although he kept his diffident composure, the young butler could not help but react to the pungent smell of hashish smoke curling in the air. He pulled his face straight, bowed slightly, and announced, "My Master and the Reverend Phipps await you in the music room. Master Crosse has prepared a demonstration of his electrical machine, and craves your attendance."

MISDEEDS UNDONE

> *Now hatred is by far the longest pleasure; men love in haste,*
> *but they detest at leisure . . . Lord Byron*

When the Reverend Philip Smith ran into the cover of the trees, he found his motley army had scrambled deeper into the woods. Here they hunkered beneath a huge oak tree whose dense crown of leaves and sprawling limbs formed such a thick canopy that few hailstones made it through.

"I be nigh on six and five and I ain't ne'er seen weather such as this," Elijah Custard moaned. "'Tis powerful unnatural!"

"Aye, I fear tis an ill omen!" Martin Compton cried upon seeing the bedraggled churchman stumbling towards them. "Ours cannot be a good cause."

"Nay," the Reverend Smith countered as he brushed hailstones from his soup bowl hat. "Do you not see? The lord has given us a sign from the heavens."

And then with with the same stunning abruptness as it had begun, the thunderous roar of falling hail slackened and fell silent as the storm cloud that had produced it lifted its black crepe skirts and tiptoed on, and the dimness brightened first into a strained twilight as the low hanging sun re-emerged and great veils of misty steam rose as bone dry fields melted the icy hailstones and the parched dry ground drank up every drop of moisture and gasped for more.

"Come," Smith proclaimed. "Gird your loins. Our job is not yet done. We must tear down the wires the blasphemer uses to draw the devils to his land. We must discover the dread engines he uses to conjure wickedness and smash them."

But when the men crept timidly from their hiding places in the forest they found all their misdeeds had been undone.

"The fire is out!" Martin Compton called back to the others.

"Aye, and the sheep have all run back into their field."

"Our efforts were for naught, Reverend," the Cornishman taunted as he lathered a mocking smile on his face.

A muscle in the Reverend Smith's jaw twitched as his teeth clenched. "'Tis unnatural." He shook his head. "The Crosse fellow uses witchcraft. Tis plain to see." The churchman remained resolute, but his doubting disciples exchanged fearful glances.

"Mebbe we should be off," Philip Yandle urged, "afore the wizard fixes upon us."

His comments was met with grumbles of approval.

The Reverend Smith sensed his army was about to desert him a second time. "See the lightning Crosse conjured. Be sure that it shall seek ye out in time. Be certain that his devils shall spawn until they overrun the county, burst in through your doors in the night and drag you and your screaming children to hell!"

At Smith's words, young Rory tugged off his cap and gnashed it between his teeth, visibly trembling as he keened with terror. The older men spat on the ground and crossed themselves. The Cornishman wore a silver crucifix about his neck and now he fished it out of his shirt and kissed it for luck. By now the Reverend's promise of free rum suddenly seemed a poor compensation for being blasted into atoms by a bolt of lightning.

COURAGE IN A BOTTLE

> *Do you not see how necessary a world of pain and trouble is to school an intelligence and make it into a soul? . . . John Keats*

KAAAAABAAAAAAAAAAAAANG!

The Reverend Smith and his posse flinched violently at the sound and all reflexively ducked into a crouch. From where they hunkered on the path, they could see the windows of the music room pulsate with an ungodly bright light and the guts of each man shuddered at the maddening detonation that accompanied it.

"The Wizard's at his devil work!" Martin Compton muttered, crossing himself.

Just then, as if in confirmation, several luminous filaments of electricity crackled and danced between the wires stung overhead, and occasionally forked down to the path as they discharged into the ground.

"Lookeee!" Walter Furse pointed, It's them devils: Cob, Dom, and Chittibob!

As one, the men shouted with fear and leapt up, backing away up the path. The Reverend Smith dithered a moment, but then stepped forward and raised the Bible high in his shaking hand. With his other hand he made the sign of the cross in the air. "Back devils! I command ye, in the name of God, his son Jesus and the Holy Ghost! Back to hell with ye!"

The sparks had been a random discharge caused by the soaring levels of static charge in the air, and now they flickered once, twice, and went out. Reverend Smith turned to face his rag-tag posse, his face flushed with certitude. "Behold, the devils shrink before my holy book. Have faith in the Lord, and ye shall not be harmed."

KAA-BAAAAAAANG! They all ducked down into a crouch at the flash of bright light and ear-ringing report of another discharge from the house below. Many muttered prayers. Young Rory sobbed with terror. All cringed as they awaited the sonic lash of the next thunder crash.

Minutes passed. The silence endured.

Smith unslung the sack from his shoulder, dug out bottles of rum and thrust them into the men's hands. "Come," he said, "drink deep. You must steel yourselves for battle against God's enemies."

Corks were yanked and rum gurgled freely down men's throats. Each man quaffed greedily, snatching bottles back and forth between them, each man anxious to drown his fear in a bellyful of Dutch Courage. When the last of the bottles had been gurgled dry and tossed into the undergrowth, Smith stood tall, his Bible held high. "Come, fellows, as you are Christians you must steel yourself for battle. Behind the shield of my holy book you can suffer no harm. We will break into the house of this vile God denier and smash his infernal machines! There must an end to this blasphemy. Follow! Follow me!"

Smith set off marching toward the house, bible held before him. The men exchanged terrified looks, but they had seen the Reverend subdue the dancing devils and he had made the horrible bangs fall silent. So reluctantly, and with a bravery borrowed from the rum swilling in their bellies, they took up their axes and cudgels and loped after; all except for the young boy, Rory, who hung back as the rest trudged away. He soon lost sight of them as they reached a turn in the path. He was terrified to follow, but terrified to remain alone, so he crawled into the trees and crouched down, where he sat hugging his knees and trembling. But after a few minutes, he heard voices speaking low and crept forward until he could see through the greenery.

The Cornish man, Ryd Thorne, had not followed the others but had lingered on the path, and now he waited as his Irish companion joined him.

"What say ye?" the Cornishman asked.

Nessan O'Rourke replied with a wicked grin. "There's a beauty I saw I coulda tumbled but for the lightning."

"Never mind cunny," Thorne snarled, "we can buy a doxy in any town if we have coin. What say you about the house?"

The Irishman turned his head and spat. "I had a peer through the winders. There's enough loot there would take but a few moments to fill our pockets with enough to flee this Bourne, but there's too many servants and fancy folk parading about. And then there's the game-keeper feller with his two dogs. They scented me right enough and I had to scarper."

"Feck!" The Cornishman said. "I heard them buggers barking. They'll get my blade if'n they come for me."

"But I seen the vicar through the window. And his church is just a short way through the trees."

"A church?" the Cornishman echoed. "There's a thought. A church has wine for communion. And I have me a great a thirst for commu-nion . . ." he leered and finished the thought, ". . . communion wine, that is."

"Aye and a church means gold crosses and silver chalices what'll melt down into jinkling coins fer our purses."

The Irishman looked both ways up the path they stood upon. "Where's that daft Godman and his army of fools?"

Ryd Thorne laughed. "Him and his Christian soldiers just marched off to the house. They're gonna smash the wizard's devil conjuring machine."

"Izzat right?" O'Rourke stood scratching his bristly cheek for a moment and then devilment flashed in his eyes. "Why don't you go pay your respects at the church? While the good Reverend Philip Smith is busy rattlin' his stick in a hornet's nest, it'll give me a chance to slip inside the house and do some mischief."

"Good idea. But ye'd best be sharp about it. God's Fool is already on his way. I'll meet ye at the church and we'll scarper from there."

"Let's be having ya then!" And with that, the two deserters hurried away on different errands, O'Rourke heading back to the house, Thorne trudging toward the nearby church.

The young boy had lain still through the exchange and heard every word. Although he didn't understand what the two were talking about, he knew they were up to no good, as was the Reverend Smith. Rory was a homeless boy whose father had run away and then his mother had died of consumption. To earn a crust, he loitered about the taverns of Broomfield, doing odd jobs, many of which he feared he'd go to hell for. He reasoned he was in enough trouble, and resolved to run away home, back to Broomfield. So he crawled farther into the trees. Under the dense canopy of leaves, it was totally dark, but then he stumbled into something soft and warm. When he groped it, the warm shape proved to be a huge leg. But then the owner off the leg stood up and Rory found himself gaping up at a monster towering over him.

Rory's girlish scream shattered the silence, and could be heard for a wide distance.

Adam moaned mournfully and did a little dance on the spot, hoping the boy would stop screaming. But the more Adam danced, the louder the boy hollered. Adam knew that the boy's screams would bring Tom and many other people, and that they would punish him when they found what he had done to Titch. How he had broken him. When the strange boy would not stop screaming, Adam clamped a huge hand over the boy's mouth to stifle his cries. And then Adam tucked the boy under one arm and crashed clumsily through the trees in a hunched over stoop, branches cracking and snapping as he lumbered through them. He at last stepped out from the trees and onto another foot path that led to the nearby church the Irishmen had spoken of. But when Adam looked at the small boy he carried, he lay limp in his arms. Adam finally took away the massive hand that had been clamped over the boy's nose and mouth and as he did so, the boy's head lolled slackly. The boy had clearly fallen asleep, so Adam shook the slack body to awaken him. But as with Titch, the boy's head lolled loosely. Adam prodded and pressed, but the boy refused to open his eyes. And then, after long minutes of trying, Adam finally realised that he had broken this boy, just as he had broken Titch and he howled with despair. Now he was more frightened than before. Many people would be angry with him. They would drive him from the village. He would have no fireplace to lie down before. No one to give him food on a plate. He resolved that no one must find this second boy and so his dim mind grappled with where to hide the body. He could throw the corpse down the kitchen well, but he might come back up with the bucket. But then Adam thought of the churchyard. It was already full of dead people. He would hide him behind a gravestone, or push him deep into a hedge. And so, carrying the small limp body, Adam lumbered away toward the graveyard.

IN THE WIZARD'S CAVE

> *Invention, it must be humbly admitted, does not consist in creating out of a void, but out of chaos . . . Mary Shelley*

The four of them followed the young butler's back as he led the way along a path to the house. Mary was still wobbly on her feet. Guessing this, Doctor Freestone had taken Mary's arm and now he steadied her. They trooped along past the glowing windows of the parlour to a door at the far side of the house. Jasper held it open and they stepped into a long, wide, high ceilinged space: the music room, although the old name belied its new purpose, for no musical instruments could be seen.

The first impression was smell. Mary's nose wrinkled at the sharp whiff of hydrochloric acid that soured the air. It commingled with the metallic odours of brass, copper, and zinc. A dozen stout benches stood arranged in rows. The bench tops in turn were strewn with battalions of glass jars gleaming in the candle light, arranged with the precision of soldiers on a parade ground. Zinc anodes jutted from the tops of each jar while their bases were submerged in a viscous amber liquid from which streams of tiny bubbles rose. Thick bundles of copper wire ran everywhere. A spiderweb of copper wires burst through a small glassless window high in the far wall and stretched down to a loom-like structure.

With his fascination for all things scientific, Percy Bysshe Shelley would have revelled in such an environment, but Mary found the room cold and brutally masculine, with its sour odours and sharp edges. Three chandeliers, each festooned with dozens of candles, blazed from the rafters overhead, and everywhere flickering candle stubs were set upon the benches and tucked into every window alcove, so that their warm light illuminated the space like a cathedral during Mass. And standing at the high altar, before a contrivance of shiny metal hemispheres, was Andrew Crosse, closely attended by the Reverend Phipps. Crosse had donned a heavy canvas robe that stretched to the ground. The robe clearly had a practical purpose to protect his fine clothes from burns and splashes of acid, but it made the electrical experimenter look like a high priest with the Reverend his humble apostle.

"Welcome! Welcome!" Crosse said, raising both arms akimbo in greeting. It was a grand gesture, and Mary could not help thinking that the "Wizard of Broomfield" did indeed resemble a sorcerer casting spells in his magical cave.

"You are all right welcome to my laboratory," Cross said humbly, but his warm and generous smile betrayed his pride. And the light thrown by the low candles and lanterns threw his shadow and the shadow of his electrical engine on the wall behind, magnifying them into grotesque giants.

Crosse gestured to the skein of wires flowing in through the glassless window. "You will notice the wires that run into the room from the high window at the far end of the room."

They all stood and regarded the copper streams that flowed like fiery filaments across the room to the machine Crosse now indicated with a wave. "My explorer wires run through the trees around here for more than a mile. They are gathered together at a pole just outside the music room, and from there they pass through a conduit in the wall to this device that regulates their flow. You will note the many glass jars sitting atop the benches—"

"They are Leyden jars, are they not?" Mary interrupted.

Crosse gaped with surprise and looked at Mary with obvious delight. "They are actually Daniell cells, which are of a higher capacity, but they are very similar to Leyden jars. What a wonderfully astute observation, Mrs Shelly. How do you know of Leyden jars?"

Mary smiled modestly. "I attended many lectures on scientific matters with my late husband."

"You amaze me with your knowledge," Crosse smiled, and then continued. "I have over 600 cells in my apparatus, all of which store an electrical flux. My explorer wires extract the electrical fluid flowing through the atmosphere, and then convey it through the window and into the cells where it is stored. The cells in turn are connected to this apparatus." He indicated the silver hemispheres with a wave. "This is my discharger, a spark gap where the fiery flux of life is unleashed. But I must warn you. Each discharge is like a small lighting bolt and is very loud and rather dramatic, as I will shortly demonstrate."

Mary studied the polished silver hemispheres. She noticed a brass plate bearing an inscription at the top of the apparatus and read it aloud, "*Noli me tangere.*" It took her a moment to translate. "Do not touch me?"

Crosse nodded enthusiastically. "Your Latin is perfect, Mrs Shelley."

Mary glanced at Ada, who returned her look with a conspiratorial smile.

Crosse chuckled at some unknown joke "Although I have a very amusing story about the inscription. I had placed the words there as a warning. The voltage emanating from the discharger is extremely high when the cells are fully charged and would cause instant death to anyone who touched it. But even with the cells only partially charged, it can give a nasty shock." He chuckled again then struggled to compose himself. "Unfortunately, when I placed that warning sign I did not consider the fact that my domestics lack a formal education. I have given explicit instructions to my servants never to enter my laboratory. But on one occasion, a maid who was new to my employ, a young girl from Bridgewater, took it upon herself to come in here and tidy . . ."

"Ha!" The doctor barked a laugh. "I have heard this story before."

"Don't give it away, Richard," the Reverend chided.

Crosse flashed a guilty smile. "As I said, although I had warned my servants never to clean in my laboratory, the new maid took it upon herself to tidy. She later told me she thought the writing said "touch me here."

"Oh dear!" Mary and Ada exclaimed at the same moment. Ashamed, Cornelia dropped her gaze to her feet.

Crosse shook his head wonderingly. "I'm afraid the poor girl received quite a nasty shock. Needless to say, she did not remain in my employ much longer."

Ada added a laugh whose cruelty shocked Mary.

"And what happened to the poor girl?" Mary enquired.

Crosse looked sheepish. "Luckily she was greatly distressed but suffered no permanent injury. Needless to say she left the house and my service in floods of tears. I packed her off in my carriage back to Bridgewater and have never seen her since."

Although Countess Ada and the men chuckled together, finding mirth in Crosse's tale, Mary and Cornelia shared a look of aggrievement.

The Reverend, noticing the disapproving look Mary shared with Cornelia, attempted to move the conversation forward. "Andrew," he said, "perhaps you should proceed with a demonstration of your . . ." He shrugged his shoulders, at a loss of what to call it, ". . . apparatus."

"Yes," Crosse said, beaming a smile. Mary thought that, like a sorcerer surrounded by his familiars, Crosse's normally subdued character seemed to be growing louder and more effusive. Crosse stepped over to a series of dials mounted on a wooden panel. "Observe," he said, pointing to the uppermost dial. "This meter is connected to my explorer wires and measures the amount of electrical fluid in the atmosphere and whether it is positively or negatively charged. As you can see it is currently showing a huge negative charge of considerable energy. The reading is already very high, but as the storm passes over it will extract even more power from the atmosphere. He slapped a hand on the wooden handle of a huge brass switch gate. "When I throw this lever, it will complete the circuit, allowing the electrical fluid to discharge between the two hemispheres." He paused a moment to fix his audience with a serious expression. "Again, I warn you, it is rather loud and extremely bright, so you might want to cover your ears and be careful not to look directly at the spark."

And with that, Andrew Crosse grasped the huge switch with both hands. He clenched his teeth and threw the heavy gate switch closed. The brass contacts touched with a fizzzzztttttt, spraying a shower of hot sparks into the air.

There was the briefest of delays and then a concussive BAANNNNNNNNNGGGGG! resounded in the eardrums of the observers as a blinding arc of raw electricity leapt the gap between the two metal hemispheres. All the women screamed, and even the doctor shouted aloud with stunned surprise.

Mary had not had time to cover her ears and her insides jellied at the cacophonous roar. Worse still, despite Crosse's warning, she had been staring directly at the hemispheres, and now could see nothing save for a luminous stroke of pure white light that sizzled on her retinas and left her dazzle-blinded for a full terrifying minute.

"And again?" Crosse asked, although his words sounded distant and muffled in Mary's ringing ears. Despite Crosse's warning she had not covered her ears originally, but now she clamped her hands tightly to her ears and squeezed her eyes tight.

Crosse again grasped the huge gate switch with both hands. His long canvas coat had had fallen open, so that his shadow looked like a man with huge bat wings, a demonic sorcerer about to once again summon the terrible thunder-stroke.

KABAAAAAAAAAAAAAAAAAAAAAAANG! a second thunderous report rang out. And even though Mary had covered her ears, pure terror surged through her veins like cold quicksilver.

Crosse paused to look at the needles of his gauges, which were kicking and twitching as they climbed back into the red as the cells recharged.

By now terror was a bird trapped in Mary Shelley's ribcage, fluttering wildly as it sought to escape. She thought she must surely go mad if forced to endure another deafening blast of the discharge. She scanned the faces of the others to see if they seemed similarly distressed, but all had their hands clamped tight over their ears and from their smiles and laughter they seemed to find the ear-splitting bangs a source of amusement. She saw the needles trembling against their stops and Crosse's hand move to the gate switch. She decided she could not live through another punishing blast so she opened her mouth and began to scream "Noooooooooooo!" just as Crosse threw the switch a third time and the world detonated in a blinding flash and a skull-quaking BOOOOOOOOOOOOOOOOOOOOOOOOOM-MMMMMMM!

USURPING GOD

> *With an anxiety that almost amounted to agony, I collected the instruments of life about me, that I might infuse a spark of being into the lifeless thing that lay at my feet. It was already one in the morning; the rain pattered dismally against the panes, and my candle was nearly out, when, by the glimmer of the half-extinguished light, I saw the dull yellow eye of the creature open; it breathed hard, and a convulsive motion agitated its limbs . . . Mary Shelley*

In the music room, Countess Lovelace smiled and purred, "The fireworks and bangs are always entertaining, Andrew, but are we to see some real magic tonight? I think you know what I'm referring to."

The others all seemed to know what Ada obliquely referenced, but Mary was nonplussed; she only knew that she was grateful for a respite from the mind-shattering bangs and blinding flashes.

At Ada's question, Andrew Crosse's face grew troubled. "I . . . No . .

. I had not considered it . . ." He threw an uncertain glance at the Reverend, whose expression was thunderous.

"Oh, please Andrew," Countess Ada continued, touching him familiarly on the shoulder. Obviously, I have read about it—we all have—but I should love to see it for myself."

Crosse clearly looked torn. It was obvious he was anxious to perform the experiment for his guests, but the Reverend's scowl was ominous and now he could no longer hold his tongue. "I strongly caution against it, Andrew. An experiment to gain scientific knowledge of God's works is one thing, but tampering with divine nature is hardly a parlour trick for the amusement of guests."

Dr Freestone, however, offered a countering opinion. "As a doctor I would be fascinated to see it for myself."

"What experiment?" Mary asked, although her voice seemed weak and muffled in her own ears, which were still ringing from the deafening bangs.

"Andrew," the Reverend insisted, his voice rising in volume and his face reddening. "I object most strongly. What you do is dangerously close to . . ." he dropped his voice and spoke the last word in a stretched taut whisper, ". . . blasphemy!"

But the Countess laid a hand on the Reverend's shoulder. "Please Reverend Phipps . . ." She looked at Mary and added, "I'm sure our esteemed guest would like to see in action what she prophesied in her book. For who else knows so much about the creation of animate life from cold clay?"

"What?" Mary asked again. "What experiment do you refer to?"

Andrew Crosse looked perplexed, his gaze flickered for a moment between his old friend the Reverend Phipps and Countess Ada. "But Josiah," he began in a pleading voice, "we have some of the best minds in England present. And if the Countess bids me—"

"It is a mortal sin . . ." the reverend insisted in a taut voice. " Again I caution you all, for the sakes—"

"Of our immortal souls," the doctor interrupted. "Yes, you've made that painfully clear, Josiah."

Ada stepped back to Mary and threw an arm around her shoulder. "It is the experiment that made Andrew world-famous."

"Or, more accurately, world-infamous," the doctor jibed, and received a reproachful glare from the clergyman.

Ada continued, "In Andrew's most famous experiment he created life spontaneously through the power of galvanism."

Mary was still baffled" Do you mean through reanimation? I have witnessed experiments where the amputated legs of frogs twitched and kicked upon being electrified."

Dr Freestone snook his head and added, "Not just the reanimation of a dead thing. Andrew used the power of electricity to spontaneously create new life." He smiled at Mary. "It was quite the sensation when Andrew announced it."

"Sadly, Andrew received many horrid letters about it," Cornelia added. "And we are quite the pariahs in local society because of it, even through you know my husband is only proving the laws of Nature that God has made."

The Reverend dithered a moment and then announced. "Very well, then. If you are committed to this course of action, may the consequences fall upon your own heads. However, I cannot be present for this." And with that, he stalked away across the music room and left via the garden door.

After the reverend's dramatic exit, the gravity of what they were about to undertake settled upon the shoulders of those remaining with the weight of a lead apron. The air became tense and now that it was about to happen, Mary felt a queasy stirring in her stomach. It really did seem as through they were all about to take a step of irretrievable transgression.

Of playing God.

As the others silently watched, Crosse busied himself preparing the experiment. He brought forth a glass bell jar which contained a geological specimen settled into a large porcelain tub half filled with a liquid Crosse described as "an electrolytic bath." The chunk of rock was studded with large, sparkling crystals. Crosse muttered to himself beneath his breath as he concentrated, brow furrowed as he connected wires from the array of batteries to large zinc electrodes semi-submerged in the solution. The wires were then connected to long copper bundles that stretched to his silvery spheres. Lastly, he set down a large brass microscope on the bench close by.

"This stone you see inside the bell jar is from Mount Vesuvius," Crosse explained. "The specimen is riddled with crystalline structures. Is is immersed in a solution of potassium ferrocyanate, an electrolyte that conducts current into the stone. When I connect the anodes to my array of electrical cells, I can pass a flux of electricity into the stone. You will see that the results are quite astounding."

Crosse moved deftly about the bench, securing the electrical connections and finally took his place at the head of bench, where his hand rested upon the handle of the large gate switch.

"And now," he announced, "I will demonstrate to you the spontaneous generation of life through the application of galvanic energy." Crosse's hand tightened upon the wooden knob of the gate switch. He was about to throw the switch when he suddenly relaxed his grip and threw a look around at his fascinated audience.

He cleared his throat and smiled. "It suddenly occurred to me that, given the esteemed company we enjoy, I should invite one of our ladies to throw the switch." His gaze settled upon Ada. "Countess, would you do us the honour?"

The Countess bounded forward eagerly and grasped the wooden handle with her slender hand. But then something occurred to her and she looked at Mary Shelley. "Oh, but I should like to share this honour. Mary, would you please assist me?"

Mary Shelley hesitated a moment, but then stepped around to the far side of the bench and placed her hand atop Countess Ada's on the handle of the gate switch.

"Ready?" Ada asked Mary, who smiled radiantly, her heart swelling with pride at being acknowledged by the Countess who now began a count-down.

"Very well. One . . . two . . . three!"

The two women threw the switch, which fizzed and sparked as the contacts touched. And then all eyes eagerly fixed upon the stone beneath the bell jar.

After several minutes the Countess noted in a disappointed voice, "Nothing much seems to be happening Andrew?"

"The process takes time," Crosse said, "but wait. You will soon see."

For several long minutes, apart from the persistent electrical hum, nothing seemed to be changing. But then Ada drew closer as she noticed something happening in the electrolyte. "Oh look" she said, "There are streams of tiny bubbles rising up from the electrodes."

"That is hydrogen gas," Crosse explained. "It is one of the elemental gases present at the formation of the primordial earth." He reached into the folds of his canvas gown and drew out a pocket watch. "The process is just now beginning. It will take perhaps twenty minutes before the effect fully manifests."

After another ten minutes, Crosse drew off the bell jar, releasing into the air a sharp whiff of ozone, such as after a lightning storm on the sea shore. He then dragged the heavy brass microscope close to the stone and squinted through it, one hand twiddling the knurled focus knob forward and back. Finally, he drew his eye away from the eyepiece and beckoned the others to move closer.

"The morphogenesis is beginning. If you would care to take turns at the microscope you can watch the process unfolding before your eyes."

The doctor was closest. He put his eye to the eyepiece and stared hard. After a few moments he let out a gasp of astonishment, then looked up at the others, with a wondrous smile upon his face.

"What is it, Richard?" Ada asked impatiently. "What do you see?"

The doctor stepped away from the microscope and beckoned with a wave. "Be my guest, ladies."

Ada sprang forward, eager to be next. She hovered over the eyepiece, intently peering. "What?" she huffed. "I don't see anything . . . oh . . . oh wait! Ah, I think . . . I . . . that's amazing!" Her head finally pulled away and then she slipped an arm around Mary's waist and drew her to the microscope. "Mary, you must see what's happening."

But while Ada had been eager, Mary was filled with foreboding, such that fear was a pulse throbbing in her throat. She was frightened to look, and terrified not to. She brought her eye cautiously to the eyepiece and turned the ferruled focus wheel until the image resolved and then sharpened. The view was dizzying: like looking down upon the earth from a high mountain. In the eyepiece, individual crystals burst up from the craggy surface like stalagmites, but then she noticed that, as she watched, the stalagmites were changing, growing. "The crystals," Mary gasped. "They're turning into tiny insects." She looked up at Cornelia. "Cornelia, you must come look, too." But Cornelia responded by covering her face with both hands and shuddering. "No. I have seen them already, and they much discomfit me."

Mary went back to the eyepiece, much absorbed by the spectacle she was observing. The mites appeared to be fastened to the stony surface by the pointed ends of their bulbous abdomens. They had a number of legs, all tightly folded and pointing forwards. But then, as Mary watched, the hairy legs began to wriggle. And then the creatures began to detach from the rock substrate, unfold their legs, and crawl about the surface.

"They . . . they're moving!" Mary gasped.

"What?" Richard exclaimed and lunged forward to take another turn at the eyepiece. "How amazing!" he cried. "There are dozens of them. All crawling about." He continued to observe until Countess Ada pushed him out of the way to take her turn.

"How wonderful!" The Countess breathed. She looked up from the eyepiece at the others. "There appear to be two distinct species. The larger ones have six legs. The smaller ones have four legs. And they are both quite hideous!" She looked up from the microscope's eyepiece at Crosse. "Whatever are they?"

Crosse smiled as he gripped the lapels of his canvas cloak. "They are tiny mites," he proclaimed proudly. "Life spontaneously formed through the action of galvanic energy. I have named them *Acarus Electricus.*"

The party chuckled to hear the name Crosse had coined.

Ada eventually relinquished the microscope and Mary took her turn. The mites were indeed hideous: spider-like and thickly covered with with long, spiky hairs. By now they were quite active, with more hatching out every second. They skittered here and there, swarming the surface of the stone. Then, as she watched, a larger six-legged mite chased down one of the smaller mites and seized it in its jaws. The legs of the four-legged mite wriggled helplessly as it was drawn into the larger mite's mouth. The smaller mite's struggles gradually faltered as it was drawn in. Eventually the wriggling legs stilled, as if the insect understood that death was imminent and so passively surrendered to its grisly fate. The six-legged mite used its extra front legs to help cram the smaller mite down its gullet, and then it too became still as it digested its meal, the mouth parts busily chewing.

The gruesome scene unfolding in the eyepiece sent a frisson of revulsion shuddering through Mary. She jerked away from the microscope, feely queasy and nauseous.

Ada took another turn at the microscope and trilled with laughter at what she saw. "Oh look!" she cried, "the little monsters are gobbling one another up! How delightfully horrid!"

By now the colour in Mary's face had drained to a bloodless white. The ghastly things she had seen through the microscope, grotesquely magnified, made her woozy and she feared for a few dreadful moments she might faint. What had seemed a wondrous conjuration of spontaneous life had quickly turned into a monstrous spectacle of cannibalism. She felt a flush of hot sweat bead upon her brow. Her vision swam and then her knees buckled as she staggered and crashed into the doctor who caught her as she swooned.

THIEF IN THE NIGHT

Satan has his companions, fellow-devils, to admire and encourage him; but I am solitary and detested. . . . Mary Shelley

W rapped in shadows, the Irishman crept up to the handsome front door of Fyne Court. The door knob turned freely in his filthy hand. As he was not the kind of man to stand on ceremony, O'Rourke slipped inside without bothering to knock. He found himself in the large entrance hall, gloomily lit by just enough candles to allow someone to navigate the darkness. He stood stock still, barely breathing, ears straining. Through years of practice Nessan O'Rourke was an accomplished thief: a burglar who could slip into a sleeping family's bedroom and steal the chains from around their necks, the pennies from their pockets, and slip the rings from their fingers without even waking the dog sleeping on the foot of the bed.

O'Rourke crept to the foot of the staircase. He could hear the servants moving about the house and calling out to one another. They mostly seemed to be in the downstairs, so he floated up the staircase to the first floor, silent as a shadow. He moved slowly and methodically down the long hallway, giving each door knob an exploratory twist. All were locked, until he passed a large ficus growing in a tall urn, and the next doorknob turned in his hand. He slipped into the bedroom. A lantern on a bedside table had been turned down to a low glimmer, and now he grabbed it and turned the wick up.

As light pushed the shadows away, he saw that the room was being occupied by a woman: a night dress had been carefully laid out on the bed. Some small framed paintings and other trinkets sat arranged on a dressing table. A canvas travelling bag sat on the foot of the bed. It would be handy to carry the things he stole and so he grabbed the bag, and upended it onto the bed. He raked roughly through the spilled contents but to his annoyance found only an assortment of woman's clothes. His eyes then moved to the trinkets atop the dressing table. The portraits of children held no interest for him, but the frames looked to be silver and might fetch a coin or two and so he grabbed them and tossed them in the bag. Then his eye fell upon the slender wooden box with the butterfly engraving. He grinned and snatched it up, sure that it must contain jewellery or something precious. But though his calloused fingers pried and twisted the box this way and that, he could not fathom the mystery of how to open it, and when he shook it all he heard was a muffled thudding and not the hoped-for jinkling of jewellery. Disappointed, his face soured in a frown and he carelessly tossed it into the bag along with the other swag, to be studied later. In the first dresser drawer he discover a bottle of laudanum. He had never learned to read and so could not decipher the letters inked upon the label, but he recognised a laudanum bottle by the shape and smoked glass. He uncorked the bottle and took a quick swig, his face puckering in a hideous grimace at the bitterness. For a moment he was going to place it in the bag along with the other swag, but then he thought better of it and jammed the bottle in the pocket of his coat. Maybe he would share with the Cornishman, but maybe there wouldn't be enough for two. He continued on, rifling through the drawers and chortled when he discovered yet another slender bottle. This one was under a pile of clothes, a lame attempt to hide it. Again, he couldn't read the black letters the apothecary had scrawled on the label, but from its slender shape he had no doubt it held the same content. When he shook it he discovered the bottle was full, and so he slipped it into his other coat pocket. Maybe he would share the almost empty bottle with the Cornishman and keep this one for himself. In the third drawer he found a few more boxes of jewellery: earrings and a necklace and he cackled as he tossed these into the bag. But the remaining drawers were empty and quick snoop around the rest of the room found nothing worth stealing—not even the candleholders on the dresser, which he accurately guessed were gilt and not solid silver. Still, he grabbed one of the heavy candlesticks and tossed it in the the bag—it was heavy and may come in handy to cudgel the brains out of a servant if he met one as he crept back down the stairs. He was about to quit the room when he froze at the sound of voices from downstairs. He waited in a sucked-in-breath silence for the sound of feet stomping up the staircase, but nothing came. Still, the servants were stirring and he decided it was time to quit the house. He was about to leave when his eye fell upon the extinguished candles on the dresser and a smirk twisted his face. He may as well have a bit of fun to make up for his meagre takings, and he had an idea that might prove a distraction should anyone challenge him as he tried to slip out the front door again. He found an extinguished tapir, lifted the lantern glass and kindled it to a yellow flame, and then lit the candles in their cheap gilt holders. Then he slid both candle-holders to the very edge of the dresser, so that their naked flames flickered dangerously close to the heavy curtains. It would take a while, but the heat from the candles would no doubt eventually catch the curtains on fire. Maybe they would all catch alight. Maybe they wouldn't. Maybe the whole house would burn to the ground. Either way, he hated the English and it would be a well-deserved payback if everyone in the house burned to death. His mischief done, he padded to the door and cracked it, his ear held to the opening, listening. When he heard no voices for several long seconds, he slipped out of the room and crept back down the hall to the staircase. Minutes later he slipped from the house and loped away into the woods, Mary Shelley's canvas travel bag swinging in his grip.

TRAGEDY BEGETS TRAGEDY

The dew of compassion is a tear . . . Lord Byron

A fter returning Zeus to his kennel, Tom stopped by the kitchens on an errand and finally walked into the stable carrying a over-filled tankard slopping ale. He expected to find Adam where he'd left him: sitting patiently on the hay bale, but instead, the Goliath was nowhere to be seen. Tom cussed softly under his breath; the simple boy had probably become curious and wandered off to peer in at the windows at the fine people. The gamekeeper stalked to the middle of the stable and looked around. "Adam?" He called out. "Adam? Where are you? Show yerself!"

Tom had been gone longer than he had expected. He was unconcerned at first, but then he noticed that Titch was also missing and his unease quickly turned to fear. He was still peering around when a large drop of something wet fell from above and splashed on his cheek. Tom wiped it away with one hand and examined his palm.

Blood.

Thick.

Red.

Arterial.

As Tom looked up to see where it was coming from, another fat gobbet dropped from above and splattered on his forehead.

His mouth went dry when he saw where the blood was coming from. Snagged in the eye-hook was a clump of bloody hair.

Blonde hair.

The breath tore from Tom's lungs in a terrified gasp. The tankard of ale he was holding slipped from his grip and splashed itself empty on the ground. Pins and needles swarmed Tom's face. In a taut, terrified voice he called out: "Titch? Titch my bonny boy, where are ye?" He stood and listened, but was answered only by silence and restive snuffles from the horses. "Adam?" He shouted in a strangled voice. "Adam! Answer me! Answer me, damn you!"

Again, only silence. He looked desperately about the stable, still clinging to the forlorn hope that the blood was somehow nothing, that Titch and Adam were playing tricks. That both were hiding somewhere, straining to hold in their laughter, and that they would burst from their hiding places at any moment. But then Tom's eye fell upon the ladder up to the hay loft, and an icy flood of dread surged into his belly.

Blood. And more blood. The rungs of the ladder were stained with bloody footprints that gorily recorded a large set of feet clambering up the ladder, and then smearing the bloodstains as they climbed back down the ladder. Tom had to force his feet to stir and moved with the slow motion of a man walking along the silty bottom of a river. He reached the ladder and slowly began to climb. The blood painting the rungs was growing sticky as it congealed, and stained the palms of his hands. He stepped off the ladder into the dim light of the hay loft and peered around, fearful of what he might see. And to his horror, there it was: a child's bare foot protruding from beneath a heap of straw clumsily dumped to hide a dreadful secret. Tom swept the straw aside to uncover the little boy's face, gory with blood. A keening cry ripped from Tom's throat. His faced twisted into a mask of grief as he lifted the tiny body into his arms and cradled it. Then sobs ripped from him with a severity likely to tear him in two.

"Oh my poor laddie. My poor little lad!" Tom wailed. He could easily guess at what had happened: it was the game he had forbidden them to play. It had not been deliberate.

In the end, not knowing what to do, Tom took the tiny body to the horse trough and washed the blood from Titch's face. Then he kissed Titch and wrapped his cooling body in a horse blanket and laid it on the soft straw bed of a hay wain.

But as he crossed the stable Tom's shaking legs gave way and he fell to his knees, his head hanging slack. A storm of grief raged in his mind as he agonised over what to do. It felt wrong to leave the child alone in the haywain. Little Titch had always been afraid of the dark and didn't like it when Tom left him on his own to do his rounds before locking up the horse stable. But Tom reckoned that, as Titch was dead, he wouldn't mind being left for a short spell. Then Tom grappled with the terrible need to notify Mister Crosse of the death, and wondered what he would say. It was an accident, but Tom had been remiss in his duty, leaving the young boy alone with Adam. Still, he decided he needed to find Adam first, and fetch him back to the house. Tom clambered shakily to his feet, his body numb. He could not fathom a way to undo the loss, the damage, or the heartache that was to follow.

First he must find Adam. So Tom strode back to the kennels and looped a rope around Zeus's neck. Then, with the dog in harness, Tom led him out to the pathway that plunged into the dark woods. Another wave of storm clouds was fast approaching. He made sure not to look at the moon when it chanced to tear free from the rags of black cloud, lest it spoil his night vision. He led the dog out and then clucked his tongue and said, "Find Adam. C'mon boy, find Adam."

At his encouragement, Zeus surged forward, straining at his lead, so that it was all Tom could do to hold him back. The lurcher had picked up a fresh scent, and Tom had to lean back and dig his heels in to resist being dragged along the steep and loamy paths. They set a cracking pace and Tom was racing up the path toward the church yard when he stumbled on an unseen tree root and his grip momentarily slackened on the leather lead. It was enough for Zeus to snatch free of his grip and the dog bounded away, dragging its lead behind.

"Zeus!" Tom bellowed after the dog. "Zeus, damn ye, come back!" But the dog had clearly caught a scent and was bounding away in pursuit.

～

The Cornishman had scoured through the discarded rum bottles the Reverend Smith's tribe had flung aside, and now he tipped up the final bottle, hoping to catch a last mouthful, but all that remained was a trickle of silty dregs. He cursed and pitched the bottle into the undergrowth. His Irish crony had been gone for a quite a spell and Ryd Thorne decided it was time he set off toward the church. If the Irishman was taken, Thorne figured he at least might have a sack-full of altar dressings and a jug of communion wine to set himself up at the next town. As storm clouds smothered a blood-red setting sun, dizzily pitching the world once more into pseudo night, the woodland paths darkened until they became nigh unnavigable. But eventually, the Cornishman found the dry stone wall that surrounded the churchyard and was just easing himself through the lychgate when the ferocious barking of a dog warned him that the gamekeeper was fast approaching. As a long-time poacher Thorne had many a scar to show from dog bites. And so he fumbled the knife from his pocket and ducked down behind a gravestone to keep watch. He had cut the throats of many a gamekeeper's dog before, and knew the trick was to hold your nerve, ignore the flashing teeth and gouging claws, hold the blade ready, and wait for your moment.

But as the barking drew ever closer, Thorne stopped to consider his position. The gravestone he had ducked behind was a scant five feet from the Lych gate. The dog would leap the low gate and be upon him in seconds. He stood up and looked around, his heart pounding and his mouth dry. He saw a large tomb another fifteen feet away, and prayed he could reach it in time. But as he hurried toward it he dodged around a gravestone and found a vast black rectangle of shadow at his feet: an open grave freshly dug and awaiting a body. He teetered on the crumbling precipice of the grave, arms windmilling for balance as he fought not to fall in. It was a near thing, but he barely managed to keep his balance. Had he fallen into the open grave he would have been taken and no mistake. Now he hurried past the open pit, figuring it was one more obstacle to slow the hound.

He reached the large tomb and ducked behind in the nick of time, for when he looked he saw the grey blur of a lurcher galloping up the path toward him. It cleanly vaulted over the lychgate but then something unexpected happened: the dog's trailing lead caught in the top of the gate and catapulted him backwards. The dog whined a moment but then it shook itself and scrambled back to its feet. It lurched forward, only to be snatched back once again by its lead.

From his vantage point behind the tomb, the Cornishman had watched it all happen, and could not believe his good luck.

He jumped up from his hiding place, knife clutched ready in his hand. He would have to strike first, and make sure he did major damage, or the dog would rip him to bloody tatters. With a howl he rushed at the dog. The lurcher leaped up for his throat, but was jerked back again by its trapped lead. Thorne surged forward, slashing at the dog's eyes with his blade. Blood splattered the back of Thorne's hand. The lurcher howled and whined and shook its head. Thorne laughed as he watched the dog thrash and wrestle against its trapped lead. His knife had taken one of its eyes. The army deserter watched its frantic struggles, and when the moment was right, he leaped forward again and slashed for the dog's exposed throat. Zeus let out a dreadful howl and fell to the ground, thrashing wildly. Blood spurted from its gaping neck wound, splashing hot and viscous on the dirt. A sick shiver passed through the lurcher, and then the dog grew suddenly still and a final whimper escaped it as the dog lay its head upon the ground; the body shivered a final time and moved no more.

Ryd Thorne was shaking with adrenalin, but he had bested the beast. He wiped the bloody blade on his trouser leg and laughed. But then a voice spoke from the darkness that turned his inside to jelly.

"I could have forgiven you anything, poacher . . . but not killing my dog."

When the Cornishman looked up, he saw Tom standing on the other side of the Lych Gate, breathing hard. His face was shadowed and unreadable in the gloom, but the blunderbuss cradled in his arms had its flared muzzle pointing straight at Thorne's heart.

"Step forward," Tom said in steely voice. "Let me see your face."

The Cornishman swallowed and twitched with fear, but his knees were locked and he could not unlock them.

"I'll not ask again," Tom said quietly.

Thorne saw the gamekeeper's finger tightening on the trigger and urged himself to take two staggering steps closer.

Now separated only by the Lych gate, Tom swept his eyes over the Cornishman's face. "I know you. How do I know you?" Tom's lips were a flat line. "Ah, yes. Now I know. I reckon you work at Frank Godley's farm. You and that Irish feller. Showed up six month ago. From what I hear you're a thievin', lousy pair of troublemakers, izzat right?"

Thorne would not answer, knowing anything he said might result in having his face blown off by a blunderbuss. But then he saw his partner in crime, the Irishman, stealing silently up behind the Gamekeeper. Nessan O'Rourke put a finger to his lips, signalling Thorne to keep quiet and then flashed a wicked smile.

"Cat got your tongue?" Tom asked. "Don't matter, I reckon you'll do plenty a'talking afore you take the drop at Bristol. We hang poachers in this county."

Nessan O'Rourke crept closer. He still clutched the candlestick he had stolen from Fyne Court and now he raised it high in the air.

Tom gestured with the Blunderbuss. "The knife. Throw it away . . . far away."

The Cornishman smiled, happy to comply. It would help distract the gamekeeper and give O'Rourke a chance to get close enough. He held up the knife to show Tom and then tossed it away into the woods.

At the last moment, Tom had seen the Cornishman's eyes flicker to look at something behind his back and sensed a presence behind him. But it was too late, as O'Rourke brought the heavy candlestick crashing down on the back of Tom's head with a sickening *thwack!*

The gamekeeper staggered forward, doubled over, head drooping. The Blunderbuss dropped from his slack fingers before his knees buckled and he sprawled face-first onto the ground.

"What's that ya got, O'Rourke?" Ryd Thorne asked, nodding at the object gripped in his crony's hand.

The Irishman held up the candlestick he had cold-cocked Tom with. "Taint proper silver, but it came in handy for whackin' skulls, now didn't it?"

Nessan O'Rourke tossed aside the candlestick and stooped to pick up Tom's Blunderbuss. He tarried a moment while he admired the firearm. "Now that's a fine bit o'work, now that it. That'd fetch a pretty shilling or two in Bristol." He stepped over to where Tom lay slumped on the ground, put a boot against his ribs and gave his limp form a kick to turn him over. Tom groaned as he rolled onto his back, where he lay, eyes heavy-lidded and half-conscious. The Irishman stood over him and brought the muzzle of the Blunderbuss within an inch of Tom's face.

"Wait!" The Cornishman said, "Whaddya doing?"

"Killin' him with his own gun," O'Rourke grinned. "Now there's a fitting' end—"

NO!" Thorne cried. "They'll hear the gunshot over half the county. You'll bring the hue and cry down upon us and there's a dead man to prove it."

At that moment both men stiffened at a ghostly moaning coming from the darkness.

"What the feck was that?" The irishman asked. His eyes flickered up to the surrounding trees, scanning left and right.

Both stiffened and stood alert, staring wildly at the darkness surrounding them.

"I think it came from over there," Thorne said in a whisper, pointing.

And then, as if to prove him right, something came lumbering out of the darkness toward them. It was huge. A giant man. A bear. No, worse, a monster!

Both men screamed with fright and staggered back. The figure clumped forward until it stood over Tom, holding its arms out, trying to shield him.

"What the hell is that thing?"

"A monster! Shoot it!"

The Irishman raised the Blunderbuss and fired point blank into Adam's chest: *BANG!* The load, nothing more than fine pebbles and rock salt, blew a hold in his shirt and the powder flash burned Adam's chest so that he howled with pain, but the wound was only superficial.

"Feck! He didn't even feel it!"

"Quick," O'Rourke shouted. "Use your knife. Stab him!"

"I don't got my knife no more."

The Irishman snatched up the candlestick and whacked Adam across the head, which made him shriek and flail about. His thick arm caught the Irishman across the throat and sent him sprawling. Thorne leapt forward and punched Adam in the face over and over, but it had no effect and then Adam swung a trunk-like arm which smashed into Thorne's face, breaking his nose and snapping his head backward. "Help!" he screamed. "He's killing me!"

The Irishman jumped onto Adam's back and rode him for a moment, pummelling his head with both fists until the two of them tumbled to the ground in a tangle of flailing limbs.

The Cornishman stood watching the melee at a loss. He had lost his knife and searched the ground for a weapon, but then he remembered his scarf and snatched it from around his neck and quickly looped it around Adam's throat. He cinched it tight and then twisted. Adam released a hissing scream, but continued to flail out and kick, delivering bruising blows to both of them. He finally staggered to his feet, pulling the Cornishman off his feet as he clung to both ends of the scarf.

"Help me O'Rourke!"

The Irishman staggered to his feet and leaped forward to grab one end of the scarf. Together the two deserters heaved and strained to pull the scarf ever tighter, so that it dug deep into the muscular folds of Adam's neck. The giant staggered this way and that, dragging the men across the ground. The struggle went on for far longer than it ought to, but finally, his oxygen cut off, Adam's struggles began to falter. Eventually, he staggered and and sank to his knees. The two low-lifes retightened their grip upon either end of the garrotte, and then each put a boot to either side of Adam's face and heaved with all their might. Adam made a horrible choking sound, as the giant body fought for life. But with a plaintive gargle he finally succumbed and toppled like a great stone idol face-first to the ground. The two army deserters kept the choker tight until their arms wearied and they judged that Adam was finally dead.

Exhausted, the two sprawled on the grounded, sucking lungfuls of air.

When he could finally draw breath Ryd Thorne glared at his partner-in-crime. "What kind of soldier are you? Ya had him point blank and ya missed him!"

"I shot him square in the chest. It didn't so much as startle him."

The two staggered to their feet and crouched over Adam's body.

"Best make sure he's dead," O'Rourke said, and then to make sure, he gave Adam hard in the kick in the temple. The hydrocephalic head lolled back and forth and then fell slack. The eyes were wide open, the mouth gaping.

"Well he's dead sure enough. Now what?"

"We best be movin' on. The gunshot would've been heard a mile away."

"What about the thunder? They'll likely think its just thunder."

"Any fool who's shot a gun can tell the difference a'tween the two."

"We'd best be for the off. Before the hue and cry."

"What about the gamekeeper?"

"In fer a penny, in fer a pound."

"So we kill him, too?"

"May as well hang fer two as fer one! Find yer knife, Thorny."

But when the Irishman looked at where they'd left the unconscious Tom, he was nowhere to be seen.

"Shite!" The Irishman swore.

"What?"

"He's gone!"

"Feckin' hell! Gone? It can't be!"

"Look for yourself!"

Thorne leapt up and ran over to where Tom had lain stunned upon the ground. There was nothing there. He darted a desperate look around at the darkened trees.

"We must find the bastard and finish him off."

"We've got to be off, O'Rourke. The game keeper saw my face. He knows who we are. We'd best take to our heels before they raise a posse and come for us with the dogs."

The Irishman looked thunderstruck. He nodded at Adam's body. "What about him?"

"What about him? He's dead. Leave him!"

"No. If they know we've killed the hue and cry will chase us the feckin length of England. We'll swing for sure if they know we've killed. If we hide the body, they'll just think we stole."

"Where do we hide a dead body? Especially that big a dead body?"

The two looked around and saw the open grave waiting.

"He's dead ain't he?" The Cornishman asked. "He belongs in a grave, and there's one waitin' right there."

Grunting and swearing, the two ex-soldiers dragged Adam's body to the edge of the open grave. Then both put their boots to the body and gave it shove. Adam's body gurgled as it slowly rolled into the grave and hit the bottom with a dull thud. The Irishman yanked the spade from the pile of dirt piled beside the grave and tossed it to his crony.

"What?" Thorne said. "We don't have to feckin' bury him, do we?"

"Like you said, the longer it takes afore they know we've murdered, the farther we can be afore they raise the hue and cry."

And with that, the two took turns kicking shovelling and pushing as much earth into the grave as they could. When the grave was nearly filled, Thorne thrust the spade into the heap of earth and wiped his hands on his shirt. "Come," Throne said. "That's good enough. Let's be for the off."

But his Irish comrade hesitated. "Best if we don't travel together. You take the road. I'll take the fields. We'll meet at the bridge at Broomfield. But first, I've an errand to run."

"What? Yer goin' back to that house after all that's happened? With the gamekeeper lurking about. Are ye mad in the head?"

"I left a bag full of swag near the house. I'll not be leaving' it. We'll need coin when we get to Bristol."

The Cornishman threw his comrade a sour look. He turned and spat, then wiped his mouth on his sleeve. "Aw right. I'll wait for ye at the crossroad in Broomfield. But if yer more than an hour late—"

"If I'm not at the crossroads before ye then I'm already dead and buggering the Devil in hell."

"Most like he'll be buggerin' you!"

And with that the Irishman traipsed off down the gloomy forest path. The Cornishman waited another five minutes and then set off in the same direction, stealthily following his crony, as there was no trust among thieves.

After another five minutes, the bushes stirred and Tom painfully crawled from the undergrowth. He was still alive, but his head throbbed violently with each pulse of his heart so that he saw flashes of light if he tried to move too quickly. He staggered to the loamy pathway and dropped to his knees, dizzy and sickened. And then his head lifted as he scented something on the breeze.

Smoke.

At first it was faint, but then then the acrid taste of burning filmed his mouth. It was a fire, a serious fire, and the smoke was blowing from the direction of Fyne Court. He'd been unconscious and so he hadn't seen what had transpired with Adam. He thought about looking for him, but now there was a far more urgent need, so he turned and shambled in the same direction the two low-lifes had taken, keeping a watchful distance.

STRANGE STAR SURPASSED

> *If such lovely creatures were miserable, it was less strange*
> *that I, an imperfect and solitary being, should be wretched. . .*
> *Mary Shelley*

The rattle of the doorknob in the darkness awakens me. An eye-watering slash of light opens and then dilates as someone pushes the door wide and steps into my bedroom. Once again, acting on some instinct I say nothing and lay still, my eyes mostly shut so that I can dimly perceive shapes filtered through my eyelashes. Floorboards creak as a shadowy silhouette floats into the room. It moves first to the fireplace and stands looking down at something that burns smokily in the grate. The silhouette is slender—clearly that of a woman—but in the darkness, I cannot tell whether the figure is a maid or my hateful step-daughter. The figure then turns and moves toward the dresser, but as it does the figure seems to notice my presence in the bed for the first time and gasps loudly, putting a hand to her throat, as if surprised to see me lying in my bed.

I sit up quickly, my eyes flying open as I hiss at my tormentor, "So, step-daughter, are you so impatient?" I spit. "Have you come to watch me die?"

"Oh, excuse me. I am so terribly sorry," the woman blurts. "Wrong room."

I lurch forward and grab at the woman. In response, the figure reels back a step, so that the light from the fireplace falls across her face for the first time. To my astonishment, the light reveals features that I know only too well. It is my own face, younger by a decade or so. Before I can utter another syllable the woman hitches her skirts and flees from the room.

For several moments, I sit stunned. From the other side of the door I can hear women's voices conversing and recognise the words I once spoke when I visited Fyne Court and walked into my bedroom only to find an old woman lying in bed, and the place in darkness like a sick room.

With sudden dread I realise that I have just seen my own doppel-gänger. I know that coming face to face with one's doppelgänger is at best a sign of bad luck, and at worst an omen of death. My dead husband, Percy, had seen his own of doppelgänger on many occasions, including an encounter on a beach. The doppelgänger had raised its arm and pointed to the sea. Percy drowned in a sailing accident not long after that, when he made the rash decision to sail his brig in the lake with too much sail in the teeth of a building storm that drove all other ships to shore.

"That was me I saw," I say aloud to the empty room, "an old woman on her way to death."

THE DEATH OF MARY SHELLEY

> *Life and death appeared to me ideal bounds, which I should*
> *first break through and pour a torrent of light into our dark*
> *world . . . Mary Shelley*

I n the music room, the spontaneous generation of life demonstration had been concluded. The Reverend had returned from outside, and the strong smell of tobacco on his clothing suggested he had spent his idle time enjoying a pipe. Now came the therapeutic use of electricity, which he presumably approved of. A shocking table had been set up at one end of the room. Atop the table was a pair of brass grab handles. The middle of the table was occupied by a large rotary dial that could be turned from right to left, and on the clock face was a dial that indicated the level of current being delivered to the handles. The zero position was off, with 10 being the maximum, although the numbers from 7 through 10 were shaded with red, to show the extremity of the voltage.

Crosse smiled and drew the sleeves of his canvas gown back to his elbows. "And now Mrs Shelley, you have witness the destructive power of electricity and the life-creating power of electricity. Now I shall demonstrate the healing power of the electric fluid." He looked at the Countess. "Ada, would care to demonstrate to our guests?"

"I should be happy to do so," the countess purred and released a pleased smile as she slinked over to the far end of the table. She gripped a brass handle in either hand, before turning her gaze to Mary Shelley. "I suffer from a number of ailments, principally of the digestive system. The best efforts of conventional doctors have failed me. But Andrew and his electrical treatments have relieved me of considerable suffering." She turned her attention to Crosse. "Andrew, why don't we start at three? At my signal we may go further."

Andrew Cross bowed his head to the countess. "Very good, countess." He threw a small gate switch which sparked and paused one last moment to check with Ada. She slipped something out of her silken sleeve—a short wooden stick—and then, to Mary's surprise, placed the stick in her mouth, much as is done with an epileptic. That done, she grasped both handles and gave a quick nod.

Cross turned the large dial from zero. Immediately a low hum filled the air. As the needle crossed number one, Ada's hands visibly clenched upon the handles. A muscle spasmed in her face. "More!" she muttered around the stick.

Crosse slowly turned the dial higher and the hum grew louder with it. The needle swung past three and settled at four. When Mary looked, she saw that Ada's lips were twitching from the current surging through her. "More!" she mumbled around the stick. Crosse paused a moment to share a questioning look first with Cornelia and then with the doctor, who nodded his assent. And then Cross turned the dial until the needle pointed at five.

By now the hum had amplified to an ominous drone. When Mary studied Ada's face, she saw that the Countess' eyes were shut tight, her lips twitching, face contorting. It struck Mary as obscenely sexual, like a woman's face in orgasm, and Mary felt her own face flushing with shame. Studying the men only made it worse. Crosse retained the composure of a serious scientist, but the looks of the doctor, and even the reverend, were hungry and libidinous, the aroused expressions of bawds greedily watching a scene of copulation. Seeing Ada's beautiful face spasming with what could be agony or ecstatic pleasure was deeply disturbing. But then Mary glanced at Cornelia, and to her shock saw the same excited look of wicked engrossment on her face.

"More!" Ada mumbled. By now her whole body was shaking and convulsing. Her face dewed with sweat. A blue vein bulged at her temple and throbbed dangerously.

"Enough!" Crosse cried. And he began turning the dial slowly counter-clockwise. When it reached zero, the hum died away. Ada's hands unclenched from the brass handles, she took two staggering steps backward before falling into a slight swoon. Luckily the doctor quickly stepped forward and caught her, while the reverend dragged forward a chair and they settled Ada into it. All crowded around the countess, concerned for her safety. But after a moment of catching her whirling senses, she looked up at the others with a beaming smile and said, "I feel wonderful. She jumped to her feet and pushed the others away as she began to skip, dance, and twirl about the laboratory. "I feel as if my soul has been purged . . . emptied of poison . . . filled with liquid light. I feel . . . " she shook her pretty head in wonder, ". . . reborn."

Mary moved quickly to where Andrew Crosse stood. She seized his hand and pressed it earnestly between her own.

"I implore you, Mister Crosse," Mary said. "Might I try? I believe this may be the balm my soul has been crying out for."

And so, a few minutes later, the scene was repeated, only this time it was Mary Shelley who gripped the brass handles.

"Ada is well-used to the therapy," Crosse said, as he readied his hand on the shiny brass gate switch, "and she is used to the current. With you, Mrs Shelley, I shall proceed with more caution. Should you feel undue discomfort, simply cry out and I shall stop the procedure immediately." He paused before throwing the switch and looked to Mary. "Are you ready?"

Mary nodded her assent, and sparks flew as Crosse slapped the gate switch shut, allowing the contacts to touch. He put his hand upon the dial and slowly turned. The audible hum began as the needle crossed the first number. He paused again and checked with Mary. "Shell I go further?"

"Yes," she replied, "I feel nothing. Pray go higher."

Crosse slowly turned the dial to two and checked again. Mary nodded and so the dial was advanced to three.

"Nothing," Mary muttered around the stick in her mouth. "I feel nothing."

So Crosse advanced the dial still farther unit the needle rested upon four. The humming pitched to a threatening drone. Mary's hands tightened their grip on the handles and trembled visibly, but her face remained determined, but calm.

Crosse's face showed a mixture of concern and surprise. "This is as high as I have ever gone with Ada. Are you quite well, Mrs Shelley? Shall I stop now?"

"No! Mister Crosse. Do not stop!" I feel nothing but a pleasant tingling," she replied. "I pray you go higher still. Much higher."

"Wait!" Ada shouted. "She stepped forward and pressed her stick into Mary's mouth.

Crosse shared a momentary look of unease with the others in the group, and then slowly rotated the dial to five, six, and then seven, at which Mary began to tremble with the forces of the electrical flow. Within her the sensation was of a flowing to and fro of energy, like a rushing stream within her body pulsing to and fro.

Crosse put his hand back upon the dial began to turn it still further. By now the hum was like a hive full of angry bees. As the dial almost reached eight, Mary unleashed a shuddering groan, which drove Crosse's hand off the dial. He shot an alarmed look at the first the doctor and then the vicar.

"More!" Mary managed to mutter between tightly clenched teeth.

Crosse frowned deeply, he threw an importuning look at the others, as if to ask for their blessing and then inched the dial slowly higher.

As the needle swung toward nine, Mary felt something like roots ripping. Snapping. Tearing free. She felt something begin to split away from her soul, like an insect shedding a carapace. She heard a agonised moan from within. A cry of something she was moulting, something that had fastened itself to her soul and that the electricity was now peeling away. Instinctively, she knew what it was: the thing that had flown in through the window that night at the Villa Diodati, ridden in on a lightning bolt. The malevolence that had fastened itself to her soul and brought her so many years of sorrow and suffering.

Her monster.

"Mu-mu-mu-more," she mumbled through her tight sealed lips, half afraid she would bite her own tongue off.

"That's enough, Andrew!" the doctor shouted.

"Yes," the vicar seconded. "Cease now, Andrew. I fear you will destroy her!"

Ada said nothing. She knew the allure of the electricity, and she watched with envy. Mary could clearly tolerate more current than she could. Much more. Would it not be foolish to abandon the experiment now?

For Mary, the figures of Crosse, Cornelia, and Ada were a shaking blur as her body shuddered and convulsed constantly. And then she saw it: a huge shadowy figure standing beside Ada. The others could not see it, but it was just as she had glimpsed that night: a hulking promethean figure in the fiery core of the storm-blasted tree connected to her by an umbilicus of silvery light.

Mary knew instinctively that once the umbilicus was severed she would be at last free of it.

She wanted to beg for more, for Crosse to turn the dial still higher, but her back teeth were savagely compressed and the surging flux would not let her straining jaws unclench. In desperation, she turned her eyes to Cornelia, and though she could not focus for shaking, she implored Cornelia with her eyes for help.

Mary tried to plead for help but it came out as a torn moan.

"Did you hear that, Andrew?" the doctor said, "She is suffering horribly. You must stop this now!"

"Yes!" the vicar urged.

But then Cornelia lunged forward, seized the dial, and snapped it all the way over, so that the needle plunged deep into the red zone, until it hit a metal stop past ten and could advance no further.

The humming sound climbed to a sizzling drone and the pungent smell of ozone, singed flesh, and hot electrics swirled in the air. The higher voltage ratcheted Mary's muscles into full spasm, so that her back arched backward in a bent double pose the most skilled contortionist would have found impossible. There was a cracking sound as Mary's back teeth snapped the wooden stick in two and the pieces fell from her mouth.

"Cornelia!" Crosse cried. "What have you done?"

"Quick man!" Dr Freestone shouted. "For God's sake, shut it off!" Cornelia grabbed the wooden dial to turn the current down, but the dial came off in her hand and she fumbled to fit it back onto its spindle.

Crosse pushed her out of the way and struggled to replace the knob, but his hands were shaking so badly he could not.

At that point Countess Lovelace stepped forward, grabbed the wooden handle of the gate switch, and jerked it open. The circuit broken, the humming abruptly stopped. Released, Mary crumpled to the floor unconscious.

At that moment the doors to the music room crashed open as the Reverend Smith and his posse burst into the room.

"What ungodly rite is this?" Smith shouted as he strode toward Crosse, his staff raised high. "Blasphemer!" he bellowed. "Even now they celebrate unholy Mass. Destroy it!" he urged his men. "Smash and destroy the toys of the devil."

Smith swung his shepherd's crook across one of the low benches, sweeping aside the rows of electrical cells which crashed to the floor, shattering glass, splashing acid and exploding in a volley of sparks as anodes clashed and short circuited.

"Stop this!" Crosse shouted, arms outspread as he moved forward to shield his delicate apparatus. "Get out, you fools!"

But then one of the old labourers from Broomfield struck Cross across the face with a walking stick so that he recoiled and staggered backward.

There followed a confused melee as the Doctor and Reverend Phipps battled with the interlopers. Although the doctor knocked a few of the men down, most were armed with clubs and staves and scythes with wicked keen blades. The Doctor, the Reverend and Crosse actually held their ground gamely for a time, although they were mostly on the defensive, fending off blows from staves and clubs with whatever piece of scientific apparatus they could snatch up. In hysterics, Cornelia screamed and clung to her husband, while Ada was quick witted enough to snatch up several of the broken electrical cells and fling their acid contents in the men's faces, which set them to howling and screaming. Blinded, they staggered about, crashing into tables and upending them, sending acid spraying and sparks sputtering and crackling. But though they fought gamely, Crosse's coterie were outnumbered by the armed brutes. A standoff finally ensued, with Crosse and his party cornered in a part of the room, with the Reverend Smith and Martin Compton beside him, in control.

"Godless blasphemer!" Smith proclaimed pointing out Cross with a ramrod—straight finger. "Today you will witness the destruction of all your unholy instruments. Never again will you summon devils to dance upon the wires and affright the good people of this Bourne."

Forgotten where she lay slumped on the floor, Mary began to stir. She listened for several moment and then her eyes snapped open. When she peered between the table legs, she saw overturned benches and the Reverend Smith and his posse.

Smith's eye was drawn to the shiny hemispheres of the discharger and he read aloud the Latin inscription: *"Noli me tangere."* Do not touch me!" a sardonic smile twisted Smith's hawkish face. "Here be the devil's own dread engine." He snorted with contempt. "I will not just touch thee, I will smite thee with my rod. In the name of the Almighty I will smash thee. I will destroy thee!"

Smith stepped forward and raised his crook high in the air, ready to bring it down with crushing force.

"No," Crosse shouted. "Stop! You don't know the danger you're in!"

"Oh, I know evil when I see it. And I know how to exact the Lord's vengeance.

Once again, Smith raised his staff high and was about to strike when Mary burst up from the floor. "No!" she shouted and flung herself forward just as Smith swung his shepherd crook. At the same moment, her free hand touched the lower of the silver hemispheres. There was a tremendous flash as the full electric current surged though her body and through the staff into Smith's body. The power of the unleashed current flung them both high into the air. Mary fell to the ground in a crumple. Smith was knocked backward ten feet, crashed to the floor, rolled over and and also lay still. In an instant, a section of Smith's staff the length of a man's forearm had been vaporised and now a pall of silvery wood smoke swirled in the air.

"She's killed him!" Martin Compton yelled. "The witch threw fire and has killed the reverend right enough!" The words were enough to drive the posse into a panic and now the men fled the music room even faster than they had burst in.

Everyone rushed to where Mary lay slumped on the floor. The doctor put his head to Mary's chest and listened. He felt at her wrist end then palpated her throat, searching for a pulse. Finding none, he called for his medical bag. The Reverend found it and rushed over to the Doctor with it. Richard Freestone fumbled in his black bag and dug out a small mirror.

"Dear God, she must survive this!" Andrew Crosse fretted. His wife clutched his arm and buried her head in his shoulder, weeping.

The Reverend stood over Mary's body, his face tragic as he made the sign of the cross, and began to recite last rites. Ada Lovelace lifted one of Mary's limp hands and held it to her cheek. The hand was already growing cold, the warmth fleeing.

The doctor held the small mirror beneath Mary's nostrils for several long moments, but the glass refused to mist. Finally he looked up at the others with stunned eyes and muttered. "All life has left her body. She is dead. Mary Shelley is dead."

UNHOLY RESSURRECTION

 I beheld the wretch—the miserable monster whom I had created . . . Mary Shelley

When young Rory awakened he was lying up against a slab of hard, cold stone. When he timidly reached out a hand and touched it, his exploring fingertips traced the engraved letters of someone's name and then he saw it was a gravestone. Rory squealed and rolled away only to find, to his greater terror, that he was in a graveyard. He had fainted when the monster picked him up. Or maybe he had died and now he was was an earthbound ghost haunting this terrible place.

Lightning forked overhead, followed immediately by the boom of thunder. Rory screamed again. He sat, knees together, shaking hands covering his face, terrified and bewildered. The storm front preceding the thunderstorm had arrived with gusting winds stripping green leaves from the churchyard elms, and thrashing the tree tops that hissed and seethed like banshees.

With trembling reluctance, Rory raised himself in a half-crouch and peered over the edge of the gravestone. His eyes flickered left and right, looking for the monster, sure he must be lurking somewhere near and would soon return to tear him apart. Close by, a shovel stuck up from the shoddily filled grave near the church wall. And just then, a bolt of lightning flashed down from the thundercloud overhead and struck the handle of the spade. A deafening boom ripped the air asunder and Rory cowered as clods of freshly shovelled dirt pattered down upon his head. The intense flash temporarily blinded the boy, so that he dare not move from the spot. But then, as the swarming afterimages faded, he saw that the lightning had struck the shovel handle, vaporising it. The surging current had melted the spade's metal blade and a spatter of molten metal had set fire to the dry grass which burned in places here and there. And now as Rory watched in wide-eyed terror, the steaming pile of grave dirt erupted with giant beetles and spiders scurrying away while fat, blood-red earthworms burst up from the fresh-churned dirt, driven out by the heat and electricity to writhe in their death-throes. The uneven fill of the grave seethed with rising steam and then the earth suddenly heaved up, as if a giant mole were digging its way to the surface. A sudden whirlwind arose, swirling about the churchyard and sucking up a vortex of leaves. Static electricity made Rory's hair stand on end. Skeletal leaves scratched his cheeks.

The earth on the grave collapsed, sucked back into itself. And then it heaved up mightily, as something buried beneath the dirt stirred from its unnatural slumber. The earth shook and danced, until it became clear that something truly was digging itself out of the grave. The earthen mound swelled again, the clods splitting and cracking apart, and this time a naked hand burst out, clawing at the dirt. Then, with a violent jerk an entire arm tore free, and then a second arm. And as Rory watched in wide-eyed terror, a head burst out, followed by a pair of massive shoulders, as if, from the cold womb of the grave some monstrous child was birthing itself. Finally, a hulking form dragged itself loose from a caul of dirt until it staggered upright on the thick pillars of its legs and and stood erect. It was the monster he'd seen earlier. But no, it appeared different. Half the flesh of the face was charred black while all the hair on the head had been burned to a frazzle of singed black wires prickling from the livid scalp. The monster had torn its clothes to rags as it dug itself loose of the grave and now steam rose from the muscular torso. The huge head pivoted on its broad stump of a neck, scanning the churchyard, and then the monster turned and shambled directly toward the gravestone Rory was hiding behind. The boy curled into a tight ball and squeezed his eyes tight shut as he was too terrified to look. He heard footsteps lumber closer and stop. Suddenly, a reek of burning hair and scorched flesh sizzled in his nostrils. He took a chance and cracked his eyes to slits, peering up.

And instantly regretted it.

The monster was standing over him, looking down. Set into the ghastly face, its dead eyes were a vivid yellow. At the dreadful sight, hot urine gushed down Rory's trouser legs, his lungs emptied of breath and he was unable to take another. It seemed certain that the monster would lean down and smash him with one fist.

The monster's yellow gaze locked with his own for long seconds, as if peering into the darkest recesses of his brain. But then the monster broke its gaze as the huge head raised, looking off into the distance, as if sensing something. Then, abruptly, it turned and lumbered away until it was swallowed up in the unfathomable shadows of the woodland paths. And then Rory, his body quaking, unable to stand, unable to move, rolled onto his side, curled into a foetal ball, and lay there whimpering.

STRANGE STAR UNSPOKEN

> My spirit will sleep in peace; or if it thinks, it will not surely think thus. Farewell. Mary Shelley

I am awakened by voices.

Familiar voices.

They are close by. In the hallway outside my room. I hold my breath. Listen.

"Oh, there you are Mary."

"Baron, I was just about to change your mother's sheets."

"Could you do that later? I wanted to sit with Mama for a while."

"Very good, sir. I'll go help Ruth in the kitchen."

"Thank you, Mary."

I hear my doorknob rattle. The door open. Footsteps enter. Heavy footsteps. The steps of a fully-grown man.

"Hello, Mother," a male voice says. It is filled with kindness and affection, and my heart swells to hear it. I know instantly whose voice it is.

My son, Percy Florence Shelley.

The bed sags as he sits on its edge. I feel him lift my hand and gently squeeze it between both of his.

I must open my eyes. I must tell my son that I am at last awake. That I am getting better.

But though I search the ruined palace of my body, I cannot find my eyes. I cannot claim my voice. I crawled to the doorstep of death. And for two months I lay there. Slumbering without dreaming. Dead yet alive. And then I awakened, and could open my eyes, but pretended I could not when Jane visited me. Now I wish to open my eyes but cannot. The homunculus in my head is growing larger. Soon it will kill me. I am slipping backward. The darkness has its claws in me and is eager to reclaim me.

Percy Florence lifts my hand to press it against something warm and soft: his cheek.

"Oh mother," he says, "You have sacrificed everything in your life for me." His voice is thick, lachrymose, choked with emotion. "I wanted to be a good son to you. I wanted to be as great as my father . . . but . . . I know I have fallen short. Still, I hope you know I have always loved you . . . and always will."

I'm here my darling son, I want to reply. But I cannot find my eyes to open them. Cannot find my voice to speak to him. I am like a blindfolded woman in a darkened room, groping without a sense of touch.

A voice calls from the hallway, "Percy? Husband where are you?"

It is Jane's voice. My hated daughter in law. Despair surges through me. She always seems to know when Percy is in my room. I know she resents him spending time with me. Even now, when I am mute and unresponsive.

"Please, mother, do not leave without saying goodbye," he says softly and kisses the back of my hand. I feel the warm wetness of his tears.

I love you, my child. I will try to say goodbye—if I am able—before . . .

"Ah, Percy, there you are." Jane has entered the room and her cloying perfume poisons my nostrils, sweet and sickly as she is.

I imagine my son still has tears in his eyes because Jane quickly says, "Ah, I see you are distressed. I will leave you. We must finish the latest manuscript of your father's work. I will wait in the parlour. Please try not to let the servants see you so . . . discomposed. It is unfitting in a man."

She leaves the room, dragging her cloud of poison with her.

The bed shifts as it takes Percy's full weight. I feel his lips kiss my forehead. And then his voice whispers in my ear, "I love you, mama." He gives my hand a final squeeze. I know this simple act of love is a premonition of what will happen again, when he enters this room and finds me dead. It is not far away.

The bed rebounds as he stands up. I hear his footsteps walk to the door, open it, and close it behind him.

I feel my body sink into the bed, pass through it, and fall in a descending glide toward the centre of the earth.

MEETING WITH THE GODDESS

But I am a blasted tree; the bolt has entered my soul; and I felt then that I should survive to exhibit what I shall soon cease to be – a miserable spectacle of wrecked humanity, pitiable to others and intolerable to myself . . . Mary Shelley

The next thing Mary knew she was floating somewhere near the ceiling of the music room, looking down upon a disturbing scene. Doctor Freestone crouched over a figure sprawled on the floor with the others huddled around. She saw the doctor pull something from his leather bag and bring it toward the face of the recumbent form. But then he moved to one side and Mary saw that it was her own body, eyes wide and unblinking. With a jolt of despair she realised they all thought she was dead. She called down to them, "No, I am not dead! I am up here. Please help me!"

But no one heard.

Then Mary felt herself bump up against the underside of the

ceiling and gently bounce, like a helium balloon. She bumped against the ceiling a second time. There was a moment of resistance, and then she passed through the ceiling effortlessly. She saw the beams of the rafters and suddenly she was outside the music room, looking down on the slate roof tiles.

No! She cried helplessly. Something was drawing her upward. She continued to rise so that soon she was looking down on the rapidly diminishing house and stables of Fyne Court. She glanced toward the woods. Even though it was dark, she could see everything clearly, including the group of shabby men stumbling along the pathway: the Reverend Smith's army, running away in terror.

She soared higher, toward a massively overgrown thundercloud boiling high into the sky. As she neared its base, sheets of wind-driven rain lashed the air around her and then the world faded and dimmed as she soared up past vaporous jellyfish tendrils of black cloud and was drawn inside. She found herself in a vast space, larger than the largest cathedral. Black and grey striations of cloud spanned the huge dome of cloud like flying buttresses. Dazzling bolts of lightning ran jagged through the air around her as the vault of heaven resounded with a cannonade of thunder.

She continued to rise, and soon burst through the top of the cloud and into clear sky where the ruddy glow of a sun already set limned the cloud tops with fire. And then her ascent slowed and stalled as she began to move horizontally, only able to judge her progress by the Somerset fields and hedgerows drifting below.

For the first time Mary realised she was still connected to her body by a silver cord that emerged from her navel and stretched away. Soon she started to descend and found herself over hilly terrain, deeply wooded.

On the hillside ahead she noted a great tumble of giant stones; at their base, the jagged black orifice of a cave leading underground. But then she noticed that she was drifting toward the cave opening and recognised with dread the same place in the story Reverend Phipps had told: Ruborough, and the ancient camp of the Romans where the malevolent force had attacked him and tried to drag him underground.

With time and the weather, the bricks that Reverend Phipps had used to seal the cave opening had collapsed inward, leaving a snaggle-toothed maw that Mary was helplessly being drawn into. Although it was totally dark inside the cave, Mary could still see plainly and watched helplessly as she down down the stony throat deeper and deeper into the earth. The air was thick with the stench of corruption and the cave floor was littered with the rotting carcasses of sheep and foxes and badgers that had crawled inside and died there. And then she heard a cacophony of horrible shrieks and moans resonating within. The cave narrowed to a vertical shaft that plunged miles underground and ended in a huge cavern where something hideous awaited.

It looked like a giant spider, only with a hundred twitching legs, but as she drew nearer she saw that it was no spider. Rather it was a squirming pile of worm-like creatures that slithered and roiled. They were a grey colour with heads like lamprey eels and when they opened their gaping mouths she saw rows of wicked, backwards-facing teeth. The eels writhed and squirmed and then the hideous mouths would gape and they would bite into one other and squirm inside the other's body only to obscenely burst out from another place, constantly devouring and being devoured. As she watched, the face of the nearest creature melted and flowed into that of a despairing human face. Mary realised with horror that these were human souls, writhing in torment. She was being steadily drawn nearer and realised that she would soon become one of the slithering things and shuddered with utter dread at the terrible fate awaiting her.

Suddenly she saw something ahead: a door incongruously set into the wall of the cave she was plummeting down. It looked like a door that might be found in anyone's house. As she hurtled toward it, she focused her desperate gaze upon the door and willed herself to move toward it. But at the last minute, she feared it might be a trick, and that the door would likely open onto something darker and even more dreadful. And yet the door seemed to offer hope, and so she willed herself toward it with all her being. As she passed, the door flew open and she was drawn inside.

Suddenly and without transition, she found herself in a room that seemed strangely familiar. She looked around dazedly, and saw much that she recognised—the tall bookcases crammed with leather jacketed tomes. The writing desk piled with books and loose manuscripts. And there on the wall behind the desk was a portrait she had spent many hours of her youth staring at.

It was the portrait of her mother.

And then she heard the sound of a pen scratching on paper and became aware of a figure hunched over the desk, feverishly scribbling away at a manuscript.

It was a woman's form. At that moment the figure became aware of Mary. The scribbling stylus paused, the woman looked up, and their eyes met.

It was her mother: Mary Wollstonecraft.

For a long moment, Mary could not summon speech, and then finally she managed, "Mother?" in a fragile whisper.

Wollstonecraft stood up from the desk and stared at Mary in puzzlement. Then she finally asked, "Who . . . who are you?"

"Mother. Mother it is I. Mary. Your child."

The stylus Wollstonecraft had been writing with slipped from her hand. Her mouth fell open. Confusion swarmed her features. "But I have no daughter."

"You do, mother. I am your daughter. Mary. You . . . you . . . we never . . ."

Wollstonecraft stepped from behind the desk and cautiously approached, her eyes frantically searching Mary's face. She stopped an arm's length away and stared in disbelief, her lips quivering. After moments of baffled wonder, she took a stumbling step forward and placed her hands on either side of Mary's face. "You . . . you have my eyes . . . my cheekbones. How is this possible . . . ?"

Tears flooded Mary's eyes, her lower lip quivered. "Oh mother. At last we are together." A sob broke loose from Mary and she flung herself into her mother's arms and the two embraced and trembled with upwelling emotion.

"Oh my child!" Wollstonecraft sobbed. "I never saw you. I never held you. I never kissed you."

"Then kiss me now, mother, for I have waited a lifetime to see you."

The two embraced crushingly, their bodies quaking as they sobbed, arms fiercely embracing one another, afraid to ever let go.

"I have been lonely for you my whole life," Mary sobbed.

They moved to a mirror on the wall and the two women stared at their side by side reflections. "You have your father's nose, but you have my eyes." Wollstonecraft marvelled. "I despair that I was not there for you."

"But you were, mother. In your writings. In your poetry. In your stories. In your philosophical writings. All through my youth I read them all. Many times. Your voice has guided me through my life. You have always been with me . . . in my heart."

"Oh my beloved child." Wollstonecraft paused a moment and finally asked, "But why are you here?"

"I died, mother. I died and was being drawn into a place of dread and terror. A death that brought no peace. No release. But then I thought of you."

"No. You are still in danger! We are in the Bardo. It is a temporary place. An anteroom. But you cannot remain here. Your soul faces further challenges. You must prepare. You must be strong."

"But mother, I want to remain here. With you."

Wollstonecraft shook her head, her face tragic. "That cannot be so. Every soul faces its own trial. Your journey on earth is not yet done."

From behind came a loud bang as the door to the room sucked open and a strong wind rushed inside, peeling the pages from the manuscript on the writing desk and whirling them around and around the room in a cyclone. Mary shrieked as she felt a tidal pull tugging at her, trying to drag her away from her mother. "No!" Mary screamed. "I won't leave you. I won't!"

"Hold fast to me." Wollstonecraft screamed. "I will not lose you a second time."

The two women tightened their embrace, but the pull was monstrous and irresistible. Slowly, gradually, the two women were pried apart. They clutched hands in a desperate struggle, but the forces working on them were too powerful. Soon they only held on by their fingertips.

"You have my love," Mary Wollstonecraft shouted above the roaring wind. "Remember that. You will always have my love."

And then their grip upon one another failed and Mary was dragged backward toward the open door.

"Mother!" Mary Shelley screamed as their fingers slipped loose.

It was the last Mary Shelley saw of her mother's despairing face as she was pulled to the door and then sucked from the room. The door slammed and Mary lost sight of her mother. She had thought she would be drawn into the hideous pile of tortured souls, but to her surprise she found herself ascending, moving up the throat of the tunnel with increasing speed. She flew out of the cave mouth at Ruborough and then was drawn back up into the seething black morass of thunderclouds.

Lightning flashed jagged around her. Waterfalls of rain swirled in up-currents and down drafts, lit by flash after flash of lightning. She burst through the top of the cloud, high enough to see the entire county spread before her in the livid light. And then she began to move backwards, back toward the tiny buildings of Fyne Court.

It was then she saw that she was being towed backward by the silver umbilicus. Soon she hovered over Fyne court and began to plummet toward the rooftops. The drops of rain evaporating before they hit the slate roof tiles of the music room. She passed through the roof, the attic, and plunged back into the music room. Her body had been lain upon one of the benches, a handkerchief draped over her dead face. She saw Crosse and the others, hugging one another in consolation and weeping. In their fits of mourning they failed to notice the hulking shadow waiting at the head of the bench. Mary knew exactly what it was: the malevolent shadow that had followed her through the years and which was now drawing her back into her body.

Reluctant to surrender her ... even to death.

STRANGE STAR FALLEN

 Roll on, deep and dark blue ocean, roll. Ten thousand fleets sweep over thee in vain. Man marks the earth with ruin, but his control stops with the shore . . . Lord Byron

With rising dread, I twitch the curtain open and crane to look out the window. On the foggy street, a hulking form loiters beneath the halo of a Gaslamp. As if sensing my gaze, the grizzled head lifts and the merciless yellow eyes fix upon me. By long habit I recoil and jerk my hand away. Somehow I know that the monster's presence means my time is growing short. That I am close to death. A cyclone of emotions whirls in my chest: fear, dread, anger. But suddenly, the cyclone stills and my fears evaporate. At long last, I have no more fear left within me. Instead, surging in to fill the void is a reckless emotion, not bravery but an utter absence of fear. I have already lost everything, so now there is nothing left to lose. A reckless determination stirs again, gathering force like a nascent storm. It is my monster in the flesh. He has tracked me down. Run me to earth.

If I can no longer run away, I think, *then I shall run toward. And if I die in the monster's embrace, it will be my choice.* A grim smile twists my lips as my own words echo back from across the years: *I am fearless, and therefore terrible . . .*

My body is weak from months of being bedridden and I struggle to heave aside the heavy bedclothes My feeble grip on the sheets slips and my flailing hand knocks over the pot of ink and quill on the bedside table splashing blue ink across the pillowcases. My green journal tumbles from the bedside table and slaps the floor. Finally, I pull my emaciated legs free and touch the soles of my bare feet to the cold rug. For a triumphant moment I rest, panting and dizzy. As I fight to catch my breath I hear the voice of my daughter in law, loud and close, immediately outside the door

"You may go to bed, Florry," Jane announces. "Mama still sleeps. I will check on her myself before the marquess and I retire for the night."

I freeze, expecting my hated daughter in law to walk into the room and catch me out of bed. But then floorboards creak as Jane's ponderous tread trudges away, no doubt on her way downstairs to the parlour. I wait a full minute and then struggle to stand on my quivering legs, leaning heavily on the bedside table for support. The tabletop is pooled with spilled ink and I plant my left palm in it, feeling the wetness ooze between my fingers, viscous and sticky as blue blood. I absently wipe the hand upon my nightgown spreading a huge stain. The bedroom door is three staggering steps away, but I reach it, and grasp the door knob with both hands for support as I lean my forehead against the cool wood, and wait for the room's giddy carouseling to slow.

The glass door knob is ink-slippery in my feeble hands, but I manage to twist until the latch releases and door gasps inward. Clinging heavily to the doorframe, I gather my strength and then push away from the door and totter down the hall to the top of the staircase. The stairs are precipitous and a fall might snap my brittle spine. I clutch the handrail and ease down the stairs, one perilous step at a time. Miraculously, I encounter no errant servants as I reach the lower landing. As I shamble past the door to the front parlour I can hear my son's voice and his wife's clumsy piano playing stumbling over the arpeggios. Finally, I reach the entrance hall and the front door leading to the square outside.

The bolt has been shot tight in its fixture and takes all my strength to yank and wiggle and ease the bolt loose. Fortunately, the domestic staff have not yet locked the door and the cold brass doorknob turns in my hand.

The front door swings open onto the night, and suddenly I am free, standing on the front door step while clutching the doorframe for support. A frigid breeze blows through my sweat-dampened nightgown and I shiver in the chill. At the other side of Chester Square, the hulking figure still lurks beneath the gas lamp, a form only sketchily glimpsed between panes of seething fog.

Risking a broken hip or worse, my feet slither down the slippery marble steps and I only just manage to catch myself on the Greek columns that frame either side of the entrance. This is my last available support. Crossing the cobblestone square will require my efforts alone. Here, I rest awhile, waiting for my galloping heartbeat to slow. And then, like a lone sailor casting off the ropes to cross a wide ocean, I let go of the column and set my first unsteady foot upon the rime-slippery cobbles of Chester square.

FYNE COURT BURNS

> *Invention, it must be humbly admitted, does not consist in creating out of a void, but out of chaos . . . Mary Shelley*

In the music room, one of the benches had been cleared of electrical cells and Mary's body lay carefully arranged upon it, her face covered by one of Ada's fine silk handkerchiefs.

Nearby, the other members of the party stood arranged in a tableau of sorrow. Andrew Crosse sat collapsed in a chair, shoulders slumped, head hanging in despair—the wizard whose magic had failed. His wife, Cornelia, sat on the floor at his feet, hugging his knees and weeping. The other members of the party, Countess Lovelace, Reverend Phipps and Doctor Freestone stood gathered around them, their eyes wet and their faces pale with shock and grief.

"I wanted electricity to enlighten the world," Crosse despaired. "But instead of life I have brought only death!" He looked up at the others, tears flowing, his face a mask of remorse. "I will smash my machines. I will destroy every last piece and foreswear swear dabbling in matters no man has right to." He threw a desperate look at the

Reverend. "You were right to doubt, Josiah. I have trespassed upon the holy ground of the almighty and and now an innocent soul has paid the price for my transgression."

"Andrew," the doctor spoke in a gentle voice. "This was not your fault. This happened because we were attacked by that madman Smith and his gang of ruffians. He is the one responsible for Mary's death. Not you!"

The others murmured their assent, but Crosse was inconsolable.

Unseen by them, the linen handkerchief covering Mary Shelley's face and begun to suck in and out and then, suddenly, with a ferocious intake of breath, Mary sat upright on the bench and the handkerchief fluttered away.

Cornelia screamed and the others reacted with shock and terror. Mary looked about herself, bewildered, unable to tell if she still dreamed or was dead.

While the others held back in fear, Doctor Freestone slowly approached, his face amazed."Mu-Mary . . . Mrs Shelley?" He stuttered.

Mary looked about herself. "I had the strangest dream," she said. "I dreamt I was dead. My spirit soared high above the landscape, through the midst of the mightiest thunderclouds."

"You . . . you were dead," the doctor stammered. "No heartbeat. No pulse. No breath. Quite dead."

The Reverend pushed forward and took Mary's hand. He threw an amazed look at the others. "Her hand is cold as death." He gazed intently into Mary's eyes. "Did you see heaven? Did you meet God? You must tell me!"

Still dazed, Mary spoke haltingly. "At first I floated among the clouds. But then I felt a force pulling me in, drawing me back down to the earth."

"Dear God, no!"

"I found myself above a landscape strewn with large stones of a Roman camp." She looked at the Reverend."And then I saw the cave you spoke of at Ruborough. And though I tried to resist, I was soon drawn inside."

The Reverend Phipps released a hiss of astonishment. He immediately dropped hold of Mary's hand, stood up, and backed away from her, crossing himself.

"And were you taken to hell?" He asked in a quavering voice.

I was drawn deep into the earth. At the end of the shaft was a cavern filled with hideous shapes: human souls writhing in torment . . ."

Phipps crossed himself furiously and drawing he crucifix he kissed it repeatedly.

"I sensed the creatures wanted me. Wanted to devour my soul, to join them in their wretched suffering. I was being pulled toward them, powerless to resist. But then I saw a door in the wall of the tunnel."

Phipps looked puzzled. "A . . . a door? What kind of door? A celestial door? Did you see angels flying in and out?"

"It was a door from the house I grew up in. The door to my mother's study. I willed the door to open. I passed through and was in my mother's study. And there I met my mother."

All looked at one another in amazement.

"She is in shock," the doctor muttered in a low voice. "It was naught but a fantasy of the mind . . . a dream."

Mary shook her head wonderingly. "No, this life is the dream. What I experienced was the true reality, bright and brilliant and more vivid."

"And your mother helped you find your way back?" Cornelia asked.

"We embraced and kissed as we had never chance to do in life." Mary held her sleeve to her face and inhaled deeply. "Oh, God, I can still smell her! It was real! We were together!"

Mary's wondering face collapsed into a expression of dread. "But then I was torn from my mother's arms and dragged back here by my nemesis."

The Reverend Phipps blurted, "You mean the devil?"

Mary shook her head. "The creature. The monster who has dogged my life since that night at the Villa Diodati." She shot a fierce look at the others. "It is here now. In this room."

Her words spooked the others, who looked about themselves with fear, searching for unseen spectres.

"My monster will never let me rest. It will pursue me to the last breath I draw. It will ruin and murder all those around me."

Countess Lovelace stepped forward and laid a comforting hand on Mary's shoulder. "My poor Mary, yours has been a life of sorrow and loss, but there is good that may yet happen—"

She was interrupted as the door to the music room crashed open and Tom rushed in. His face was streaked with blood and dirt and his clothes disheveled. "Suh-sir," he gasped, fighting to catch his breath.

Crosse sprang up from the chair. "What is it, Tom? Is the Reverend Smith and his rascals still up to their mischief?"

"Mister Crosse, sir. You must all come outside. Quickly. Save yourselves. The house is ablaze and I fear we shall never put it out!"

MONSTERS IN THE FOG

*Life, although it may only be an accumulation of anguish, is
dear to me, and I will defend it . . . Mary Shelley*

Tom and Andrew Crosse dashed from the music room and
the others followed. The doctor and the Reverend Phipps
supported Mary beneath each arm and half-carried her
from the room. As they stepped outside, a wave of heat crashed over
them and they choked on air turgid with smoke and burning debris.

A room on the second story of the house was engulfed. Large
flames licked from the window, and roof above was smouldering in
places where the fire was starting to burn through. After a moment's
study, Mary realised with horror that the burning room was her room
and she was stricken with terrible guilt. Had she left the candles burning? She seemed to remember blowing them out and turning the
lantern low. But now, looking up at the fire blazing from the shattered
window . . .

The doctor threw an arm around Mary's shoulders and dragged
her away from the burning house, past the stables, to the beginning of

the paths that led into the woods. Here he sat her down on the stump of a felled tree, far from the flames.

"Stay here, Mrs Shelley," Doctor Freestone said, "You will be safe. The Reverend and I must assist." And with that the two men ran back toward the house.

Despite her recent ordeal, Mary could not sit still. She rose shakily to her feet and looked on in horror at the chaotic scene.

Crosse, Tom and the household retinue milled about the burning building. Servants ran forward with ladders and leaned them up against the house so that the window of the burning room could be accessed. More servants came running with overflowing buckets slopping water. Tom clambered up the ladder carrying a bucket of water which he threw into the open window and then quickly retreated as the intense heat forced him to back away. Soon a bucket brigade formed with servants passing along buckets of water drawn from the well. Andrew Crosse stood at the foot of the ladder, waving wildly and shouting instructions. The women huddled in a group close by. Cornelia was screaming in hysterics, but Countess Ada was with with her, a restraining arm thrown about her shoulders to stop her from running to be at the side of her husband.

Mary studied the window from which yellow flames gouted, and covered her face with both hands. Cornelia had warned her about the care that needed to be taken with candles. Had she left them burning? Had she caused this fire? She seemed to remember Cornelia blowing out the candles, a hand cupped behind the flame. Or had she imagined that? Her mind was so scattered. Had she caused this calamity?

The terrible uncertainty forced her to break her gaze and look away into the dark woods, but then she saw something, someone, standing a dozen feet away on the gloomy woodland path: a woman. Was she from the house? Was she a servant? The woman was barefoot and scantily dressed in a white nightgown lit by the fire's ruddy glow. Her long grey hair was unpinned and bedraggled. Her left hand and white nightgown were stained with blue ink. She was looking straight at Mary, her eyes reflecting the flames. Mary realised she had seen the woman before. It was the same woman she had seen lying in her bed, the woman she had taken for an invalid houseguest. But then the light from the leaping flames lit up the woman's face and Mary's eyes widened with stunned recognition.

It was Mary's doppelgänger—only this one was of her older self, her hair turned white with age. The two women stared at one another in horror, wide-eyed, lips quivering with fear. After breathless seconds, the older Mary let out an anguished cry and then turned and ran away, back into the gloomy depths of the woodland. Terrified by seeing her older double, the younger Mary turned and hurried back toward the fire, eager to return to the company of people she knew. But as she as she stepped clear of the trees, she saw to her despair that the once splendid house was by now a hopeless conflagration, with screaming people running aimlessly, hither and yon, in blind confusion.

But she had only gone twenty feet when she tripped on something lying in the middle of the path. Among the looming trees it was too dark to make it out, but when she groped the shape she was amazed to find that it was her travelling bag. How had it come to be here? She had left it in her room? Hadn't she?

"Ah, be sure ye've found me bag," a voice purred in a Cornish accent. "And here I tawt I'd gone and lost it."

She spun to find herself face to face with a strange man. A rough man, and Mary instantly guessed he was not part of the Fyne household.

Ryd Thorne casually stripped the scarf from his neck, wound it around Mary's throat and used it to pull her close, so that his vile-smelling breath washed over her face. He gathered the scarf up in one hand, and with his free hand gripped her breast and squeezed it. "Looks like your friends are all busy with the fire, so you and me have time to get acquainted."

Mary's eyes widened with fear. When she tried to pull away, he twisted his grip, tightening the scarf into a garrotte, choking her.

"'At's right," he leered. "Fight if ye want. Struggle. It adds spice to the dish. Dead or alive, yer body will keep warm for another hour. Which is plenty of time for me to poke about inside. I like to see tears while I'm about my business. A woman's tears are like salt on me porridge."

His eyes hardened. His breathing slow and shuddering with lust. His mouth slackened into a wet-lipped leer, and Mary felt the scarf tightening around her bare throat until she fought to draw the next breath. Her hands flew up to her throat and her fingers scrabbled to loosen the scarf digging into her throat, but it continued to tighten until her eyes bulged and her straining heartbeat thundered in her ears.

The Reverend Smith loped painfully along the forest path, peering cautiously into the darkness and flinching at phantom shadows. He had lost his hat and his Bible—both left behind in the wizard's unholy cathedral. He had hoped to find his faithless flock, but it was soon clear they had all scattered and run for home. When the young zealot had come to his senses in Crosse's devilish chamber, he had listened long enough to hear that the witch was dead, killed by the same fiery spell that had knocked him senseless. He had crawled from the place back outside, only to find that the house was on fire—surely an act of divine retribution for the godless going's on. Only as he limped though the dark woodland paths did Smith feel the pain and discover that his right hand—the hand that had gripped the staff he had sought to smite Crosse's infernal machine with—had been badly burned with several fingers fused together. The hand he held the Bible in while reading aloud the scriptures was now clenched in a frozen claw he could not open. Despite this, Smith welcomed the pain and reasoned that if the hand never healed, he would preach about his battle with the devil's own witch and hold up his withered hand to the congregation—proof of his sacrifice in the cause of righteousness.

But then he heard the crash of feet from somewhere ahead, and the sound of ragged breathing. As his wide-open eyes strained to filter the darkness, he dimly made out something moving his way: a white amorphous blob. It soon resolved itself as the uncanny figure of a woman. But as she approached he saw to his terror that it was a dead woman, barefoot and dressed in a burial shroud, as if she had just climbed from her own coffin.

Smith froze in place, and could only stare in terror until the dead woman was almost upon him. She also stopped and stared, her face wild and near demented. And then she pointed a finger at him and spoke: "You! I know who you are. I remember you now. You are the Reverend Philip Smith of Bridgwater."

It was the witch! She had been killed by the fiery spell she had flung at him. But now she had risen from the dead, and was walking the earth again, seeking him out.

Smith shrieked with fear and turned to run away. But the woods here were dense and in the wan light the way forward near-unfathomable, He tripped and stumbled over tree roots and snarls of ferns, or slammed a shoulder bruisingly into the trunks of trees bordering the path. The path turned a sharp corner and he dashed around it, only to collide face-first with something huge and soft. He rebounded, staggered backward, and sat down hard, his head spinning.

When his senses cleared he looked up to see what he had run into and quailed with terror. It was a monster, huge and hulking, its face burned and blackened. The huge form exuded a gagging reek of charred flesh and burnt hair as if it had just stepped, hot and smoking, through a portal from hell. It was the monster, just as the undead witch had prophesied, come to rend him limb from limb. At the sight of the creature, Smith's bowels emptied in a hot gush. The monster bent over, bringing its face close to Smith's, and the dead yellow eyes raked curiously across his face, but then the monster seemed to lose interest. Instead, it grasped him by the front of his jacket, lifted him so that his feet dangled in thin air, and then hurled him away. Reverend Smith tumbled head over heels, arms and legs failing, and crashed down into a dense thicket of blackberry bushes. And then, as Smith lay there blubbering, the monster shambled on. When the religious man was certain the monster had gone, he fought to clamber free of the prickly blackberries, howling with pain as the thorns tore and bloodied his flesh. When he finally dragged himself back to the path, Smith staggered to his feet and began hobble along as fast as he could, anxious to return to Bridgwater where he resolved never again to preach in a pulpit nor speak of devils and witches.

~

Mary was clawing at the scarf as is it tightened around her throat, but Ryd Thorne's grip was like iron, no matter how she dug her nails in. Mary tried to plead with him, to beg, but her voice came out as a rasp.

The Cornishman flashed his gap-toothed grin, his eyes alive with lust. But then he let out an astonished gasp, his eyes widening as he looked up at something looming up behind her. His grip relaxed, the scarf slackened and Mary was able to suck in a choking breath. The army-deserter's face contorted with naked terror. He stumbled a half step backward just as a huge fist smashed down upon the top of his head with a nauseating crunch. Ryd's neck concertinaed with the force of the blow, which drove his skull down with the force of a sledgehammer, so that his spinal column speared upwards into his brain, killing him instantly. A gout of blood shot out his nose and sprayed from both ears. The Cornishman's stunned eyes flared wide before his knees buckled and he toppled backward onto the path, already dead before he hit the ground.

When Mary spun around to look, she blanched with fear to see the owner of the huge fist.

A monster. Or rather, what had once been the idiot boy, Adam, the face now transformed, burned and disfigured, the dead eyes a hideous yellow, but lit within by a hideous intelligence. It was a face Mary had seen before. A face she was familiar with. The face of her monster. She covered her mouth with both hands. Took a faltering step backward.

The monster had been born into the world by a second fiery bolt, and with the face half-cooked and the hair burned to a frazzle, it still smouldered like something forgotten in the oven. Over the years it had worn many guises, but it always remains recognisable.

As the Reverend Phipps had prophesied, evil had found a vessel into which it could pour itself.

Despite the terror she felt upon first glimpsing him, Mary suddenly became calm. She knew she was about to die, and was reserved to her fate. The long chase across the years was at last over.

"So," Mary said, finding her voice. "You've come to kill me? To murder me?"

The monster responded with dark laughter. "Murder? You speak of murder? I was not born from love as most humans are. I was born from murder, stolen from the sweet oblivion of death and dragged screaming into a life I never coveted."

"It was you who killed my children. My husband. My family. It was you, wasn't it?"

Something like a smile twisted the hoary features. "Yes, because I am a jealous child and will share you with none."

"So my reward for creating you was the curse I have carried my whole life?"

"The curse was not because you created me; the curse was because you abandoned me."

"I did not abandon you. The story ended. It had to end somehow. All stories must have an ending."

The monster leaned into Mary's face, glowering with rage. "Your story left me lost and alone, wandering in a frozen wilderness. You would not give me a partner, and so I stole from you all that you have ever loved. But *our* story has not ended. Not yet. I will kill you, but slowly. I am within you, a homunculus . . . a malevolence growing in the brain that spawned me."

"My headaches? That is you? Why are you punishing me? Why torture me when I merely wanted to tell your story?"

"You want sympathy?" The monster asked. "I have no tears to shed, because you put none in me. I am a living-dead thing, and the dead have no pity . . . and no remorse."

"But you are just a story I wrote. You aren't Not real."

"What is real? What is not real? There is nothing but stories. All life is naught but a story."

The two faced each other in silence. Mary expected a violent, painful death. But the monster turned and tromped away. But before it vanished into the shadows it turned back a final time and spoke. "Your bones will turn to dust, but I am made only of words, which can never die. But know this: your name will be shackled to mine for eternity, nameless though I be."

"Mary? Mary are you there?" It was Countess Ada's voice, calling to her.

Mary turned to see a feminine form hurrying toward her, her fluttering silk dress limned by firelight. "Ah, I see you now." Then Ada Lovelace gave out a little cry of fear and a hand flew up to mouth. She paused a moment and then crept forward, approaching cautiously. "How strange?" she said breathlessly, peering into the darkness. "For a moment I thought . . ."

Mary turned to look back at her monster, but it had vanished. She stood alone on the woodland path.

The Countess laughed shakily. "For a moment I thought I saw something horrible." She shook her head as she reached Mary and they embraced. "No. It was just a trick of the light."

Mary gripped Ada's arm. "The house . . . is it?"

"The house is lost," Ada answered. "It is so sad. But I have come to collect you. Mister Crosse has asked us all to gather on the road. Carriages and wagons from the nearby farms have been sent for. We will all be conveyed to Taunton." Ada's eyes pooled with tears. "Oh what a calamity. I grieve for poor Mister Crosse. And poor Cornelia. To lose one's home . . . and at his age. Surely this will kill him."

Mary replied with a sad smile and shook her head.

"Come," Ada said. She took Mary's hand and began to lead her away. Mary stooped to retrieve her travelling bag, and threw one last look behind her.

Her monster was gone, but the woods seemed full of its baleful presence, for death seemed to darken every shadow.

MEETING THE DEVIL

> Devil, cease; and do not poison the air with these sounds of malice. I have declared my resolution to you, and I am no coward to bend beneath words. Leave me; I am inexorable . . . Mary Shelley

Nessan O'Rourke lurked in the shadows of the arched stone bridge on the outskirts of Broomfield cursing his luck. On the way back to retrieve the travelling bag full of swag he'd stolen, he been greeted the welcome sight of Fyne Court burning. Just moments earlier he'd smelled smoke and then, at a turn in the forest path, he'd seen the quavering light and saw ahead the white two storey building with tongues of flame billowing out a second storey window. Recognising his own handiwork from earlier, he cackled with glee, but then he saw the canvas travelling bag where he'd set it down at the foot of a tree. It was but twenty feet away, but by now a great many servants were running to and fro, carrying buckets of water they were dousing on the flames.

O'Rourke gambled that he wouldn't be noticed amid all the hullabaloo and crept closer. He waited for an opportune moment and then stood upright and walked briskly toward the bag. He was about to pick it up when a servant ran up to him and pressed an empty bucket into his hand shouting, "Hurry, make yourself useful. Fill this at the well!"

As soon as the servant ran way, the Irishman tossed the bucket away and retreated back up the path where he dropped into a crouch and watched the chaos unfolding. But after ten more minutes he decided the meagre swag was not worth the risk of being caught— especially not with the dead man they had murdered filling a fresh grave in the churchyard. And so feeling cheated of his prize he skulked away into the forest and soon came out at the dirt lane where he trudged all the way to Broomfield empty-handed and cursing.

Now he had been waiting in the shadows under the bridge for what must have been an hour, but there was no sign of the Cornishman.

O'Rourke was not a sentimental man. He and Ryd Thorne were good thieving partners and had had some roistering times together. But all good times come to an end. Besides, when the hue and cry went up, as it would when they found the giant they had murdered, it would best if Thorne took the drop for the crime alone. He would not need any company on the gallows.

The Irishman left the shadows of the bridge and walked to the crossroads where he cast a glance in either direction. A carved mile- stone set in the weedy verge read "Bridgwater 2", not that O'Rourke could read. Still he stared along the dirt lane a long time, his wildly dilated eyes straining to sift a walking human shape from the shad- ows. But after another twenty minutes he gave up. No sign of the Cornishman. Ryd Thorne was not that clever a fellow. He'd probably been taken.

Ah well, the Irishman reasoned, he'd waited long enough.

O'Rourke suddenly remembered the bottle of laudanum in his pocket. He fished it out and smiled as he yanked the cork. The laudanum was cold and bitter as he swigged a mouthful, which puck- ered the insides of his mouth. He shuddered as he gulped it down and then raised the bottle a second time and sucked down the dregs, wiping his lips on the filthy sleeve of his jacket before hurling the bottle away where it shattered somewhere in the darkness.

After only a few minutes, a welcome warmth surged through his belly and wrapped a blanket of warm relaxation about his shoulders. And then he remembered the second bottle. Still fearful that Thorne might shuffle from the darkness at any moment and claim his share, O'Rourke dug out the second bottle. Even if he could read, O'Rourke would have been unable to decipher the apothecary's scrawl of faded blue ink that identified the contents as "Prussic Acid."

The Irishman yanked the resistant cork with his teeth and hovered a nose sprouting hairs over the open neck. It smelled sweet, and if O'Rourke had ever eaten almonds, he might have recognised the tell-tale smell of Prussic Acid. He put the bottle to his lips and swilled a mouthful. This bottle was even more bitter than the first and he grimaced as he choked it down. Still, he knew that all medicine tasted like poison but he was anxious for the effects, so he chased the first swallow with a second, long, Adam's apple-bobbing guzzle that emptied most of the bottle.

He swivelled his eyes to the sky, where the throb of amber light and rising shower of firefly sparks streaming up into the night sky confirmed that the Crosse house still blazed. By now his mood was mellowing and he no longer cared if Thorne had been taken by the hue and cry. Maybe he would cheekily wave to Thorne from the crowd as the poor fool climbed the scaffold at Bristol.

But then a very strange feeling began to creep over O'Rourke. It began as a vague sense of unease. And then he sucked in a sudden gasp as he became short of breath. It would only last a few seconds, he reasoned, and so he tipped up the bottle and drained it dry before hurling it away into the night.

Suddenly his stomach clenched and O' Rourke doubled over as if kicked in the guts by a horse. "Steady, there!" He managed to gasp before another spasm ripped through him, stronger than the first. Now his legs were quivering so that he reeled and fought to stay upright. Suddenly his knees buckled and he sat down on the iron-hard lane. His vision swam as currents of ice cold mercury surged through his veins.

"What the feck?" he bellowed aloud. "What'd I just drink?"

By now he was shivering uncontrollably. Unable to sit up by himself he flopped with his back propped against the milestone.

It was then he heard the slurred stir of footsteps on the road, moving toward him.

"At last, you're here!" He bawled aloud, thinking it must be the Cornishman. "But yer too late!" He laughed. "I done already drunk it all down."

He lifted his head and peered that way.

On the dark lane, a shadowy human form, only huge and hulking, shambled toward him.

O'Rourke's belly clenched painfully and he vomited black bile down the front of his jacket.

When he looked up the hulking form was upon him.

It was huge. A monster. It could have been the giant man they killed, only this one looked different. One half of the face was burned into a blackened and livid mass of swollen flesh. The hairs of the head had been scorched to a frazzle of black wires. Worst of all were the murderous eyes, which gleamed a bright yellow.

By now O'Rourke's body was limp and he could not move anything save to lift his head.

The monster stood at his feet and now it stooped down and brought its dreadful face close as it studied him. O'Rourke recognised the face instantly.

"You . . . you're the devil!"

The dead yellow eyes roved over the Irishman's face. Without anger. Without hatred. Only a disinterested curiosity.

"You're the devil, aren't ye?" The Irishman gasped. "Come to drag me off to hell?"

O'Rourke twitched with a violent spasm as he opened his mouth and vomited up another belly full of black bile. And then he felt cold death creeping through his body, like a nest of newly-hatched spiders bursting open and skittering in all directions.

"I'm dying! I'm dying!" He breathed as the dread realisation broke over him. Knowing that death was imminent, in his final moments O'Rourke tried to summon up a memory from his childhood in Ireland. A comforting image from a church service. A carved wooden saint. An angel from a stained glass window. Anything. But all he found when he looked inside was an empty, echoing darkness.

Instead, the monster's yellow eyes were the last thing he saw.

STRANGE STAR PURSUED

> *The whole series of my life appeared to me as a dream; I sometimes doubted if indeed it were all true, for it never presented itself to my mind with the force of reality ... Mary Shelley*

Mary's sole surviving son, Percy Florence Shelley was trying to read his book (Wilkie Collins', *The White Lady*) but his wife's piano playing, her fingers stumbling across the keys, stopping and starting every time she made a mistake (which was often) meant that he had read the opening paragraph five times without absorbing a scintilla of meaning. He finally snapped the book shut and hurled a look of exasperation at his wife (which, fortunately for him, she could not see from where she was seated at the piano). Percy Florence cleared his throat with phlegm-rattling irritation, then reopened the book and paged back to the beginning to try again . . . for the sixth time.

Although his easy chair was drawn up close to the fireplace he shivered as an frigid draught traced its icy fingers down his entire left side. He threw a puzzled look at the parlour door. It was closed, but a chilly gale was whooshing in from under the door jamb. With reluctance, he set the book down on an end table and got up to attend to the fire. Although the heaped coals glowed cheerily, the fireplace was doing little to actually warm the parlour with its high ceiling. Percy scooped another shovel full of coal from the brass bucket and tossed it on the fire. It was then that he noticed the draught again, which was so strong it was causing the fire to flare up. The draft was ferocious like a Niagara of icy cold air flowing into the room. He reached up for the bell pull beside the fireplace and gave it two sharp tugs. After only a few seconds the footman, a youth by the name of Atkins, entered the room.

"Ah, Atkins," Percy said. "There's a terrific draught in here. Go around the house and check that no windows have been left open."

The footman blinked stupidly, then said, "Uh, yes, Viscount Shelley. Right away, sir." The youth looked puzzled. It was December and no one in their right mind would be opening windows at this time of year, but he ducked a bow and left the room. Moments later he dashed back into the parlour, his face flushed with alarm.

"Su-Sir!" he stammered. "The front door's been left open. Wide open!"

Jane Shelley's dreadful piano playing arpeggio'd to a halt. "My word," she said. "Have we been burgled, Percy?"

But just then the maid of all work rushed into the room, wide eyed and wringing her white pinafore in both hands. "Sir, Ma'am, I just went to check on Mrs Shelley, but her bed's empty. She's gone, sir! And she ain't nowhere in the house!"

Percy Florence and his wife shared a look of utter bewilderment and then as one, everyone jumped to their feet and rushed through the house to the front door which was flung open to the night. There they found an inky handprint on the wallpaper next to the door, and more ink on the doorknob. When he touched it, Percy Florence found that the ink was still wet. What had happened was immediately obvious. His ailing mother, who had scarcely been conscious for the last two months, had somehow clambered from her bed, navigated the stairs, and escaped the house.

Percy Florence stood in the open doorway peering out at the roiling miasma. The fog was a London Particular, so dense he could scarcely make out the ghostly glow of the Gaslamps on the far side of Chester square.

And now his invalid mother was out there. Wandering somewhere in the bone-chilling fog.

Clad only in a thin nightgown.

Barefoot.

Alone.

Lost.

LOST AND FOUND

> *From you only could I hope for succour, although towards you I felt no sentiment but that of hatred. Unfeeling, heartless creator! You had endowed me with perceptions and passions and then cast me abroad an object for the scorn and horror of mankind . . . Mary Shelley*

Mary staggered, one arm outstretched, half blind in the dense fog, that she suddenly realised stank horribly of burning coal fires. No, not coal, she thought. Something else burning. Walking on the icy cobblestones froze her feet numb, but with her next step the ground suddenly felt warm and loamy. She stooped and touched her fingers to the ground and came up with a handful of dirt and dry leaves. *Where am I, she wondered? Have I passed through the square without reaching the streetlamp? Am I now in the small park at the square's centre? How did I get through the park gates? Were they somehow left wide open so that I chanced to pass through them?*

She looked left and right, but the view in all directions was screened by the dense roiling fog. And then she noticed that the air was warm. Fireflies danced in front of her face but then she saw that they were not fireflies but sparks and hot embers. And then she saw it in the near distance: a great fire. A grand house of two stories alight, orange flames leaping into the sky from the ruined roof. At the base of the house, she could see small figures scurrying about in a mad panic.

Where am I? She wondered. Her mind tumbled in free fall, thoroughly disoriented. She dallied for a moment, looking behind her. Perhaps she should try to retrace her steps, to get back to the cobbled square and her house. But the burning house provided the only light, and frightening though the spectacle was, she shuffled toward it.

When she drew close she saw a great many fine people and servants all fighting the save the house. *Wait* she thought. *This happened years ago when I visited Fyne court. But that was fifteen years ago and two hundred miles away in Somersetshire. How did I come to be here? What is happening?*

As she looked on, she saw the people she new fighting to save the doomed house. Andrew Crosse was helping his gamekeeper Tom battle the blaze. Servants had formed a human chain and were passing along buckets of water to Tom, who then scaled a ladder and hurled the water through an open window billowing with flame. Through the smoke and the panic and with charred embers falling from above, Mary noticed that none of them seemed to see her. But then she saw the women hanging back from the flames. Cornelia was wailing and weeping hysterically and being comforted by Countess Ada. And then she saw the woman standing at Ada's side.

It was herself, only younger, before her hair had gone to grey. Her doppelgänger was staring at her, mouth open, eyes wide in terror. And then she remembered the event. Remembered seeing herself standing at the edge of all the chaos as Fyne Court burned like a funeral pyre.

Ohmigod! Mary realised. *I am the doppglegänger!*

And like all doppelgängers, she was an omen of a death foretold. Her own.

~

Mary hurried along up the loamy paths deeper into the forest, her ink-stained nightgown snagging on thorns and ripping as she snatched it free. The storm clouds that had darkened the sky for so many hours had all drifted on, and now a ghostly crescent moon scythed through the scudding clouds. She hurried along the paths as fast as her faltering legs would carry her. She had no idea of where she was going. Her only thoughts were to flee. Run. Escape. She just wanted to get away. To distance herself from her younger incarnation.

And then as she ran, she heard the footsteps of someone or something moving toward her. And then a figure suddenly appeared a few feet away. It was not a monster but a man dressed in a clergyman's clothes. His hair was black and lank, and he cradled his injured right hand in his left. Mary was frightened but he was clearly more terrified of her. His dark eyes widened and a look of terror transfixed his face. Suddenly Mary remembered the young man. She pointed a finger at him and hissed: "You! I know who you are. I remember you now. You are the Reverend Philip Smith of Bridgwater."

The young man screamed in abject terror and turned to flee. Mary followed behind on the path as he bolted away around a turn in the footpath and vanished.

And as she moved further up the loamy paths the acrid smoke that had burned her straining lungs grew cool, and finally cold and no longer held the bonfire smell of burning wood and plaster, but was spiced with the brimstone tang of coal fires.

When she could stagger no farther, she stopped and leant a hand against a tree trunk for support. Only instead of bark she felt the rough texture of brick and mortar beneath her fingertips.

She looked around in puzzled wonder. She had passed without transition from deep forest into a city street, lined with handsome five storey brick houses. The hot smoke she had been choking on had become cool fog and the ghastly white orbs that hung suspended in the luminous grey veil were gas lamps. The soft forest loam beneath her bare feet had turned to cobblestones, cold and slippery with rime and frost. She looked about herself and realised that she was once again in Chester Square, somehow transported fifteen years and two hundred miles from Somersetshire to London.

She shrieked as a horrible groaning reverberated in the air. At first it sounded like the bellowing of a monster, but then Mary recognised it as a fog horn from a ship plying the Thames.

"Mareeeeeeeee!" a woman's voice called from somewhere in the fog. But the voice sounded neither like Countess Ada's nor Cornelia's. "Mareeeeeeee!" Came the disembodied cry again, but this time it was followed by a masculine voice shouting: "Mother!" And then, as if mocking the it, the first voice call called out "Motheeeeerrrrrr."

But then she saw it: a vague silhouette punching a man-sized hole in the fog as it lumbered toward her. It was her monster. It had unerringly followed her, just as it had pursued her these many years. And so she loosed her hold on the lamppost and staggered away, tottering blindly into the fog-swirling abyss.

The shape loomed toward her. Mary shrieked and swerved away into the fog, but took one stumbling step before her bare toes stubbed on something and she staggered to catch her balance. Just then the fog cleaved and the looming shape rushed forward and caught her in its arms. Mary unleashed a shattering scream and struggled to break free, but the arms would not release her and she was exhausted, her energy spent. But then she saw who had caught her: it was Percy Bysshe Shelley, her husband. He had not died after all. There had been no drowning, No mastless sailboat. No face nibbled to ribbons by fish. No hasty cremation on a foreign beach. No unburned heart snatched from the fire.

Somehow he had survived the slow grind of years. But he had grown old and bald. The once lithe body larded with fat. His youthful beauty faded into grey-bearded middle age.

"Mother!" the man gripping her by the shoulders shouted into her face. "Mother, why did you run away? You will catch your death!" And now she recognised the man. Not her husband but her son, Percy Florence Shelley.

Her energy spent, Mary's knees finally gave out and Percy Florence struggled to hold his mother up as she sagged in his arms. And then the darkness surged over her mind in a drowning wave and like a an exhausted swimmer who has flailed against the current for too long, she sank into oblivion.

STRANGE STAR DESCENDING

> *The agony of my feelings allowed me no respite; no incident occurred from which my rage and misery could not extract its food . . . Mary Shelley*

And so Mary was gathered up and carried back indoors where she was placed in the big armchair drawn close to the fire. Here she was wrapped in a blanket, a pillow placed behind her head, while Percy Florence and his wife rubbed the warmth back into her icy hands and frozen feet. Although she was peppered with questions—*Where did you get to? How did you get downstairs without help? How long were you out of bed?*—Mary did not speak or answer in any way, but passively sipped the restorative brandy when it was pressed to her lips. When she seemed fully warmed again, Mary was carried upstairs by Percy Florence and the young footman and returned to her bed where the sheets had been freshly crispened by a warming pan filling the room with the comforting smell of hot linen. When he was satisfied that his mother was comfortable, Percy

Florence kissed her on the forehead and then reached to turn down the lamp wick. Only then did Mary respond, with a protesting groan.

Percy Florence paused. "You wish me to leave the lamp mama?"

Mary made another groan.

Percy Florence paused, looking down at his mother. She had been unconscious for close to a month, which made her dramatic escape all the more remarkable. But now it seemed she had lost the power of speech. Her face was thin and near translucent. Surely the end must not be far. He reasoned that, he too, would not like to pass in the dark, and so he relented and turned the lantern wick back up.

"Sleep peacefully, mama," he said, and then quietly left the room.

Exhausted after her ordeal and lulled by the warm cocoon of blankets, Mary Shelley drifted into sleep. Memories tumbled through her mind like slow and clumsy clouds, caroming off the walls and bumping into one another. She remembered the worsening headaches. The more frequent doctor visits. What was his name? *Frankenstein? Freestone?* No, those were not the correct names. She groped for the physician's name but it was soap-slippery. She tried to sit up but her arms tremored violently as she tried to push herself up the dense wall of pillows. Too weak. How long had been unconscious? Days? No . . . more likely a week . . . or weeks!

She no longer had the headache, but she seemed to feel the presence of a throbbing void, a malevolent darkness coiled at the base of her brainstem. And it was growing until it would want all the space for itself. Mary accepted the truth that her death was imminent. She searched herself for fear. For anger. For remorse. But, chillingly, found nothing but indifference. She would die, just as everyone else had and will die. She had no fear of death because her life had been lived as well or as clumsily as any human life can be lived, and now she had come to the end of hers. She had nothing left undone. Nothing uncompleted. But then she opened her eyes and looked at the bedside table. There, waiting for her like a faithful dog, was her old friend: the green leather notebook she had carried through the years and her journeys around the world. Through the best of times and through the worst of times. It contained poetry, sketches, snatches of travel writing, and too many of the pages were stained by her own tears during the worst of times. And those, unfortunately, had been many. Far more than a woman such as herself deserved.

And then the realisation struck her like a bolt of summer lightning. She was leaving behind something unfinished: the story of how she had tried to loose the curse she had brought down on her own head, the curse of the monster that had dogged her life and brought down all the grief and loss she had suffered. Her eyes turned once more to the green journal. She drew a thin arm from beneath the bedclothes and reached for it, but her fingers closed on empty air. The leather journal lay beyond her grasp. She leaned her body over as far as the tight bedclothes allowed, but it was still out reach. She gathered herself for one final attempt and lunged. This time her fingers closed upon the concertina'd binding. But the journal was heavy, and her wasted muscles were weak. She had to pull with all her trembling might but a few moments later the journal lay open in her lap. Her quill pen stood waiting in its inkwell, but as she dragged it closer, blue ink spilled out, staining her fingers, the pillowcase, and the bedclothes. Careless of that, she wiped her hand on the sheets and then cracked the binding of the journal, turning to a page that had been marked with a green ribbon. Her eyes swept the cramped lines of her own handwriting as she read her last entry. A smile creased her face. It was her story.

Still intact.

But unfinished.

And so she drew the dripping quill from the inkwell, wiped the excess ink away, although a drop fell and blotted the page as she moved the pen to the end of the final line.

And then, with a trembling hand, Mary Shelley continued to write the end of her story.

STRANGE STAR EXTINGUISHED

> Bright star, would I were stedfast as thou art. Not in
> lone splendour hung aloft the night.And watching, with
> eternal lids apart, like nature's patient . . . John Keats

In the morning Jane Shelley entered Mary's room, threw a cursory glance at her sleeping mother in law and then snatched up the bedside brass bell to summon the maid of all work to empty the chamber pot and turn the bed down. She was about to tinkle the bell when she looked down at her mother-in-law and froze. The green leather journal lay open on her lap and her hand, which still clutched a quill, lay where it had fallen when she had dropped off.

Jane Shelley then noticed with horror the spreading stain of blue ink bleeding into the bedsheets and struggled to hold in a snarl of rage. The sheet was assuredly ruined, for she doubted the ink would come out in the wash. Cursing the old woman under her breath, Jane reached down to pluck the quill from Mary's grip. But when she touched Mary's hand she found the flesh gelid and the fingers stiff with rigor. Jane Shelley sucked in a sharp breath and lurched back.

Had it finally happened? Had she and her husband finally been released from their hideous burden?

Slowly, tentatively, Jane's slender fingers explored her mother-in-law's throat, feeling for a pulse. Finding none, she lifted the frail arm, and palpated the thin wrist. The skin was icy. Jane's fingertips traced up and down the blue arteries on Mary's throat but not even the feeblest pulse could be detected. Needing proof positive, the Baroness plucked a goose down feather from the pillow beneath Mary's head and placed it upon her cyanosed lips. Jane Shelley crouched over, her face within inches of Mary's, studying intently. For a full minute she watched. The feather did not move. A cautious smile spread across Jane's lips. And then a laugh burst from her and she clamped a hand over her mouth to stifle it.

Jane Shelley paused a moment to ready herself, composing her face in an expression of shock and grief. She even tried squeezing a few tears into her eyes, but they would not come. She turned her head to shout aloud—a cry of distress for the servants, a call for her husband to hurry to her aid. But then Jane's eye fell upon the green leather journal open on Mary's lap. It was nearly full, the pages filled with precise rows of her mother-in-law's neat handwriting. As Jane's eyes traced across the blue lines and squiggles, a single word jumped out:

Monster.

Curious, Jane struggled to pry the journal loose from Mary's rigor-stiffened fingers. Her eyes flickered up to the beginning to the page and she started to read. But after only a few words what she read caused her to suck in a breath. Her mouth went dry. Her head quivered atop her neck. She stopped reading. Thought a minute. And then she stepped to the bedroom door and quietly turned the key in the lock to prevent a servant from barging in on her. Jane Shelley returned to the bed and perched on the edge, next to the cooling body of her dead mother-in-law. Then she turned to the front of the journal, and began to read. And as she read her expression changed from smirking self-satisfaction to one of dread and dismay.

Jane Shelley read page after page, and soon lost track of time. She only came back to herself when she heard her husband's voice in the hallway. He was talking to the maid-of-all-work, asking her if she knew where her mistress was.

Jane Shelley slammed the journal shut and leapt up from the bed. Like a burglar caught in the act, she dithered with the journal in her hand, looking around the room for a hiding place, but then her eyes were drawn to the fireplace. She rushed to the fireplace and tossed the journal in. By now, the fire had burned low, with only a few glowing red coals still burning in the grate and the book threatened to smother them. Dense grey smoke plumed up from beneath the green leather. She grabbed the iron poker and lifted the journal in the grate, so that air could reach the coals and rekindle them. Soon, the coals reddened and began to burn. Jane propped the book at an angle on the andirons and after a few seconds, smoke rose again from the book and then red flames licked about its edges as the book began to burn. But then she heard her husband's voice just outside the door. Loud. Very close. She dropped the poker and hurried to the bedroom door, eased the key to unlock the door and then rushed to the bedside to strike a pose before he entered.

When Percy Florence Shelley entered the bedroom, he found a tragic tableau awaiting him.

His wife knelt at the bedside, his mother's limp hand pressed to her cheek, his wife's face a studied portrait of grief.

"J-Jane," he stammered. "Mother . . . is she . . . ?"

His wife blubbered, "My dearest husband, our beloved Mama is at last at peace . . ."

A long gasp of sorrow tore from Percy Florence's lungs. He tottered to the bed, his expression wretched, his eyes pooling with hot tears. He laid a hand upon his mother's forehead and said in a voice torn to rags "Oh my dearest Mama!" He grabbed his mother's hand and kissed it. Jane Shelley tolerated the lachrymose display, which curled her lip as excessive and unmanly, before she said, "Come comfort me, Husband, for we have lost our wonderful mother."

Percy Florence threw his arms about his wife, who stiffly accepted his embrace. But then he broke away and returned to his mother's body.

Noticing something amiss, he reached down and lifted his mother's hand, which still was frozen around her missing quill. "But look at my mother's hand. The ink! She must have been writing something."

Jane Shelley could not face her husband and looked away as if distracted.

"But what could she have writing?" He glanced around the room. "Where is my mother's green journal?

And then, for the first time, Percy Florence looked up toward the ceiling and noticed the areabesques of fine grey smoke curling there. "Something's burning!" He cried, and then his eyes were drawn to the fireplace and a horrified gasp tore from him.

"My mothers' journal!" He cast a baffled look at his wife. "But how did it come to be on the fire?"

Jane Shelley flustered a moment. "I cannot imagine . . . it . . .it . . . it" Her brain grappled to summon a believable excuse, but finally she realised it was futile, and so she said. "I placed it on the fire."

"What? You placed it . . .?" his voice broke in astonished exasperation. By now he had grown red in the face, his breathing rapid. "Why? Why would you burn it? Why would you do that?"

"I did it . . ." Jane struggled to think of a reason. "I did it . . . to protect you . . . beloved husband"

"To protect me? What on earth do you mean: to protect me? What kind of writing did it contain, wife?"

She shook her head carelessly. "In truth, I could not say" she turned her face away, lest he read the lie in her eyes. "I did not read it. Well, all of it. But it did not seem to be finished."

"If you did not read it, how on earth could you tell it was unfinished?" her husband demanded, his voice hardening. "What do you mean, unfinished? What was it about? What was the subject matter?"

Jane Shelley had the face of a liar who knows she has been caught in an untruth and is trying to lie her way free. "I . . . I noted that the handwriting seemed fresh and yet . . . I could scarcely read it for the ciphering was so tortured. Oh, but what little I could make out . . ."

She shook her head dismissively. "It was nothing. A trifle. Some nonsense about a trip to Somersetshire."

"A trip to Somersetshire?" Percy repeated the words and grew thoughtful.

His wife unleashed a careless laugh. "Yes, as I say, it, it, it seemed to be a story of some kind. A fiction. Oh, but it was very silly. The ideas were much muddled. Impossible to follow. For she was in a great home one moment and a castle the next and then wandering in a dense fog with bad men chasing about . . . and a monster—"

"A monster?" Percy Florence interrupted. "The same monster as in her novel Frankenstein?"

"Yes, no . . . I, I imagine . . . perhaps . . . " She trailed off. Forced another laugh. "Really, husband, do not look so concerned. Your poor mother has been an invalid these two years now. She has scarce been awake for much of the last two months. Her mind was in tatters—"

"The times she has been awake my mother's mind has been as keen as ever," Percy Florence Shelley fumed. "And now I seem to recollect some talk of her visiting Somersetshire. I was at Cambridge at the time. It was some ten or fifteen years ago. . ." he trailed off, eyes darting to and fro as he wracked his memory. "I seem to remember there was a purpose to her visit. Though later she claimed it was just to visit with friends in Bath. But at the time I was surprised and wondered at why she would undertake such an arduous journey with her health already declining." He thought long and hard as his wife turned away and pretended to be looking out the window. The morning light was beginning to sketch blurred outlines. In the foggy square a hulking form lurked in the splash of light beneath a street lamp, but Jane's fevered brain was too busy ravelling the knot of lies she was spinning to notice.

"I seem to recall her mention a gentlemen's name," Percy Florence said. "I think it was . . . Crosse . . . or Croft . . . or something very like that . . ."

Jane Shelley's head raised and her back stiffened at the mention of the name. Percy Florence noticed the change in her demeanour.

"Was that the name she wrote of?" He demanded. "Crosse?"

She hesitated before answering. "I, I . . . cannot precisely recall. Perhaps . . ."

"Perhaps?"

Jane Shelley's lips quivered. It was clear she could not meet his eye. "I'm not certain, but yeessssss. I believe it was."

"So was the journal entry an account of her visit, a travel piece? Or was it a story? A fiction?"

"I, well, it must have been a story. Yes. Clearly. A work of fancy. A fiction."

"But you just told me you read of bad men chasing people about? A monster? And yet this Crosse fellow was a real person?"

"No, husband, you are quite mistaken. I am sure it was all just a story."

"My mother told of me her and my father going to see a lecture given by a Mr Crosse when they lived in London. He was a gentleman scientist, an electrical experimenter who lived in Somersetshire."

"Again, I tell you husband. It was all naught but nonsense and silliness."

"And you burned it? Without letting me see it?" For the first time she met his gaze and saw anger flare in his face.

"Do not concern yourself, husband. It was not by your father. I made doubly sure of that. It was in your mother's hand. I knew it at first glance."

He shook his head wonderingly. "I had no idea my mother still wrote fiction."

"I . . . I have caught her scribbling a few times. Well, not caught. I should not say that. No, I should not use that word: *caught*. Only, a few times, when I came in to check on her, I noticed ink on her fingers. Often the journal would be open on her lap and the quill in her hand."

"What? I did not know this. And you never told me? Why did you not tell me?"

"I did not wish to trouble you. Beloved husband, your mother's illness has been enough for you to bear."

"And the journal, did you read what was in it?"

"You just said you didn't read it!"

She waved away his anger. "No . . . I meant merely that I did not read the *entire* book. I . . . I merely skimmed here and there."

"And upon that basis you took it upon yourself to burn my mother's writing?"

She forced a strained smile. "In truth, darling, it was no great loss. If anything, you should thank me. Your mother's powers as a writer had waned considerably with the years—"

"What was the novel about? What was the subject of the story?"

"I cannot for certain say. I, I, I seem to recall . . . I mean I am not sure, but I did see a reference or two to, to . . . a monster."

Thunderstruck, Percy's mouth fell open. "A mu-monster?" He stammered "As in the creature in *Frankenstein*? My mother wrote that when she was still but a girl. And this was a new story about her monster?"

His wife drew out her answer, fearful of saying too much. "I . . . suspect so. But it was a shallow imitation of the original. Let's be brutally honest, husband—your mother's only triumph was *Frankenstein*. She was probably trying to recapture a spark of that success. And your father, no doubt, was the true author of that horrid story." Her shoulders twitched with a dramatic shudder. "No *woman* could ever conceive of such dreadful things—"

"That's a bloody lie and you know it!"

"Husband! Do not profane in our house! Why do you treat me with such violence?"

"Because you have burned my mother's book and so silenced her voice forever!" Percy looked wildly at the fireplace. The notebook was still burning, the edges of the green leather jacket curling as he watched. He rushed to the fireplace, snatched up a poker, and used the hook end to drag the burning book from the coals. It tumbled out upon the hearthrug, where the ruined book sat smouldering. Soon its heat charred the rug beneath, filling the room with smoke and the eye-watering stench of burning wool. He dropped the poker on the hearth tiles with a ringing clatter. The pages were still alight and he batted at the flames with his hands, singeing his fingers and smudging them with black soot. But when he used the poker end to flip the smouldering covers open, Mary Shelley's words flew out as embers of burning paper, all her words turned to smoke and ash.

He let out scream of anguish. And though he batted at the book, feverishly, it was clear that only the very inward edges of pages, those closest to the binding, remained intact. The rest had been rendered into smokey ghosts. In the odd dozen or so partial pages remaining, Percy Florence's eyes scanned the rows of his mother's neat handwriting, sifting half-words, partial sentences, snatching tantalising references from the sad remains. He found familiar names and words like Crosse, Lovelace and monster, but most of each sentence had been erased by burning. He finally gave up and dropped the book and looked up at his wife with eyes red and smarting from smoke . . . and rage. His breathing was quick and ragged, his face visibly purpling like a darkening thundercloud.

Percy Florence Shelly rose slowly to his feet slowly and glared at his wife. It was an utterly murderous look that said, *I know what you have done and why you did it.* It was a look of pure poison that declared, *nothing between us will ever be the same again.*

"What you have done, wife . . . "Percy Shelley said in words cast in lead, ". . . is unforgivable. By burning her words you have killed my mother more certainly than her illness, because her writings are immortal."

Because Percy Shelly had been mollycoddled since birth by his mother, Jane Shelley had always dominated her weak-willed husband. Now she decided, wrongly, that standing up to his anger was the best strategy. She threw her head back and glared at him with haughty disdain. "Husband, do not assume such a tone with me—" she could say no more as in flash Percy Shelley had snatched up the poker with one hand and seized his wife by the throat with his other. His face was mottled with red spots of anger. Spittle foamed upon his lips. He raised the poker in his trembling hand high above her head, ready to fall like the hammer of a cocked pistol, ready to smash her skull and dash her brains to the walls.

Percy's grip on his wife's throat tightened until her eyes bulged and she released a choking sound. He suddenly came back to himself, and realised what he was about to do. Slowly, he lowered the raised poke, and finally released his grip on his wife's throat.

She tore away from him and rushed from the room, emitting a horrible squawking noise.

Clara, the maid-of-all-work, rushed into the room. "Sir!" She cried. "Whatever's amiss?"

Percy Florence looked at the young maid's startled face with resignation. "My dear sweet mother has passed. Send for the undertaker . . . and a doctor. We will need a death warrant."

ALL STORIES MUST END

M ary awakened into darkness.
    Total.
    Absolute.
No . . . not quite.

After several moments, she discerned that this darkness had depth, darker currents flowing within the sea of blackness. As if she was at nexus in a collision between darknesses: the one from without and one from within her mind.

She looked about. Desperate. But this time there was no companion star. She tried to open her eyes, but felt a pressure on them. A weight. when she put a hand to them, two coins fell away and her eyes sprang open.

She was in her bedroom in her house on Chester Square.

Alone.

For a moment she wondered: *Why had someone placed coins on her eyes?* And then the dreadful truth came to her.

Am I dead? She wondered. I*s this Is this how it feels to be dead? But it feels no different. Or does it?*

She looked about her room. The events of the previous night continued to play out in her mind. She had run toward her monster only to run back to the time and place it had taken physical form, back in Somersetshire and that fateful night the Crosse house burned to the ground. But as she looked back on it, the events seemed silly and fantastic. Surely that was all just one of her airy nothings.

Andrew Crosse,

Ada, Countess of Lovelace.

Dr Richard Freestone.

Were those real people or just characters in one of her made up stories? Just more of her airy nothings. And then she thought of her husband, Percy Byssshe Shelley, young and handsome in his drop front trousers and tight-waisted jacket. Her sister Claire Claremont. Dr Polidori. Lord Byron, with his exquisite curls and cruel beauty.

Were these real memories or just characters in one of her stories?

Her life. Her past . . . seemed unreal. A story. A fiction. A tale.

She caught a sudden motion in the corner of one eye as a child ran past her bed. She looked but found nothing. Had she imagined it? Was she in a dream of death? Or had her life been just a dream?

But then a small head rose up at the bottom of the bed, shyly peeking at her over the bedclothes. Then it ducked out of sight, only to appear again at a different corner of the bed. The head belonged to a little boy with fine blonde hair. He peek-a-booed again and flashed a delighted smile, giggling as he ducked out of sight again. And then Mary realised that she knew that giggle, that devilish smile.

"Willmouse?" She called out. "Willmouse is it you?" The boy jumped up in full view laughing and clapping his hands as he darted around the room, only now he was being chased by two little girls. Mary's heart surged as she recognised them. Her two girls, Clara, and the child who had died as a mere babe. The children giggled as they joined hands and ran into the corner of the room, where they plunged into the shadows and vanished. It was only then she noticed the young man sitting in a straight-backed chair at the foot of the bed. The figure smoked a pipe as he hunched over a sheet of paper upon which he was scribbling lines of writing. The quill he held in his ink-stained fingers scratched across the vellum but then he paused a moment as if to reflect upon the line he had just penned. He seemed to become aware of her gaze and looked up, smiling a familiar smile. It was her husband, Percy Bysshe Shelley, as she had known him in their early days, years before he slipped from his sailboat and drowned in the Gulf of La Spezia.

Mary realised what was happening to her: *My brain is dying, emptying itself of a lifetime of memories.*

She suddenly noticed a figure lounging against the mantlepiece. It was Lord Byron, his noble head bowed as he studied a manuscript, his Byronic curls lit by the ruddy glow of the fire. At that moment Byron looked up from the manuscript he was reading and his eyes locked with Mary's. He lifted the manuscript slightly and nodded, a mocking smile playing about his lips. Then she recognised the sheaf of papers he was reading, It was the rough pages of her fist rough draft of *Frankenstein* and Byron's gesture had been a salute of recognition.

Byron strolled across the room and handed the manuscript to another young man. It was Doctor Polidori, who took the manuscript, smiled, and bowed slightly in Mary's direction. Then he turned and walked into the shadows of the corner of the room and melted away.

Now Mary was alone, as all the phantoms of her past had vanished. Her vision seemed to darken and her heart leapt up with fright. But then she realised that the room was dimming while the fireplace was growing, widening, expanding until it filled the far wall. The sad remnants of her green journal still burned on the fire grate, reduced now to the final remnants of the blackened binding. And then she realised the back of the chimney breast was retreating, as the fireplace stretched into a long, sooty tunnel.

And then she felt a change. A shift in gravity as the room distorted around the gaping fireplace and something dreadful approached. She saw a distant figure approaching through the darkness, and She recognised it instantly from its shambling gait as the stuttering walk of corpse sewn together from arms and legs of odd sizes. At last it reached the end of the tunnel and stepped over the burning fire grate and into the bedroom.

Her monster.

The face, as always, changed with each incarnation but remained hideous. The body was a butcher shop assemblage of limbs of disparate sizes, so that the crooked creature hobbled on legs of unequal length. Apart from some ragged clumps of matted hair, the grizzled head was criss-crossed by train tracks of stitches zig-zagging across a necrotic face sewn together from random slabs of corpse meat. It tottered forward with its ponderous mass until it stood at the foot of Mary's bed, looking down upon her with its pitiless, yellow-eyed gaze.

"You are too late," Mary said. "I am already dead."

The creature slowly shook its hoary head. "Not dead yet . . . dying."

"Then destroy my body, but I have already been destroyed by the the loss and grief you have visited upon me."

The creature tilted its head as it looked down on her. "You want sympathy? I have no tears because you put none in me."

"Go on. Murder me. Take your revenge."

"I murder *you*? It was you who murdered me. I was born from murder, stolen from death and dragged screaming into a life I never sought by a thunderbolt's violence. I have not come to kill you. You will die and your bones will turn to dust but you and I are bound by an umbilicus you can never cut. Your name will forever be shackled to me, nameless though I be.

I who have never lived can never die. But as my name is forever shackled to yours, neither can you die."

"Why haunt me? What torment me? My whole life? I created you!"

"You who are my creator ask me that? You abandoned me as my story tells."

"What do you ask of me?"

"One thing I always asked for and was never given in my story . . . to be loved. That is all. The same thing you have always asked for yourself."

"Yes, that is true. To be loved is all I have ever craved."

"Then come, we must love each other."

The Monster crawled onto the bed and folded his great limbs so that he could lay his head upon her breast.

"Am I not your child, too?"

"Yes."

"Though I am unlovable."

"No. That is not true. I love you as a mother must love all her children."

The bed shook as the monster convulsed as sobs wracked the great frame.

Mary said, "Your eyes are wet. So you do have tears to cry?"

"Yes, Before I had only rage in my heart, but now you have given me the gift of sorrow."

"I had much sorrow to share. A lifetime's worth."

"But sorrow is sweet, because nothing speaks more true of the loss of love."

"Yes. But shush, I am dying now and must prepare for the long journey into death."

"No, you are not dying. You are becoming immortal. Together you and I can never truly die."

"Yes . . . yes . . . yesssssss . . .

As she exhaled the word the monster held his lips close to hers to share her final breath.

Where are we going, monster?

Into the darkness.

I am afraid.

Be not.

Yes.

The End

PLEASE LEAVE ME A REVIEW

Did you enjoy this book? If so, please leave a review. Reviews really help build readership and ensure more books like this in the future.

Thank you in advance and warmest wishes.

Vaughn Entwistle, Cheltenham, England 2019

ABOUT THE AUTHOR

Vaughn Entwistle grew up in Northern England, but spent many years living in the United States, first in Michigan, (where he earned a Master's Degree in English at Oakland University), and then in Seattle (where he worked as an editor/writer and also ran a successful gargoyle sculpting business for ten years. Yes, really!). He currently lives in the English spa town of Cheltenham.

Find out more about the author and his books at his website:
www.vaughnentwistle.com

GET A FREE SHORT EBOOK!

Get a free copy of my short ebook, *The Necropolis Railway,* by signing up for my occasional newsletter at my author website:
www.vaughnentwistle.com

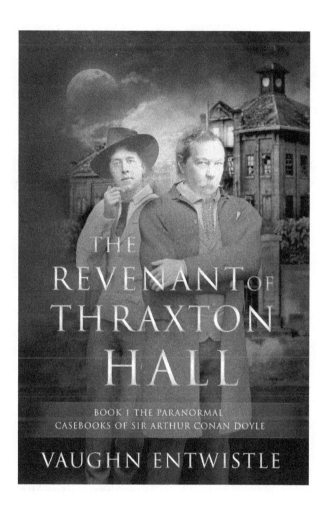

The Revenant of Thraxton Hall

"My murder will take place in a darkened séance room—shot twice in the chest." The words are a premonition related to Arthur Conan Doyle when he answers a summons for help from a mysterious woman who identifies herself only as "a Spiritualist Medium of some renown." The house is a fashionable address in London. The woman's voice is young, cultured and ethereal. But even with his Holmesian powers of observation, Conan Doyle can only guess at her true identity, for the interview takes place in total darkness. Suspicious of being drawn into a web of charlatanism, the author is initially reluctant. However, the mystery deepens when he returns the next day and finds the residence abandoned.

1893 is a tumultuous year in the life of the 34-year old Conan Doyle: his alcoholic father dies in an insane asylum, his wife is diagnosed with galloping consumption, and his most famous literary creation, Sherlock Holmes, is killed off in *The Adventure of the Final Problem*. It is a move that backfires, making the author the most hated man in England. But despite the fact that his personal life is in turmoil, the lure of an intrigue proves irresistible. Conan Doyle assumes the mantle of his fictional consulting detective and recruits a redoubtable Watson in the Irish playwright, Oscar Wilde, who brings to the sleuthing duo a razor-keen mind, an effervescent wit, and an outrageous sense of fashion.

"The game is a afoot" as the two friends board a steam train for Northern England to attend the first meeting of the *Society for Psychical Research*, held at the mysterious medium's ancestral home of Thraxton Hall—a brooding Gothic pile swarmed by ghosts. Here, they encounter an eccentric mélange of seers, scientists, psychics and skeptics—each with an inflated ego and a motive for murder. As the night of the fateful séance draws near, the two writers find themselves entangled in a Gordian Knot that would confound even the powers of a Sherlock Holmes to unravel—how to solve a murder *before* it is committed."

"Marvellous fun . . . delightfully swift reading, and when all is said and done, rather spiffy too."—**British Fantasy Society**

"Grand Guignol fun. Entwistle is an original who has assembled a delicious, extravagantly eccentric cast of characters."—**Open Letters, An Arts and Literature Review**

"London's gaslights sputter and the game's afoot in The Revenant of Thraxton Hall, a witty, atmospheric tale featuring the unique detecting duo of Arthur Conan Doyle and Oscar Wilde." – **Cara Black**

"The Revenant of Thraxton Hall is a delight. It's a treat to meet the great detective's creator (Arthur Conan Doyle) as a sleuth in his own right. And partnered with Oscar Wilde—what a bold and wonderful conceit!"—**John Lescroart**

EXCERPT—CHAPTER 1: A VOICE IN THE DARK

Sherlock Holmes is dead ... and I have killed him.

The smartly dressed Scotsman stared blindly through raindrops beading down the hansom cab window. Submerged in reverie, he did not notice that the cab had stopped. He did not see the limestone residences with marble steps guarded by iron railings. All he heard, all he saw, were the misty wraiths of the world's greatest consulting detective and his arch-nemesis, Dr Moriarty, as they plummeted into a cataract of roaring waters, grappling in a final death-struggle.

A hatch in the ceiling above his head opened and the driver of the hansom cab rained down a patter of gravelly syllables: "We're here, guv'nor."

The words jolted Arthur Conan Doyle into awareness. The seething vapours of the Reichenbach Falls evaporated and a London street materialised before him. He blinked, at a momentary loss. Where was he? Why had he taken a cab? Then he looked down at his lap and the torn envelope curling in the grip of his rain-dampened gloves.

A courier had delivered the letter that morning to his South Norwood home in the suburbs of London. He drew the creamy paper from its envelope and shook it open. The handwriting was elegant and unmistakably feminine. For a moment Conan Doyle's soft brown eyes traced the loops and whorls of the penmanship.

> *Dear Dr. Doyle, I crave an audience with the noted author of the Sherlock Holmes stories on a concern of the utmost gravity. This is a matter of mortal peril, and I believe that only an intellect such as yours can prevent a tragedy. Please visit me at number 42 Tivoli Crescent on Tuesday morning. Arrive no earlier than 10:00 a.m.*
>
> *Please, help. I am a lady in desperate straits.*

In place of a signature the letter was signed with an elegant flourish.

An anonymous address.

A nameless summoner.

But as he tilted the page to the light, a phoenix watermark floated up from the fine stationery. Despite himself he felt the stirrings of a coalescing mystery that would have intrigued his Sherlock Holmes.

A figure brushed past the cab window—he caught a vague, rain-blurred impression of a man in a hat, walking head down, a hand to his chin. No, holding something to his mouth—a cigarette or a pipe.

It was the briefest of glimpses. A momentary flash. And then it was gone.

The cab driver yanked a lever; the cab door flung open and Conan Doyle stepped down from the hansom. As he rummaged his pockets for loose change, a spectre of tobacco smoke still swirled in the damp London air. His head snapped up as he caught a whiff. He threw a quick glance to his side, but saw only rain-puddled pavements and the endless parade of city traffic: black two and four-wheelers drawn by plodding horses, their breath pluming in the damp air, hooves clop-clopping on the wet cobblestones.

The smoker had vanished.

He shook the image from his head and handed up two shillings to the driver. As he turned and took a step toward the glistening marble steps, it occurred to him to ask the cabbie to wait.

But too late—the driver whistled, shook the reins, and the cab clattered away.

Conan Doyle paused to peer up at the elegant, six-storey Mayfair home. But when he raised his head, an icy March rain needled his eyes. He dropped his gaze and, in a fashion surprisingly nimble for a big man, skipped up the rain-slick steps, anxious not to dampen his best top hat and coat.

The entrance of number 42 Tivoli Crescent featured a magnificent, eight-panelled oak door painted a deep, Venetian red. A large brass knocker provided the door's centrepiece—a phoenix rising from its nest of flames.

The exact double of the notepaper's watermark.

His gloved fingers grasped the knocker, raised it, and brought it sharply down upon its anvil with the percussive report of a pistol shot. He was about to knock a second time when the door flung inwards, snatching the brass phoenix from his grasp.

A red-turbaned footman—a Sikh gentleman—swept the door aside as if he'd been lurking behind it.

Waiting.

Wordlessly, the servant drew Conan Doyle inside with a low bow and a beckoning wave of his white-gloved hand. The entrance hall, though opulent, was a gloomy snare of shadows. His breath fogged the air—it was colder inside than out. The footman took his hat and coat without a word, hung them upon a naked coat stand, and led the way to a closed set of double doors.

"Please to wait inside, sahib," he said in heavily accented English.

The servant bowed again and held the door open. Conan Doyle stepped inside—and recoiled. The room was some kind of windowless antechamber, sparsely furnished with low couches and bookshelves. But further detail was hard to make out, as the room was even darker than the entrance hall. The only illumination came from the stuttering light of a single gas jet turned low.

"Just one moment!" Conan Doyle began to protest, "Am I to be cast into the darkness?"

Despite his complaints, the door was softly but firmly shut in his face.

"Wait! What? What is the meaning?" he yelled and snatched at the door handle, which refused to turn.

Locked.

Outraged, he rattled the handle and banged a meaty fist on the door.

"See here, you fool, you've locked me ..." Conan Doyle fell silent as he tumbled to the truth: it was no accident.

In rising dudgeon, he strode across the room to the far door and seized the knob. But a firm yank revealed that, it too, was locked. The young doctor released a gasp of astonished umbrage and looked about. For several seconds he wrestled with the notion of seizing one of the end tables to use as a battering ram. But then the words of the letter ran through his head:

This is a matter of mortal peril and I believe that only an intellect such as yours can prevent a tragedy.

Already half-convinced that he was being drawn into a web of charlatanism, Conan Doyle hitched up the legs of his trousers and dropped onto a cold leather couch, nostrils flaring as he gave a snort of indignation.

Minutes passed. Anger turned to curiosity as he idled, peering around the room. It became an interesting sort of game, trying to fathom what was going on—the kind of game that Holmes—*NO! That part of my writing life is over. Holmes is dead and I am finally free to write the serious books I wish to write.*

In the room beyond he heard a soft bump followed by the snick of a key turning in a lock. His eyes remained fixed upon the door, expecting it to open, but it remained closed.

"Doctor Doyle," a high, musical voice trilled from the other side. "If you would be so kind as to join me."

Conan Doyle sprang to his feet, dithered a moment, then strode to the door and flung it wide. To his surprise, the room beyond was even darker. The guttering gas jet behind him threw only a wan slab of light that sketchily illumined a hulking leather armchair. Everything else—the remainder of the room and its mysterious occupant—lay drowned in umbrous shadow.

My God! He thought. *It's a trap! I'm being kidnapped.* He owned a pistol, but seldom carried it.

Now he very much wished his service revolver was tucked into his waistcoat.

Every instinct told him not to enter the room. Undoubtedly a gang of ruffians crouched in the shadows, waiting to spring upon him. But then the memory of the kohl-eyed servant conjured more exotic visions: a Thuggee assassin with his knotted silken kerchief, anxious to slip it around a white man's throat and snap his neck.

"Now see here!" Conan Doyle barked, hoping the steel in his voice would mask his rising fear. "I trust I have not been sent on a fool's errand. I am a busy man and have many pressing affairs—"

"Please, Doctor Doyle, forgive the unorthodox greeting. If you would kindly take a seat, I can explain."

Despite his fear, there was something about the voice, an earnestness that made him wish to linger, to find out more about its owner. He stiffened his posture and harrumphed noisily to show that he was not a man to be trifled with, then threw back his shoulders and strode into the room, his large hands balled into fists, ready to hurl a punch. When he stood before the armchair the voice spoke again: "Please sir, be seated."

In the gloom, the chair proved lower than he estimated, the drop farther, and he thumped into the cushion with a spine-jarring jolt, expelling air with an "oof!" The door, which he had left ajar, groaned slowly shut under its own weight and latched with a clunk. Darkness blindfolded his eyes. Shadows bound him to the chair. Arthur Conan Doyle found himself a prisoner of obsidian night.

Total.

Absolute.

He gripped the arms of the leather chair, feeling suddenly off-balance.

"I beg you, sir," the voice soothed. "Do not be alarmed. I-I owe you an explanation: the reason we must meet in darkness."

The leather arms creaked as he slackened his death grip.

"You are obviously at great pains to conceal your identity," Conan Doyle said, his mind racing ahead. The attempt at anonymity was pointless—it would be a simple matter to trace the owner of such a distinctive house.

"No," the woman said. "The reason is that I suffer—" Her voice grew taut, "I suffer from an affliction."

"An-an affliction?" Conan Doyle started at the sudden loudness of his own voice. Hideous visions flashed before him. The woman must suffer from a disfiguring disease. "An affliction?" he repeated, affecting a neutral tone.

"Do not be concerned," she hurried to reassure. "It is not contagious. It is, rather, a disease carried through the bloodlines of my family. For me, every ray of sunlight is a needle dipped in arsenic. Even the wan glow of a lamp is a cloud of slow poison oozing through my skin."

For moments, Conan Doyle did not speak, his pulse quickening. As a doctor he had heard talk of such an ailment: *porphyria*, a congenital disease. There was even a rumour that this malady touched the family of the royal personage.

Think, Arthur! He chided himself. *Think as your Holmes would do.*

By now Conan Doyle was finding the total darkness oppressive and a rising sense of vertigo told him that the chair and the floor beneath his feet were rotating slowly backwards and to the left. The sensation was strengthened by the impression that the woman's voice seemed to be moving around the room, first left and now right and then, most disturbingly, floating up to where he imagined the ceiling to be.

He blinked and his vision swarmed with ghosts. As a medical man and student of the eyes, he knew the spectres were a natural phenomenon—the light receptor cells on the surface of the retina firing spontaneously like mirrors bleeding light in a darkened room. Deprived of sight, Conan Doyle opened his other senses to sieve every possible clue. First, the voice. Female. Definitely. He had seen convincing fakes on the stages of the less-reputable music halls. And while strolling in the most dangerous parts of London, seeking physical sights and sounds and sensations for his mysteries, he had been solicited by lissom creatures who dressed in daring women's fashions but who possessed Adam's apples and husky voices.

No, he was certain. The voice sprang from feminine lips. But there was something about it, an uncanny aspect. His mind summoned the word from the shadows around him—ethereal.

"I understand you wish to protect the good name of your family," Conan Doyle said. "But might I know at least your first name?"

A momentary silence followed as the woman mulled his request. "Forgive me, but I wish to remain anonymous. However, should you find it in your power to assist me, I will reveal all."

He cleared his throat. "I am a writer, madam, a mere scribbler of tales. I do not know what I could possibly—"

"It is a case of murder," she said bluntly.

The words cradled on Conan Doyle's tongue languished and died. "Murder?" he repeated.

"Murder. Violent. Sudden." Her final words came out in a strangled voice, "And premeditated."

Conan Doyle cleared this throat. He had somehow known this was coming and dreaded it. "I am afraid I cannot help you, madam. I am no policeman. Nor am I a detective. However, I do have many contacts at Scotland Yard—"

"I have already spoken to the police," she interrupted, disdain icing her words. "As to the detectives at Scotland Yard, they were—I am afraid to say—unable to offer the least assistance."

"But as I said, I am no policeman."

"And yet you have created the greatest detective of all time?"

There was a time Conan Doyle would have been flattered by the compliment, but now he felt only irritation. "A trifling fiction, madam. It is a common misconception held by my readers. Sherlock Holmes is a mere phantasm of my imagination. A bit of whimsy. All my adventures, I am afraid, have taken place at my writing desk. All in my mind."

He did not bother to inform her that he had recently killed off the "greatest detective of all time." All of London would soon be buzzing with the news.

"And is the mind not the most dangerous battlefield one can explore?"

It was a penetrating observation and left him momentarily groping for a rejoinder.

"As I previously stated, madam. I am not with the police. If you believe a murder has taken place—"

"No, Mister Doyle," the woman hastened to explain. "That is my problem. I need you to solve a murder … that has not yet taken place."

Leather squeaked as he shifted in the armchair. He fought the giddy sensation that her voice had swooped above his head and she now stood behind his chair, a hand hovering over one shoulder, ready to alight.

"I am sorry, I do not understand you."

"I will be murdered in two weeks time."

"Has someone threatened your life? How can you possibly know—?"

"I am a spiritualist medium of some renown. I have moments of clairvoyance. Visions of events that have yet to happen. For the last two years I have had the same premonition. The details loom sharper with time. In two weeks I will be murdered during a séance—shot twice in the chest."

The fiction writer in Conan Doyle immediately saw the logical flaw in such a story. "But if you can foresee the future, then surely you must see the face of your murderer?"

"Unfortunately, no. That is hidden from me. The room is lit by only a single candle and the faces of the sitters are little more than smudges of light and shadow. There is, however, one face that is recognisable—the face of the sitter on the murderer's left hand. Until a year ago, I had no name to put to that face. But then I saw a photograph in the *Strand Magazine* of an esteemed author. It was your photograph: Doctor Arthur Conan Doyle, the true genius behind Sherlock Holmes. You are the man I see in my visions."

Moments passed before he found his voice. "Madam. Many people have dreams, visions—what you will. Most are silly, illogical and only have a meaning we ascribe to them. Few truly foretell the future."

His words marched out into the darkness and tumbled over a cliff into silence.

When the woman spoke again, there was a hitch in her voice. "I believe these dreams, Mister Doyle. I believe I will be murdered. I also believe you are the only one who can prevent my death. Will you please help me?"

The voice seemed to be moving, gliding past his left shoulder. A faint breeze caressed his cheek. His nostrils pooled with the musk of perfume. He heard the swish of silken thighs brushing together, a sound that sprang prurient visions into his mind. He imagined a young woman, dressed in northing more substantial than the diaphanous pantaloons of a harem girl. He found himself becoming aroused and wiped his sweaty palms on the arms of the chair, struggling to empty his mind of such thoughts.

After all, he was a married man. A gentleman. A doctor.

"What do you say, Doctor Doyle?" He started as he felt warm breath lick the bowl of his ear. She must be standing next to him. Touchably close. "Will you help a young woman in distress?"

Something in her voice made him want to believe. Want to help. Want to save her.

But then he thought of his wife. Of the impropriety.

The year just passed had been the most turbulent in Conan Doyle's thirty-five years. His father, Charles Altamount Doyle, had finally died in a madhouse after a life-long battle with melancholia and alcoholism. His beloved wife Louise had been diagnosed with galloping consumption and, despite the advances of modern medicine, her lungs were shredding to rags. He could not help this young woman for many of the same reasons he had killed off his most successful artistic creation, Sherlock Holmes, for Arthur Conan Doyle no longer believed in a world where a man—even a man with advanced powers such as a Consulting Detective or a Medical Doctor—could alter Fate.

"I-I am afraid I must decline," he stuttered. "But as I said, I personally know many of Scotland Yard's best—"

"Thank you for your time, Mister Doyle," the woman interrupted, her voice cracking with disappointment. "You have been most kind."

"No, I beg you to reconsider. My offer is genuine. Inspector Harrison is a personal friend—"

"I will detain you no longer. Please forgive the imposition."

He felt a stir in the air currents and heard a soft bump followed by the rasp of a key turning in a lock. The mysterious woman has slipped silently from the room.

He was left to grope his way out in the darkness.

Alone.

～

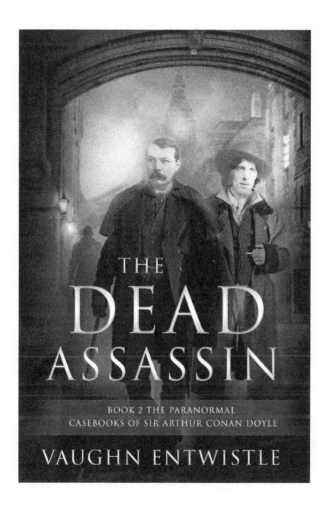

1895. Victorian England trembles on the verge of anarchy. Handbills plastered across London scream of revolution and insurrection. Terrorist bombs are detonating around the capitol and every foreigner is suspected of being a bomb-throwing Anarchist lurking beneath a cape. Even Palace officials whisper warnings of a coup-de-tat.

Dr. Arthur Conan Doyle is summoned from a peaceful dinner in the palm-room of the Tivoli restaurant to the scene of a gruesome crime that has baffled and outraged Scotland Yard's best. A senior member of Her Majesty's government has been murdered—assassinated—in the most brutal and savage fashion. The body of his attacker lies several streets away—riddled with pistol bullets that inexplicably failed to stop him from carrying out his lethal mission. More perplexing, one of the attending detectives recognises the dead assassin as Charlie Higginbotham, a local Cockney pickpocket and petty thief. Higginbotham is not just an improbable suspect, but an impossible suspect, for the young detective collared Charlie for the murder of his wife and watched him take the drop two weeks previously, hanged at Newgate Prison.

Conan Doyle calls in his friend Oscar Wilde for assistance and soon the two authors find themselves swept up in an investigation so bizarre it defies conventional wisdom and puts the lives of their loved ones, the Nation, and even the Monarch herself in dire peril.

The murders continue, committed by a shadowy cadre of seemingly unstoppable assassins. As the sinister plot unravels, an implausible theory becomes the only possible solution: someone is reanimating the corpses of executed criminals and sending them shambling through the London fog ... programmed for murder.

"With a truly likeable detective duo, a very strong plot, and a marvellous grasp of characterisation, *The Dead Assassin* is a marvellous read."—**Book Bag.**

"The main reason I like this series so much is the steam-powered London setting, the kooky nature of the narrative and the outright cheek of the author with his fast, fun-tastic dialogue throughout . . ."—**British Fantasy Society**

"... a mesmerising combination of mystery elements and delightful British humour."—**Rising Shadow**

EXCERPT—CHAPTER 1: MURDER
MOST 'ORRIBLE'

A murder. Something nasty. Something twisted. Something baffling and bizarre. Why else would the police have sought me out?

Such thoughts rattled through the mind of Arthur Conan Doyle as he watched Detective Blenkinsop of Scotland Yard step into the palm-room of the *Tivoli* restaurant and sweep his blue-eyed gaze across the crowded tables, searching for something.

Searching for him.

Go away blast you! Not now. Not tonight!

Thanks to the fame Sherlock Holmes had bestowed upon him, Scotland Yard often consulted Conan Doyle on crimes that eluded the capabilities of conventional detection. They dragged to his door the most difficult cases. The inexplicable ones. The conundrums. The impossibly knotted yarn balls the clumsy fingers of the police could not unravel. Ordinarily, he was flattered to be consulted on such cases. But on this occasion, he wished he could throw a cloak of invisibility about his shoulders.

Determined not to make eye contact, he reeled in his gaze from the detective and lavished it instead upon his dinner companion. At just twenty-four years of age, Miss Jean Leckie was a ravishing beauty fourteen years his junior. The two had by happy accident occupied adjacent chairs at the November meeting of the *Society for Psychical Research*. In brief conversation it fell out that Miss Leckie shared Conan Doyle's fascination with Spiritualism and all things occult. After the meeting adjourned, she accepted the older man's invitation to supper, where she had just revealed—over a sumptuous repast of boiled fowl a la béchamel, braised parsnips and crab stuffed courgettes—that she herself was an amateur medium who had conducted a number of successful séances.

Throughout their conversation, Conan Doyle fought the urge to stare, but when he gazed into those hazel-green eyes, sparkling with fire and intelligence, his knees trembled like a schoolboy's in the throes of his first crush.

But it wasn't just Conan Doyle who found himself under the thrall of Miss Leckie's beauty. She was a radiant presence that coaxed furtive glances from other dinner patrons, both male and female, sitting at adjacent tables. Under the Tivoli's electric lights, her dark golden hair shone. Her long face, with its high cheekbones, strong chin and aquiline nose, evinced the classical proportions of a Greek bust. In their initial conversation, he had been struck by the musicality of her voice, and was thrilled to discover that she was a classically trained mezzo-soprano. And so, with every revelation of her wit, character, and accomplishments, Conan Doyle was drawn in deeper. By the time the bread pudding arrived at the table, hot and steaming in its tureen, he was utterly smitten.

For her part, Miss Leckie seemed as equally attentive of him, for she caught the look of discomfort that flashed across his face when he glimpsed the arrival of Detective Blenkinsop.

"Are you quite well, Doctor Doyle?" she asked. "You seem suddenly quite distracted."

Conan Doyle chanced to dart a quick look across the dining room and locked eyes with Detective Blenkinsop, who now steamed toward them with the dread determination of a mechanical homing torpedo.

"I'm afraid I have just seen someone I know."

A frown upset her perfect features. "Oh? Someone who shall be joining us?"

"Quite the opposite. Someone, I fear, who shall be tearing us apart."

Conan Doyle snatched the linen napkin from his lap, crumpled it in his fist, and tossed it down on the table. It had been a delightful meal, but the intrusion of Scotland Yard meant the evening had just crashed to an abrupt and unwelcome end. He watched Detective Blenkinsop's approach with dour anticipation, the food already curdling in his stomach.

He was not alone. Other diners recoiled at the officer's approach as a wave of shock and horror surged through the room. Women shrieked. Men shouted in outrage and lurched up from their seats. A string quartet played a subdued air in a quiet corner, and now the despairing cellos groaned into silence. A matronly woman clutched her throat and half-rose from her chair before swooning to the floor. Several chivalrous gents jumped to their feet to assist the lady, only to leap back as Blenkinsop swept through their midst like a nightmare torn loose of its moorings. When the detective drew closer Conan Doyle took one look and understood why his approach elicited so much dread:

Blood ... Blood ... Blood ...

... and so much of it—an angry, violent crimson under the palm-room's cheerful lights. The detective's regulation dark blue rain cape was drenched in pints of it, runneling fresh and sticky down his front and dribbling a crimson trail across the elegant marble floor.

As Blenkinsop arrived at their table, Miss Leckie stifled a shriek behind her hand, averting eyes rolling with horror.

Conan Doyle leapt to his feet, outraged. "Detective Blenkinsop! What on earth is the meaning of this? What are you thinking, coming into a public place in such a state? Are you mad?"

Blenkinsop stood before the table. Wavering. Unsteady on his feet. His eyes held the stunned look of crushed glass beads. It took a moment before he registered Conan Doyle's words and stammered out: "B-beg pardon, sir b-but I-I require your assistance, sir. I . . . I mean I ain't never ... I ain't never seen nothing so ... 'orrible ..."

As a physician with years of medical training, Conan Doyle recognised the signs of a man going into shock—the ghastly pallor, the sweating brow. Concern swept aside his anger. He sprang from his chair, gripped Blenkinsop by the shoulder and eased the detective into the vacated seat before he had chance to fall down.

But the uproar the young detective had caused was far from over. Diners abandoned their tables and milled in confusion. Waiters scurried hither and yon, uttering soothing words to calm frantic diners and coax them back into their seats. The ruckus even drew the cooks and cleaners from the kitchen, convinced that the restaurant must be on fire. The *Tivoli's* maître d' bustled up to Conan Doyle's table, jabbering hysterically. Instantly, the Scottish doctor became the calm eye in a swirling vortex of emotion. He was at his best in a crisis, and now he took command. Barking orders, the maître d' was bustled off to fetch a large snifter of brandy. He had the detective's blood-drenched rain cape bundled up in an old potato sack from the kitchen and hauled away to be tossed into the furnace. And then he corralled two passing waiters: the first was sent to fetch Miss Leckie's hat and wrap; the second he dispatched to alert the driver of the hansom cab waiting for them outside. Poor Miss Leckie, rather overwhelmed by It all, said little as a waiter eased her into her coat, and then Conan Doyle escorted her to the waiting cab.

The doormen held the door for them and they stepped from the light and warmth of the Tivoli into a chill November night miasmic with swirling fog.

"I am so sorry our lovely evening must end in such an ugly way," the Scottish author apologised.

Miss Leckie smiled and simpered. "I too, am sorry that our most elucidating conversation was interrupted."

"Perhaps you would allow me to invite you to another dinner, to make amends?" Conan Doyle blushed as he spoke the words, which had surged from him in an unrestrainable rush of emotion. The first dinner invite had come spontaneously. The two had struck up a conversation during the SPR meeting and the invitation to continue the exchange over dinner had seemed natural. But a second invitation smacked of an ulterior motive. He quailed, fearing he had overstepped the bounds of propriety. What he was doing could be seen as highly indecorous, even scandalous. He was a married man with an invalid wife. Miss Leckie was a single lady much younger than he. But when he looked into those doeish eyes, a trap door in his chest dropped open and his heart plummeted through it.

A brief look of uncertainty crossed her face, but then the corners of her mouth curled in a coquettish smile. "That would be delightful."

He fumbled in his waistcoat pocket, snatched free a calling card, and presented it to her. "Here is my card. Please let me know of a convenient time we might meet again."

"I look forward most anxiously," she said, plucking the card from his grip. And then, in an unambiguous sign of affection, touched a hand to his forearm. The press of her slender fingers, elegant in elbow-length gloves, lingered a moment longer than necessary.

"Until then," she said, smiling sweetly. "Avoir."

Crinoline rustled as she swept up her skirts and clambered into the hansom. Before the cab door folded over her legs, Conan Doyle checked to ensure that none of her skirts were trapped and then nodded up to the driver.

"Blackheath, George, and drive carefully. The fog is worsening and you convey a most precious cargo."

The cabbie nodded. "The worst I seen this year, Doctor Doyle. But don't you worry none, she'll be safe as houses with Iron George."

Conan Doyle handed up a sovereign coin, scandalously overpaying. The cabbie tugged the brim of his rumpled bowler in salute, then shook the reigns and clucked for the horse to pull away.

Coach lights blazing, the hansom plunged into the murk and vanished from sight before it had gone thirty feet, but the image of her smile hovered eidetically on the roiling grey fog.

And then, gallingly, Conan Doyle remembered he had forgotten to ask for Miss Leckie's calling card in return. Apart from the fact that she lived with her parents in the London suburb of Blackheath, he had no clue as to her address.

It was only then that he noticed the Black Mariah waiting at the kerbside—a hulking, four-wheeled coffin used by the Metropolitan police to haul criminals to gaol and condemned prisoners to the gallows—evidently the means by which Detective Blenkinsop had arrived. Two uniformed constables hunkered on the seat, mouths and noses muffled with thick woollen scarves to filter the choking air. Even though two large coach lights burned bright on either side of the Mariah, the blinding fog also obliged two additional officers brandishing flaming torches to lead the horses and light the way.

A convulsive shiver shook Conan Doyle's large frame as the fog ran an icy finger down his spine. The November night was too bitterly cold to tarry long without a coat, and so he slipped quickly back inside the restaurant.

In the welcome warmth of the Palm Room, Conan Doyle dropped into his dinner companion's vacated seat and waited patiently until Detective Blenkinsop finished sipping his brandy, the colour flushed back into his face, and the spark of intellect burned once again in his eyes.

"Obviously it's a murder," Conan Doyle ventured. "An extremely bloody one as I could see by the state of your raincoat."

The hand holding the brandy snifter tremored visibly. "It's a murder all right, sir. But not like nothing I ever seen before."

"It must be something along the lines of a Jack the Ripper to have distressed a detective used to witnessing the worst of humanity's deeds."

Blenkinsop shook his head. At twenty-six he was alarmingly boyish-looking. He had been promoted to detective just six months previously, in recognition of a feat of bravery—a deranged gunman had walked into the crowd gathered outside the gates of Buckingham Palace and began firing his pistol at random. Two Italian tourists had been shot dead as other constables looked on helplessly. But then Blenkinsop single-handedly tackled the madman to the ground and disarmed him. In recognition of this act of valour, he had been promoted to Detective, the youngest ever on the force. Too young to grow much more than the wispy suggestion of a moustache, he looked like a fresh-faced schoolboy summoned to the headmaster's office to receive a caning.

"I'd rather say as little as possible. I figured to fetch you so you can see for yourself." He tossed back the dregs of his liquor, nostrils flaring as he snorted brandy fumes. "I recommend you have a stiffun yourself, afore we go, sir. I believe even a doctor's nerves will need steadying."

Stepping into the chill night was like an open handed slap across the face. For days, a pestilential fog, known in the popular vernacular as a "London Particular," had suffocated the capital city beneath a yellow-green blanket. Appearing each evening at the mouth of the Thames, the fog surged slowly up the river and spilled over onto the surrounding streets, submerging all but the tallest church spires. Fogs were common at this time of year, but rather than abating after a few days as most fogs did, the mephitic cloud seemed to worsen with each evening. After a full week of such fogs, the night air was cold and abrasive, a gritty cloud of pumice swirling with ash, soot and firefly embers that burned the lungs and needled tears to the eyes. The fog muffled sound and shrank the sprawling metropolis to a murky circle of visibility, scarcely twenty feet in any direction.

Detective Blenkinsop snatched wide the battle-scarred rear door of the Mariah and gestured for the Scottish author to step aboard. "Forgive the means of transport, sir. Uncomfortable, I admit, but she'll get us there, no bother."

As Conan Doyle climbed into the boxy carriage, a strangely familiar smell assailed his senses—Turkish tobacco smoke—and he was surprised to find that the Mariah already had an occupant.

"Ah," spoke a salubrious voice, "it appears I am not the only prisoner tonight. I bid you welcome, fellow riff-raff."

It was only then Conan Doyle realised that the shadowy shape he had at first mistaken for a small bear was in fact a large Irishman.

"Oscar!"

Oscar Wilde was wearing a gorgeous fur overcoat with an enormous fur collar and cuffs. Atop his head perched a fur hat fetched from his North American travels. Conan Doyle had ridden in Black Mariahs before, which invariably bore an aura of abject despair and reeked like public urinals in the worse part of London, but Wilde's expensive cologne and piquant tobacco smoke bullied the air of its malodorous stink while his insouciant gravitas commandeered the space and made it his own. A small oil lantern swung from a hook in the ceiling, and in the wan pulse of amber light the Irish wit resembled the Sultan of some exotic country being carried to his coronation in an enclosed sedan chair.

Conan Doyle slid in beside his friend and Detective Blenkinsop dropped onto the bench opposite. The door of the Mariah banged shut and a constable standing outside shot the bolt, locking them in. The driver gee'd the horses up, and the Mariah rumbled away on wobbly axles squealing for a lick of grease.

"I am always happy to see you, Oscar," Conan Doyle said. "But I confess you are the last person I would expect to meet in a Black Mariah."

The hot coal of Wilde's cigarette flared red as he drew in a lungful and jetted smoke out both nostrils. "Scotland Yard's best have been combing the city for you, Arthur. Detective Blenkinsop recruited me to assist in the search. We stopped at the Savoy, Claridges, and then your club. When you were discovered at none of them, given the hour, I plumped for the *Tivoli* and am gratified to see my guess was correct." Wilde swept Conan Doyle's dress with an appraising gaze and his full lips curled in a supercilious smile. "And now I understand why you were avoiding your usual haunts."

Conan Doyle stiffened in his seat. "I, ah. I was supping with a friend . . . a fellow member of the Society for Psychical Research."

"A fellow member, but not a *fellow*, per se?" Wilde remarked in a deeply incriminating voice. "You are quite the dog, Arthur. I suspect you were entertaining a lady!"

Conan Doyle blanched as Wilde pierced the bull's-eye with his first arrow.

"I . . . how on earth did you know that?"

Had it not been so gloomy in the Black Mariah, Conan Doyle's companions would have seen his face flush bright red.

"Your dress reveals much, Arthur. You are wearing a very fine bespoke suit—beautifully tailored might I add—rather than your work-a-day tweeds. You sport a beaver top hat, a fresh boutonnière, and have obviously spent a great deal of effort on your toilet, including taking the time to wax your extravagant moustaches, which I must confess positively coruscate in the light. Were we actually heading to gaol you would be the talk of the prison yard. A man as practical as Arthur Conan Doyle does not take such pains with his attire to dine with an old school chum or a chalk-dusted academic. You have clearly dressed for a lady friend. A young and fetching lady, I would wager. Another good reason to dodge your usual haunts to avoid wagging tongues." Wilde turned to Detective Blenkinsop and smirked knowingly. "Arthur hates it when I play Sherlock Holmes to his Watson."

"Yes, thank you, Oscar," Conan Doyle interrupted. "And I think that's quite enough. I assume you were carousing at the Savoy, as usual?"

Wilde trilled with laughter. "Au contraire. It is scarcely ten o'clock. Oscar Wilde does not *begin* to carouse until midnight at the very earliest. No, I was visiting the Haymarket Theatre. My new play is in its third week. I look in on the production from time to time. To boost company morale. To thrill my audiences with a personal appearance . . . and to count the box office receipts. Plus I am a great aficionado of my own work. I love the sound of my own voice. And I love to hear the sound of my own voice coming out of someone else's mouth. It is the primary reason for my connexion with the theatre; it ensures I am never far from the thing I love most."

"Well, now you've found me," Conan Doyle said and turned his attention to the policeman sitting opposite. "Can you reveal, Detective Blenkinsop, what has prompted Scotland Yard to search for me so diligently?"

Blenkinsop drew the homburg from his head and held it slackly in his hands, turning it slowly by the brim. "There's been a murder—no, not a murder. That ain't right. I guess you'd properly call it . . . an assassination."

Conan Doyle and Wilde exchanged stunned glances.

"Are we permitted to know whom?" Wilde asked.

The young detective's expression grew tragic. "The whole world will know soon enough: Lord Howell."

Both Wilde and Conan Doyle grunted as if gut-punched.

"The prime minister's Secretary for War," Conan Doyle muttered in shocked tones.

Wilde leaned forward, his expression tense. "An assassination, you say? Do you suspect the party or parties responsible for such an act?"

Blenkinsop shook his head, "Not a clue. Right now all we got is the body. But it's not just the murder. It's *how* he was murdered. The murder scene . . ." A gasp tore loose from Blenkinsop, whose eyes lost focus as he stared blankly into space. "I can't tell ya no more. I can't describe it. I seen some dark doings in me days as a copper. But I ain't never seen nothing like this. When I shut me eyes, I can still see it."

With Blenkinsop unwilling to reveal more, the men fell into a tense silence for the rest of the journey. Held to a slow walk by the fog, the horses clop-clopped through deserted streets, at times narrowly avoiding horse-less, abandoned carriages that loomed like shipwrecks in the fog. And so the Black Mariah took thirty minutes to travel less than a mile to reach its destination. When Conan Doyle and Wilde finally climbed out, the fog had grown thicker still, caging the street lamps in tremulous globes of light. Even with the Mariah drawn up to the stone kerb, they could barely see farther than the iron railings of the house they had stopped outside.

Conan Doyle, who knew London and the surrounding Metropolitan area intimately, looked about himself, utterly lost, and asked in a baffled voice, "Where the devil are we?"

"Belgravia, sir," Detective Blenkinsop answered. He nodded toward the limestone façade of a handsome residence where two constables stood guard on either side of the front gate. "That there is Lord Howell's residence."

As he spoke, a third constable came staggering out of the house. He wobbled a rubber-legged path to the pavement where he doubled over and vomited explosively into the gutter. Conan Doyle and Wilde jumped back to avoid having their shoes splashed as a second wave hit and the officer gargled up the remainder of his dinner. As he sagged to his knees, clutching the railings for support, the young constable looked up at them, his face wretched with horror and moaned, "Don't go in there!"

Conan Doyle shared a look with Wilde, whose eyes were saucered, his complexion waxen and ghastly in the otherworldly throb of gaslight.

"Oscar, perhaps it would be better if you remained outside. As a medical doctor, I am used to such sights—"

"No," Wilde shook his head. "If I do not see for myself then you shall be forced to describe it to me, and I fear my imagination excels when it comes to fathoming horrible things from nothing."

Conan Doyle looked at Detective Blenkinsop, who did not immediately volunteer to go in with them. "Right then," Conan Doyle said. "Let's get this over with."

"Boyle! Jennings!" Blenkinsop called to the two officers posted on either side of the gate. Lend the gentlemen your rain capes," Blenkinsop fixed the two friends with a dire look. "You'll be needin' them, I reckon."

With their fine clothes protected beneath long police rain capes, Conan Doyle and Wilde cautiously stepped up to the front door—or rather, what remained of it. A solid chunk of milled and planed English oak, the door had been smashed violently inward, tearing the mortise lock completely through the doorframe and wrenching two of the three hinges loose. Once painted ivory, the door gleamed crimson with spattered gore. The two friends stood goggling at the site, which bore mute testament to an act of extreme violence. Although the door had been solidly locked—they could see the exposed brass tenon—something with the force of a steam locomotive had smashed straight through it. They entered the house and found the marble tiles of the entrance hall slippery with blood. The footprints of every police officer that had entered the space tracked in all directions, like macabre steps in a dance studio from hell. As Conan Doyle moved inside, a gobbet of blood dropped from above and burst across the brim of his fine top Hat. He looked up at a crystal chandelier dripping red. He snatched a linen handkerchief to wipe his hat, and then took Wilde by the sleeve to guide him clear of the ghoulish centrepiece. He cast a doubting look at his tall Irish friend. "Really, Oscar, I don't think there's a need for you to see this—"

Wilde, who had yanked a scented handkerchief from his breast pocket and had it pressed over his nose and mouth shook his head violently. "No," he said in a muffled voice. "Proceed. I have witnessed the dreadful prologue. I must see how the act ends."

Their feet slithered across blood-slick tiles to a front parlour where the same maniacal force that had smashed down the front door had also ripped the lighter parlour door to splinters. Inside the room, toppled chairs and broken furniture testified to a dreadful struggle. Sometime earlier in the evening, a fire had been set in the fireplace. Left untended, it had burned down to a few smouldering coals so that the tepid air of the parlour roiled with a darkly ferric tang of blood. Beside an overturned divan, a body lay on the floor. Conan Doyle stepped around a broken end table to inspect it.

The corpse had a face both men recognised from the newspapers: Lord Montague Howell, hero of the battle of Alma and the siege of Sevastopol—amongst a score of campaigns in Crimea. Miraculously, the handsome features had escaped unscathed; the blue eyes retained a calm gaze, the lids drooped slightly, a rictus-smile drawing back the lips, showing strong white teeth beneath a scrupulously groomed brown moustache. However, Lord Howell's head was unnaturally kinked upon his neck, like that of a hanging victim.

With his years of medical experience, Conan Doyle was used to blood and death, but as he stepped closer, his gorge rose and invisible needles tattooed his face as he saw, to his horror, that the body was lying chest down.

The head had been twisted through one-hundred-and-eighty degrees, so that it pointed in the wrong direction.

"Dear God!" he gasped. "His neck has been wrung like a pigeon's." He crouched down to examine ten finger-sized bruises, five tattooed on either side of the neck. "And by someone with a demon's grip."

Wilde made a dry heaving sound and gripped a drinks cabinet to steady himself. "I think I shall look for clues outside," he said in a squeezed-tight voice.

"Yes," Conan Doyle agreed. "Detective Blenkinsop, please help Mister Wilde."

Blenkinsop took Wilde firmly by the arm and walked him out of the room.

As they left, two new constables crowded in through the parlour door, gawking at the corpse.

"Lumme! What'd I tell ya, Alfie?" the first said, elbowing his companion.

"Yer right, Stan. Won't nobody be sneakin' up on him from behind now!"

The prospect of the horrifying tableau becoming a macabre attraction struck a nerve with Conan Doyle. He rose to his feet and bellowed at the young constables: "Show some respect, damn you! This man was a hero of the British Empire. He was at the Charge of the Light Brigade and earned the Victoria Cross for valour!"

Detective Blenkinsop stepped back into the room just in time to hear. He threw a scowl at the two constables and jerked a thumb at the door, saying, "Right, you two, hop it!"

The young constables skulked out, heads lowered in shame. Conan Doyle took in a deep breath, bracing himself and then dropped to his knees and rolled the body over. Once turned upon on its back, he took the noble head in both hands and turned it the right way around. The corpse wore evening dress, the once elegant tuxedo jacket glutinous with congealing blood.

"Dressed for dinner," he noted. "Lord Howell was evidently about to go out."

He paused and sniffed in deeply. A bitter tang of cordite spooled in the air. He looked down to see the fingers of Lord Howell's right hand still curled about the trigger of a pistol—a Webley Mark IV. Conan Doyle eased it from fingers stiffening with rigor and snapped open the revolver's chambers with a practiced flick of the wrist. He dumped out a handful of spent shell casings into his palm.

"All six rounds have been fired."

Conan Doyle gripped the corpse's wrist. The body was cold and when he lifted the arm, it bent like a strip of India rubber—both the radius and ulna had been smashed to fragments. The left arm was the same. He unbuttoned the tuxedo jacket and peeled open the blood-soaked fabric. A moment's palpation revealed that the sternum and every rib were broken. He concluded his examination by patting down the stomach and legs, searching for bullet wounds. To his astonishment, he found not a one.

And then he looked up and his mouth dropped open in astonishment. One wall bore the bloody imprint of a body. He rose and stumbled closer. Something had hurled Lord Howell's body at the wall with tremendous force, leaving a man-sized dent in the plaster and a ballistic spray of blood.

"What on earth could have done this?" Conan Doyle breathed.

Blenkinsop shook his head, baffled. "Now you know why I fetched you, sir. I can't fathom none of it."

The Scottish doctor finally turned away from his ghoulish task, wiping sticky blood from his hands on a handkerchief. He flashed a grim look at Detective Blenkinsop. "I can find no bullet wounds. Not a single one. That can only mean—"

"All this blood? It's not his?"

"Unbelievable, but yes."

Conan Doyle continued to numbly wipe his hands.

"There must have multiple assailants. Lord Howell fired six shots, many of which obviously found their target. If a single man lost that much blood he would have died on the spot."

"If it was something *human* what killed him," Detective Blenkinsop spoke aloud what Conan Doyle had secretly conjectured. The smashed front door, the demolished parlour, the body hurled against the wall and then beaten to a bag of broken bones, all after six shots spilled pints of blood everywhere, defied rational explanation. It seemed more like the attack of a raging monster than a man . . . or men.

"Pardon, Detective, but I must step outside to clear my head."

When Conan Doyle emerged through the ruined doorway, Wilde

was lurking by the front gate, smoking a cigarette. The Irishman saw Conan Doyle approach and drew him farther away with a nod.

"What is it, Oscar?"

"I believe I have spotted what your fellow Sherlock Holmes would have referred to as a *clue*."

Conan Doyle's eyebrows rose. He leaned close and whispered, "What?"

"Look at the gate post on the right." Wilde drew out his silver cigarette case, opened it with a practiced flick and held it out to the two constables standing guard. "Care for a cigarette?"

The nearest constable turned his head, giving a subtle look-around. "Very decent of you, sir. Don't mind if I do." He stepped forward, giving Conan Doyle a clear view of a figure scrawled in chalk upon the brick gate post:

"Much obliged, sir. I'll smoke it later." The Constable grinned as he tucked the cigarette in a pocket and stepped back to his post, hiding the chalk scrawl once again.

Conan Doyle and Wilde turned and casually stepped away, leaning their heads together to confer.

"Just random graffiti?" Conan Doyle pondered.

"We are in Belgravia. A place where the idle scribbler and his ball of chalk seldom make an appearance."

"You are right."

Something caught Conan Doyle's eye and he tugged at his friend's sleeve, nodding at the road. "If you look at just the right angle, you can see a trail of bloody footprints leading off into the fog."

The Irish wit peered down, eyes asquint. "Ah yes, I see them now. Should we inform Detective Blenkinsop?"

Conan Doyle shook his head. "Not just yet. Perhaps you and I should investigate before the London constabulary has a chance to tramp all over them with their regulation size nines." He stepped onto the road and nodded for his friend to follow. "Come, Oscar. Let's see where they lead."

Wilde's face plummeted. "Ah, you expect me to accompany you? I had rather planned on standing sentinel at the front gate."

"I need you to watch my back."

Wilde's expression betrayed a decided lack of enthusiasm. "Which begs the question, who shall watch mine?"

"Come along," Conan Doyle said. He stepped from the kerb into the street and Wilde reluctantly followed after. The two friends had barely reached the far side of the road when the Irishman threw a timid look back. In less than ten strides, the house, the Mariah and the police officers had vanished from sight.

"I do not think we should stray too far," Wilde worried aloud, "lest we become lost in the fog."

Conan Doyle did not reply. He had his head down, eyes scouring the pavement for footprints. They reached a low garden wall daubed with a bloody handprint.

"Look! He put out a hand here to steady himself." Conan Doyle looked at Wilde and spoke in a voice coiled tight with urgency. "Come, the assailant cannot be far ahead."

"That is precisely what I am afraid of."

"Judging by the staggering gait, if the murderer is still alive, he's badly wounded and unlikely to be a danger to us."

They followed the trail of fading footprints as they reeled and staggered around a corner into a side street. But instead of petering out, the footsteps carried on. And on. And on. Until finally, in a circle of light beneath a streetlamp, they found the bloody corpse of a large man slumped on the pavement, the staring eyes opaque with death.

"Riddled from front to back with bullet wounds," Conan Doyle said. "I count at least five." He fixed Wilde with an urgent look. "Guard the body, Oscar, I must fetch Detective Blenkinsop at once."

Distress flashed across Wilde's long face. "Come now, Arthur," he gave a shaky laugh. "Are you sure you wish me to remain with the corpse? Dead bodies require little guarding. Who would wish to steal one? I have seen my share of wakes and lyings-in growing up in Ireland and I have found that the dead seldom make for good company. They are poor conversationalists, and should one actually speak, I am sure it should have nothing I would like to hear."

"Very well. You go fetch Detective Blenkinsop and I shall remain behind."

Wilde took one step away from the pool of light beneath the streetlamp and recoiled. It was clear he realised that becoming lost in the fog was a real possibility.

"On second thought," he corrected, "you are quite right. It would be better if I remained here whilst you return for help."

As Conan Doyle moved to step away, Wilde death-gripped his arm. "This would be an appropriate time for haste, Arthur."

"I shall not dilly-dally." In just three steps the fog swallowed the Scottish author. Two more and it suffocated even the sound of his footfalls.

Instantly, Wilde found himself totally . . . utterly . . . alone. A solitary figure marooned on an island of lamplight, his isolation was palpable. The street. The houses. London . . . no longer existed.

It was a bitter night. He squirmed his shoulders deeper into his fur coat, large hands rummaging for warmth in his fur-lined pockets. Cold radiated up from the pavement through the soles of his shiny leather shoes. He stamped his feet, setting frozen toes tingling. Reluctant to look back at the bullet-riddled corpse, he gazed instead into the seething greyness, shivering from more than the November chill.

Long . . . long . . . long minutes passed.

"Really," he said aloud to keep himself company, "What *is* taking

Arthur so long?" He finished his cigarette and tossed the fag end away, then fumbled his silver cigarette case from his pocket, flicked a Lucifer to life with his thumbnail, kindled another cigarette with shaking hands, and gloved them in his pockets once again. He drew in a comforting lungful of warm smoke and let it out. Then, from somewhere, a faint noise caught his ear: wisssshthump . . . wissssshthump . . . wisssssshthump . . .

It was a noise somehow familiar. He looked around, straining his eyes. The fog curled into arabesques, as though stirred by invisible shapes moving through it. A nervous glance confirmed the body was still there. But then, as he watched, the fingers of the left hand twitched.

Wilde's eyes widened.

The left leg shivered and kicked.

The cigarette tumbled from Wilde's lips.

The corpse heaved; the chest rose and fell.

Wilde's head quivered atop his neck, but he could not look away.

And then, the arm flexed. Shifted. Drew back. A bloody hand grappled for a handhold and the corpse began to push itself up from the pavement.

Wilde took a step backward.

A plume of steam shot out both nostrils with an expiring *hiiiiisssssssssss*.

Wilde stumbled backward several steps, unaware of the shape looming in the fog behind him.

The arm suddenly buckled and the corpse slumped face down to the pavement with a dying wheeze.

Wilde shrieked as a hand clamped upon his shoulder and a ghastly glowing face swam up through the fog. "It's me, Oscar." Conan Doyle was holding a police officer's bull nose lantern that lit his face eerily from below. A second wraith materialised beside him: Detective Blenkinsop.

"It moved," Wilde said breathlessly. "It groaned and moved."

"That happens," Conan Doyle reassured. "Dead bodies are filled with gases. They gurgle. They twitch. Sometimes sit up. I have experienced it myself, working the morgue as a medical student. It's simply—"

"No, you fail to understand. It struggled to rise—"

"Oscar, I assure you, the fellow is quite dead."

But despite the reassurance, the Irish wit was reluctant to approach any closer. Conan Doyle and Detective Blenkinsop stepped to the body, hitched their trouser legs, and dropped to a crouch for a closer examination. Lit from below, the glare from the bull's eye lanterns stretched their faces into black-socketed fright masks.

"I count five bullet holes," Conan Doyle said.

"Lord Howell was quite the marksman. He only missed once."

"How on earth did the man stagger this far after taking five bullets? It's almost as if he walked until he ran out of blood."

Blenkinsop shook his head. "Like I said, something awful queer . . ."

Conan Doyle did not respond. The night. The fog. The grotesque murder. Everything conspired to twist minds in an eldritch direction. Determined not to loose his grip on rationality, he asked, "When do you estimate this happened?"

"The neighbours said they heard a row about six o'clock. A lot of shoutin' and yellin'. Then shots. Five or more. A footman from the house two doors down was sent to run and fetch the police. But it took a while for a constable to arrive—what with the fog and all."

"Six o'clock?" Conan Doyle repeated. "That's nearly four hours ago!" He touched a hand to the dead man's throat and looked up at Detective Blenkinsop in amazement. "Impossible! Lord Howell's body was quite cold. But this body is still warm. Very warm. Burning up, in fact, as if the man had a fever!" He grabbed the heavy arm and lifted its dead weight. "No sign of rigor; he could not have died more than half-an hour ago."

Detective Blenkinsop leaned close, sniffed the corpse and recoiled. "Ugh! He pongs something 'orrible."

Conan Doyle had also noticed the same strange smell.

"Maybe that's a clue: he could be a tanner . . . or an abattoir worker

. . . or a resurrection man. But there's something else, something familiar about the odour."

"Garlic," Wilde said, matter-of-factly.

"What?"

"Garlic. The man reeks of it."

"Garlic?" Blenkinsop repeated doubtfully. "That's what foreigners eat, ain't it?"

Wilde released a gasp of exasperation. "Garlic, or the 'stinking rose' as it sometimes vulgarly known, has a starring role in all the world's cuisines. The fact that it is considered exotic on these shores speaks volumes about British cooking."

"So you reckon he's a foreigner, then?"

Wilde tut-tutted the question. "An assumption to which I would not leap. Although judging by his dress sense, he does not look the type to frequent the finer restaurants."

Conan Doyle leaned closer and swept the beam of his lantern across the body. The corpse was dressed in motley of tattered clothes picked from the bottom of a rag bin. Clothes too shabby even for a casual labourer. The lank mop of black hair was greasy and matted. The lantern beam swept across the exposed back of the neck and paused.

"Look," Conan Doyle pointed. "He has a tattoo of some kind. Let's see if we can't get a better look at it." He scrunched down to turn the head further toward the light.

The young Detective leaned closer and shone his light into the murder's face, but then let out a shout of surprise and sprang to his feet, backpedalling several steps.

"What is it?" Conan Doyle asked. "Do you recognise him?"

Blenkinsop nodded manically, never taking his startled eyes off the corpse. "Yeah, I know him. I'd know him anywhere. But it ain't possible. It ain't possible!"

"What is it? Speak up, man. Who is this fellow?"

"I know the face. A-a-and that butterfly tattoo on his neck. I only seen a tattoo like that once before. It's Charlie Higginbotham, that is. And no doubt about it."

"A criminal you are acquainted with?"

"Charlie's a petty thief. A dip. A cracksman. Strictly small time. It's him. It's definitely him. But it can't be . . . it just can't."

"What do you mean? Why ever not?"

Detective Blenkinsop fixed the Scottish author with an almost demented stare. "Two months ago, I collared Charlie for the murder of his wife. I even testified against him at the trial." He paused to lick dry lips. "I watched him take the drop last week at Newgate Prison. Hanged for murder. The last time I seen Charlie Higginbotham the hangman was digging the rope out of his neck. And he was dead . . . very dead!"

The Angel of Highgate

People die . . . but love endures immortal.

Lord Geoffrey Thraxton is notorious in Victorian society—a Byronesque
rake-hell with a reputation as the "wickedest man in London."

After surviving a pistol duel, Thraxton boasts his contempt for death and
insults the attending physician. It is a mistake he will regret, for Silas Garrette

is a deranged sociopath and chloroform-addict whose mind was broken on the battlefields of Crimea.

Oblivious to the danger, Thraxton's pursuit of idle pleasure leads him through the fog shrouded streets of London—from champagne soirees in the mummy room of the British Museum, to its high-class brothels and low-class opium dens. But when Thraxton falls in love with a mysterious woman who haunts Highgate Cemetery by night, he unwittingly provides the murderous doctor with the perfect means to punish a man with no fear of death.

A magnificently written, provocative novel."—**Kirkus Reviews**

"Chock-full of thrills, action, suspense and derring-do."—**British Fantasy Society**

"A heady mix of Victorian melodrama and murder mystery."—***Books Monthly***

Daringly original . . . Entwistle's cheerfully confident prose sparkles and unsettles by turns"—**Historical Novel Society**

Gothic Novel of the Year (Shortlisted) **The Dracula Society**

EXCERPT—CHAPTER 1: IN HOPES OF THE RESSURRECTION TO COME

September, 4th, 1859. It was almost seven a.m. on a Sunday morning. God was in His Heaven. Queen Victoria was on her throne. And Lord Geoffrey Thraxton was prowling the pathways of Highgate Cemetery.

Ectoplasmic mists swirled about the brooding mass of stone mausoleums. A ghostly winged form—a carved angel perched atop a grave—crooked a beckoning finger from the gloom. Thraxton ignored the summons and strode on, the fog cupping his face in its cool hands.

Despite the early hour and the somber setting, Thraxton was impeccably dressed in black frock coat and tight, camel-colour breeches, a bright yellow cravat knotted at his throat, a grey silk top hat perched at an insolent angle upon his head. In one kid-gloved hand he gripped a walking stick topped by a golden phoenix bursting forth from tongues of flame. The other hand, gloveless, stroked the cashmere lining of his coat pocket. In his early thirties, and of above average height and muscular build, Thraxton had a face that could have been said to be both handsome and noble, were it not for a certain weakness in the mouth, a hint of dissolution in the corners of the intense blue eyes.

In the still air, the only sound was the crackle of leaves underfoot, the rattle of robins in the berry bushes, and as the hour struck, the slow, dolorous clang of bells from the nearby Church of St. Michael's. To the west lay the city of London, an invisible but palpable presence in the fog, for the smoke coughed up from the sooty throats of its myriad chimneys left a bitter taste of sulphur on the tongue.

Highgate was arguably the most beautiful necropolis in the capitol, with its mixture of Classical and Egyptian influenced tombs and mausoleums, including its most celebrated architectural flourish, the Circle of Lebanon, so named for the gnarled cedar that rooted at its centre. It was a place for London's fashionable living to perambulate, as well as a final resting place for London's fashionable dead to await the Doom Crack and the body's Resurrection.

At this hour, however, Thraxton had only the latter for company. On a path leading to the Egyptian Avenue, he paused to contemplate the rain-worn face of a stone angel, its eyes cast downward in an expression of profound loss. At that moment, the bells of St. Michael's peeled a final stroke and fell mute, opening an abyss of silence wherein the world beyond the cemetery fell away, and the dead caught their breath. Then a sorrowful wail drifted from afar, faintly, as if all the stone angels of Highgate were weeping, but soon followed the rattle of carriage wheels, the jingle of horse brasses and the muffled thump of hooves on soft soil.

A rectangular shape loomed in the mist, gathering solidity until it materialised in the form of a hearse drawn by two coal-dark mares, their huge heads nodding with black plumes. Atop the hearse rode two funeral grooms in black frock coats with top hats draped in black crepe. Two more paced behind the hearse on foot, followed by four women in black mourning dresses, their faces darkly veiled. These women were the source of the weeping, which was interspersed with the occasional heart-cracking wail. At the rear of the procession strode two men dressed in daily attire but for the black crepe armbands that marked them as mourners.

The taller of the two was a handsome gentleman of about the same age as Thraxton, whose blond curls spilled out from beneath his top hat. The man that walked beside him was a full foot shorter, barely into his twenties, and whose bowler hat and shabby jacket marked him as a domestic servant. Both men wore expressions shaped by the solemnity of the occasion, yet the servant's face seemed to bear a look at once both serious and supercilious.

The hearse clattered around the bend of the narrow lane and Thraxton stepped aside to allow it to pass, doffing his top hat in respect. Such a lugubrious display was calculated to instil a profound sense of loss and mourning in all who witnessed it, yet the sight of the hearse had served only to tease a faint smile onto Thraxton's lips.

The glass sides of the hearse flashed as it drew alongside and he caught a glimpse of the deceased—a young woman in a crystal coffin, her body swathed in a white lace death shroud of intricate delicacy.

As the solemn cortege trundled by, Thraxton's presence went unacknowledged by the slightest glance from either the funeral grooms or the wailing women. But the blond gentlemen looked up as he passed, and for the briefest of moments his calm brown eyes met and held Thraxton's.

The funeral procession carried on for another thirty feet and drew up next to a stone mausoleum. To gain a better vantage, Thraxton clambered up on the pedestal with the stone angel. Setting his hat momentarily atop the angel's head, he stood with his arms wrapped around its waist, his cheek pressed up against the mossy stone as he watched the melancholy scene from a discreet distance.

The lamenting reached its climax as the four grooms lifted the coffin from the hearse. Assisted by the gentleman and the servant, they bore it into the tomb upon their shoulders, and the mourning women wept after them.

It was over quickly. The mourners re-emerged from the tomb, minus the coffin, the groomsmen led the horses around until they faced the direction they had just come from, and soon the cortege passed by heading in the other direction. The funereal wailing soft-ened into the distance. The hearse grew transparent, lost substance, and dissolved into the seething greyness. Thraxton retrieved his top hat, stepped down from his angelic perch, and sauntered toward the mausoleum.

A fresh wreath hung upon the bronze door, above which a stonemason had carved a grinning skull nestled amongst winged cherubs. Thraxton studied the Memento Mori as he stole a single white flower from the wreath and threaded the bloom into his boutonniere. He cast a casual glance first left and then right. The funeral party was long gone. Apart from the slumbering dead of Highgate, no one was about. The latch lifted beneath his thumb and a gentle push creaked the tomb door open. Thraxton slipped inside and swung the door shut behind him.

Inside the tomb, a profusion of candles burned here and there, their waxy scent muddled with the fragrance of white lilies scattered atop the coffin's crystal lid. He stepped closer. The flowers concealed the face of the deceased, so he swept them to the floor and peered in. What he saw made him catch his breath. The woman inside the coffin was beautiful and shockingly young, scarcely sixteen.

"My God," he gasped, "how perfect a bloom to have fallen so soon."

His fingers closed on the handle of the coffin lid. A gentle tug revealed that it was not fastened. The crystal lid was massive and awkward, but Thraxton heaved it off and set it down on the floor.

At last, he stood over the open coffin gazing down at the vision within. Despite the heavily applied white powder and red rouged cheeks and lips, the woman seemed young, fresh and alive. The sight of that face, like a sleeping angel's, sent a tremor through him. To disturb such beauty seemed sacrilege, but after a moment's hesitation, he reached out and caressed the soft down of her cheek with his fingertips.

"The blush of youth still lingers on flesh grown cold."

As he traced the full, rouged lips with his thumb, a muscle in his jaw trembled.

"Surely Death, your new husband, would not be jealous of a single kiss on this, your wedding day?"

Thraxton leaned in and softly kissed the corpse's lips. They were full and pliant, and parted slightly as he drew his lips away.

"How sweet. Even in death. How sweet."

The shroud was fastened at the front by a number of delicately tied bows. He caught and tugged the end of the topmost. The bow silkily unknotted and the shroud fell open, revealing an alabaster neck and chest. The remaining bows soon surrendered to his quick fingers and Thraxton drew the shroud open to reveal small, firm breasts with taut, high nipples, the soft dome of a belly, a patch of golden hair between the thighs. In the shifting candlelight, the flesh seemed marble that had flowed waxen and set in the shape of an Aphrodite.

Thraxton's eyes drank in the sight. He realised he had been holding his breath, and now let it out in one deep, languorous sigh.

"Ah, pretty one, has a coffin become your bridal bed? Will Death be the first to take your maidenhood?"

Thraxton slid out of his coat and let it fall at his feet. His fingers tore at the buttons of his vest. He yanked the fine linen shirt over his head in one quick motion, shedding several pearl buttons. By now, anticipation had tightened him into a throbbing knot, and as he peeled off the tight breeches he was already stiff and quivering in the chill air of the tomb.

Naked, he climbed up onto the bier the coffin was set upon and stared down upon the body in a state of greedy rapture.

"And now," he breathed, "a taste of the fruit new-fallen from the tree, before the worms can canker it!"

Thraxton lifted and spread the woman's legs, letting them dangle on either side of the open coffin, then slid in between. It was difficult to move in such restricted confines, but he squirmed his hips left and right, searching for an entry, until he slid in effortlessly.

"I will cuckold Death and add my little death to yours!"

As he began to thrust, the cold body moved rhythmically under him, breasts swaying. The sound of his laboured breathing filled the tomb, and the light of the guttering candles refracted through the coffin's crystal sides, threw grotesque, quivering shadows on the walls.

Outside, the morning fog was beginning to burn off under the weak September sun. The service at nearby St. Michael's had finished but a few minutes ago, and now many of those who had attended, gentlemen and their ladies, couples with their children, were enjoying a stroll in the tranquil peace of the cemetery grounds.

Inside the mausoleum, Thraxton's thrusting had intensified to the point where the woman's head was softly thumping into the end of the coffin. It could have been a trick of the shifting candlelight, but it appeared as though the corpse had the slightest of smiles upon its lips. The dead woman's legs had slid down until the cold soles of her feet pressed on Thraxton's steely buttocks. Even more miraculous was when the corpse's eyes opened slightly and a singularly delicious giggle escaped the deceased's lips.

"Was there ever a more lovely Lazarus?"

By now the pathways of Highgate Cemetery were busy with morning strollers and relatives come to lay flowers on the graves of their loved ones. The visitors now looked up in alarm and horror as the serenity of a Sunday morning was broken by the echoing grunts and moans of a man and a woman in the throes of sexual ecstasy.

Their macabre tryst completed, Thraxton collected his scattered attire from the floor of the tomb, while the woman put on clothes that had been tucked beneath the coffin's satin pillows. Dressed only in a white corset, the young woman let out a mischievous giggle as she tied the red silk bow that held up one of her knee-length white stockings.

"You took your bleedin' time, Geoffrey," she said. "My bloomin' arse was freezin' in that coffin!"

Thraxton smiled as he cinched the silk cravat into an insolent knot at his throat. "Merely showing due deference and respect for the deceased, Maisy, m'dear."

She snickered at that. "Bloomin' heck. I don't fink wot you just done to me was the least bit respectful!"

"Nonsense," Thraxton corrected, slipping an arm around her narrow, corseted waist and pulling her towards him. "What greater respect can a mere supplicant show than to worship at the altar of Venus?"

Maisy's eyes softened at his words. "I know I'm nuffink but a common tart, Geoffrey, but when you says them things it makes me feel all special and bee-you-tee-full!"

Never taking his eyes from hers, Thraxton slipped two fingers inside her, then put them in his mouth, tasting the acrid tang of their commingled essences. He sought to share it with a kiss, his tongue probing the sweet cavern of Maisy's mouth. For a moment, she sucked on his tongue thrillingly. Perceiving her renewed passion, Thraxton felt his ardor rise again. But then Maisy dissolved, once more, into titters.

It shattered the illusion, reminding Thraxton that, despite the elaborate pretence, Maisy was merely a street girl he had purchased for a few hours diversion. He broke off the kiss, gave her cheek a fond caress, and went back to pulling his clothes on.

"And so you are beautiful and special," Thraxton said, digging a heavy coin from his pocket which he pressed into her hand. "And here's a golden sovereign to keep your beautiful arse warm in the winter."

Maisy, who had never seen much more than a shilling for herself in the four years she had worked as a prostitute, gasped at the largesse. "Thanks ever so much, Geoffrey! You are a proper gent you are!"

He grabbed her roughly and kissed her hard on the mouth, then spun her around and slapped her on the bare behind.

"Now then, go my child and sin no more!"

Maisy rubbed her stinging right buttock and giggled effervescently.

"My Gawd! You are such a cut up, Geoffrey. Really you are. You oughta be on the music hall stage!"

Thraxton paused in brushing a smudge of tomb dust from his top hat. He threw his arms out expressively.

"But I am, my dear. I am. And every day of my life is merely another act I must play."

While Maisy pulled on her dress, Thraxton sat on the coffin staring into the shadows, a thousand conflicting thoughts wrestling in his mind. He was given to moodiness, and now he felt a post-coital depression settling upon him, mixed with the vague sense of disappointment that always accompanies the indulgence of a long-held fantasy.

Maisy by now had finished dressing, and with her parasol and little lace-up boots that showed when she coquettishly lifted her skirts, could have passed for the local vicar's daughter out for a Sunday promenade. On her way out of the mausoleum she turned and curtsied to Thraxton.

"Good day, milord," she said and dissolved once more into giggles.

The heavy door thumped shut and Maisy was gone.

A waft of fresh air crashed into the walls and dispersed, churning with the heady scents of candle wax, flowers and sex. Thraxton moved about the tomb, extinguishing candles, until only one remained burning. He stood close by, feeling its heat on his cheek, his face lit by the candle's amber glow. His eyes instead were fixed on the shadows that squirmed at the edge of the light.

The candle flame shivered in a sudden draft that made the shadows lunge then recoil. Thraxton gazed into their shifting depths and sensed an invisible presence hovering there. When the hairs at the nape of his neck began to rise, he knew it had arrived. The Dark Presence. His old adversary.

"Death?" he said, his voice a brittle whisper in the echoing silence of the tomb. "Can you hear me, Death? Yes?" He smiled. "Not today ... not today."

Thraxton licked his fingers and pinched the wick out with a sizzle, and with no light to hold them back, the shadows of the tomb fell in upon him.

When Thraxton finally left the family tomb, he found the harsh morning sunshine jarring, the knots of politely smiling middle class strollers an irritant. He wished to cling to his sense of gloomy isolation a while longer, so he turned away from the cemetery entrance and followed the pathways to the centre of the necropolis, the circle of Lebanon. The fog here had yet to lift and he plunged once more into its cool and welcome veil. Ahead hovered the brooding mass of the Pharaonic arch that formed the entrance to the Egyptian Avenue, a sloping tunnel, lined by mausoleums. With no lanterns lit, the avenue was an obsidian shaft. At its far end, luminous panes of silver fog swirled. He stepped inside the echoing space, a gloved hand brushing the bronze tomb doors as he trod the rising slope.

He froze as a figure appeared at the end of the stony tunnel—the silhouette of a small woman in long skirts, her face hidden by a deep cowl.

"Maisy?" Thraxton called out, echoingly. "Maisy is that you?"

But even as he spoke the words, Thraxton realised that the young prostitute had been dressed much more gaily, and would likely have left in the opposite direction, heading straight for the cemetery's front gates. His mind vaulted back to the stone angel that crooked a finger and beckoned to him from the fog. The shadow-form seemed to regard him for a moment, then slid from sight.

Thraxton quivered with nervous excitement. He scurried up the tunnel and emerged into the circle of Lebanon, twenty sunken tombs arranged around an ancient Cedar of Lebanon. Darkness clung to the place: the towering cedar flung a wide shadow; the cold stone corralled a twisting torus of fog. The silvery tissues teased apart momentarily and he saw the vague shape again, thirty feet away.

"Hello?" he called out, lumbering after. The shadow plunged into the fog and vanished and Thraxton pursued, the only sound his heavy breathing and the squeak of fine leather boots. A moment later he felt like a fool chasing his own shadow, for he had transited a complete circle and wound up back at the Egyptian Avenue. Whatever it was had eluded him. Just then the mists cleaved and a wan shaft of light broke through, illuminating a scattering of white blobs on the stony ground. He crouched and touched a finger to one. A white petal adhered to the tip of his gloved index finger. He rolled the petal between his fingertips. It seemed fresh. Had the petals been there when he first entered the circle?

The back of Thraxton's neck prickled as he sensed eyes upon him. When he looked up, a figure stood at the top of the stone stairs that climbed out of the circle, watching. As he rose from the ground, it took a step backward, pulled the fog about its shoulders like a cloak ... and merged into the seamless grey.